A Deadly Game

He'd planned it all so well: a few drops of lethal poison and she'd be dead. Neat, simple. Her money would be his—all his—and his beautiful young lover was waiting. . . .

Darkness came, the time for murder, too. The killer moved slowly. . . .

But the night was to end with a strange and unexpected twist. The hunter had become the hunted. . . .

The Allingham Case-Book

Margery Allingham

MB

A Macfadden-Bartell Book

A Macfadden Book........1972

This is the complete text
of the hardcover edition.

Macfadden-Bartell Corporation
A subsidiary of Bartell Media Corporation
205 East 42nd Street, New York, New York, 10017

Contents

The Allingham
Case-Book

PREFACE:

A Profile of Margery Allingham

Margery Allingham was born on May 20, 1904, in Ealing, a London suburb. She died of a sudden and devouring cancer on June 30, 1966.

Her parents moved within a few months of her birth to a square, white, late-Georgian house which had been the rectory at Layer Breton, near Colchester in Essex. It was here that she grew up, and for the greater period of her life she lived within a few miles of her first home.

Her father was Herbert Allingham who started his career as a journalist after leaving Cambridge and who edited *The London Journal* and *The Christian Globe*, a non-conformist weekly paper owned by his father, a white-bearded Godlike patriarch whose offices in Fleet Street were on the present site of the *Daily Express*. In his early thirties, Herbert turned to writing as a full-time profession. He became one of the great and prolific serialists at the dawn of the Northcliffe era, working usually for the Amalgamated Press, now swallowed by a takeover empire, and occasionally for the group known in the family as "The North."

It was the heyday of the penny weekly journals pioneered by *Answers* and the halfpenny comics. *Chips*, *The Funny Wonder*, *The Butterfly* and *Comic Cuts* all came from the same stable and used the same formula.

This consisted of a series of strip cartoons, the best of them drawn by Tom Browne, picturing such favourites as Weary Willy and Tired Tim, Tom the Ticket of Leave Man, the Casey Court Kids and Professor Radium. All these were designed for children, but each issue contained a fairy tale, a detective story, a schoolboy adventure and a family serial aimed at adults, which sometimes ran for several years.

Herbert Allingham wrote any and all of these with donnish precision, but he was at his best in the unending dramas which were the forerunners of TV serials such as *Peyton Place* or *The Fugitive*. His taught Margery a great deal not only about writing but about the business of it, for he never parted with a copyright and sold many of his stories six or seven times over, though he was never published in book form. He was a handsome, scholarly man whose appearance suggested an eminent theologian rather than a Grub Street hack, and his stories were worked out with the same academic interest that he gave to a chess problem. To his house came many of the successful journalists of the age. Edith Shackleton and her sister Norah Heald, G. H. Mair, Jimmy Heddle, James Parks, Richard Hearne and many others. William McFee was his protégé and most of *Casuals of the Sea* was written at Layer Breton.

Herbert had married his cousin who was also a writer of women's magazine stories and whose sister Maud Hughes founded *The Picture Show* and edited it for nearly forty years. Writing had been in the blood for several generations. John Till Allingham, a playwright of South of the River melodramas, and J. E. Allingham, a pioneer of schoolboy magazines who wrote under the name "Ralph Rollington," were among their forebears. The latter created "Jimmy Cake," the forerunner of Billy Bunter.

Against this background Margery had no choice but to join the ranks, for no other occupation was considered orthodox or indeed sane. She has recorded how when she was seven her father gave her, as a matter of normal progress, a room, a desk, a pen, paper and a plot to enable her to make her own start in life. Her first earnings, seven and sixpence from a story in one of her aunt's papers, made her a professional from the age of eight.

Like most authors she had her setbacks. At her first

10

school in Colchester an essay was publicly destroyed by the English mistress on the grounds that she could not possibly have written it herself and must, therefore, be exposed as a copyist and a cheat. The Perse School at Cambridge treated her more intelligently and for them she produced and acted in her own costume play.

During the first world war the family moved to London, though they kept a small house on Mersea Island, and when Margery left the Perse at the age of sixteen her father sent her to the School of Drama and Speech Training at the Polytechnic in Regent Street, to cure her equally of stammering and snobbery. He succeeded in both intentions.

In the meantime she had experienced an odd adventure. Her father, who kept an enquiring and open mind on everything from politics to theology, had decided to experiment with table-turning, and this may have been to keep pace with the enterprise of his wife who embraced the beliefs of the Church of England, Christian Science, Mrs. Mary Baker Eddy, Madam Blavatsky and the Vibrate-to-Colour school with alternate impartiality. At Mersea a series of table-turning sessions with several hands upon an upturned glass produced messages and stories from characters purporting to be seventeenth-century pirates and smugglers, long-dead inhabitants of the little island.

That these personalities, who made themselves extraordinarily vivid and authentic in their period, were entirely the product of Margery's dynamic imagination there is no doubt. This sort of phenomena, conjured by a young woman at the age of puberty, is not uncommon. The case of Bridie Murphy which had all America by the ears a year or two back is very close to it, and Noel Coward used the idea effectively in *Blithe Spirit*.

Having created the characters from her subconscious mind, Margery proceeded to bring them to life in the only way she knew. She wrote her first novel, *Blackerchief Dick*, the tragic romantic history which had just emerged, spelled out letter by letter across the table in the winter of 1920.

One of my earliest memories of her, still vivid as yesterday, is of her return to the flat in Bayswater after her first interview with A. S. Watt, the doyen of literary agents. She was elated with the champagne of success, a big,

11

handsome, bouncing schoolgirl of my own age, bursting with news.

"Daddy Watt said, 'Miss Allingham, I have to tell you that I have arranged today for Messrs Hodder & Stoughton to publish your work. They will pay you a modest fee in advance but this is subject to a proviso. The phrase which appears on page fourteen, "Blasting wilting swine," must be deleted.' A pity. I don't know any real oaths and pirates ought to be allowed to swear, don't you think?"

It was a triumph in which I shared, for at Margery's insistence the publishers used my design for the book jacket and this was the forerunner of over two thousand which I have produced since. It was indeed the first genuine commercial sale I ever made.

We had met only a few weeks before and in rather peculiar circumstances, for my mother had once had a romantic affair with her father during his Cambridge days when my grandmother's home at Waterbeach was open house to literary-minded students. Despite the breaking of this near-engagement they remained close friends and corresponded regularly even after both had married elsewhere. The tie was increased by the fact that we both had a courtesy aunt in common, a cousin of my mother's married to an uncle of Margery's. She was a garrulous and regular visitor, travelling much between households prepared to offer hospitality and regaling my sister and myself with tales of the achievements of the "cousin" who was our own age. "Margery is so clever. She has written several stories which have been published and produced a play." My sister and I grew to loathe the sound of this prodigy without realizing that we too were the subject of similar eulogies. "Philip is writing and editing a magazine which is *quite* brilliant. He does all his own drawings for it in exercise books. Betty is going to be *such a clever* actress, I feel sure."

When I became an art student in 1921, we met for the first time, at the insistence of my mother, with the greatest mutual misgivings, but I do not think that anyone who ever encountered Margery could be immune to her infectious, exhilarating charm. The following week we went to the gallery of the Old Vic together (Sibyl Thorndyke doubling as the first witch and Lady Macbeth) and before the winter was out we had seen every play of importance in town.

In the meantime Margery had written and produced a heroic verse-drama "Dido and Aeneas," for her fellow students in which she played the lead, and for which she made over forty costumes. My minor role was to design the scenery. This epic, which contains some amazing verse for a girl of seventeen, was performed with some success at the St. George's Hall and the Cripplegate Theatre in London, but by a merciful chance there was no popular demand for student prodigies in those days and though the press gave us a glimpse of glory it was brief as summer lightning.

The following summer we became secretly engaged on an August night at Mersea. It was a curious courtship because we were both naturally shy and completely inexperienced. We neither kissed nor held hands, but walked arm in arm like children; yet between us there was that complete understanding which makes sex of minor importance and mutual interests so paramount that other considerations appear remote and mildly funny.

It was four years before we did in fact become officially betrothed and in the interval both of us enjoyed educational romances elsewhere. Margery at her father's bidding wrote a long, unpublishable novel of student life, and I had graduated from art student to struggling commercial artist. We saw each other constantly, even discussing our love affairs, but always from the olympian angle of those whose association is unquestionable and eternal.

In 1927 we married and went to live in a minute flat in Holborn which had once been the caretaker's premises of the old Birkbeck Bank. One room of this was a bookmaker's office and on a memorable day we won a quarter's rent from him, but within the year he went bankrupt and we took over the whole floor space. Margery was earning her living by translating silent films into short stories for one of her aunt's papers, *The Girl's Cinema.* Each week a drama, whether it was *Nanook of the North,* the latest Valentino, or even *The Light That Failed,* had to be turned into an adolescent romance of ten thousand words. This she dictated to me at a single twelve-hour sitting and on one occasion we produced seventy thousand words in a week, in order to be free to go to the South of

France for the ideal honeymoon which we had not been able to afford the year before.

Like her father, Margery also wrote for "The North" from time to time, including an epic serial dealing with the adventures of The Society Millgirl and the Eight Wicked Millionaires. In those comparatively tax-free days, a party for a dozen friends could be paid for by what was called "a splendid long complete" for Sexton Blake* or a "special Love Story" for the Christmas number of a film-fan paper.

The Crime at Black Dudley, Mystery Mile and *Look to the Lady* were written during this period. The time to produce them had to be won by getting weeks ahead with the film work, which was bread and butter, and the books themselves were written in the country, for we exchanged her father's house for the flat each summer. They are gay because they reflect the mood of the time and into them she crammed every idea, every joke and every scrap of plot which we had gathered like magpies hoarded for a year. Connoisseurs of the period will find any number of unpublishable contemporary jokes delicately indicated by inference in these pages, and only last year a serious-minded German translator made a special visit to us to enquire about the correct rendering of Miss Fanny Adams.

In 1930 we rented our own house in the country, at Chappel in Essex, and in 1934 we bought D'Arcy House as a permanent home. Tolleshunt D'Arcy is a village on the Blackwater on the Essex coast, five miles from Layer Breton, and Margery felt that this was the background to which she truly belonged. The house itself she had known all her life for it was the home of Dr. Salter, the family physician, the great Essex sportsman and diarist.

By now she was accepted by the reviewers of the day first as an important new thriller writer, although the public had made this discovery long since, and later as a major creative author in her chosen field. She had attracted the interest of the best of literary agents, Paul Reynolds of New York, later a personal friend, and her sales in the United States began to climb. She had grown in stature and accomplishment and was determined to make the modern

* The English "Nick Carter."

adventure story as important and significant a work as any other piece of professional writing. "To Albert Campion has fallen the honour of being the first detective to figure in a story which is also by any standard a distinguished novel," said Torquemada of the *Observer* in reviewing *The Fashion in Shrouds* in 1938, and this was the accolade of which she was most proud.

World War II found her with a half-finished book, *Black Plumes*, which she completed more quickly than she had intended in order to produce *Traitor's Purse* with its remarkable warning about the obvious capacity of one nation to forge another's currency.

At the request of her American publishers she wrote *The Oaken Heart*, a factual account, based originally on her letters to American friends, of wartime life in an English village which is a recognized classic in its own time. It was written to attract intelligent U.S. opinion to the allied cause. In the States, Eleanor Roosevelt gave it a warm welcome, but the market for sympathy towards England had been saturated by Agnes Dewer Millars' *The White Cliffs* and America at that moment was self-conscious about its neutrality. It had a modest success in the United States but became a best seller in every part of the world where there were Englishmen who loved their country. Many years before Margery had written a contemporary play for her fellow students called *Without Being Naturally Qualified,* based on a quotation from G. B. Shaw's *Man and Superman.* She sent him a copy and he acknowledged it with a long letter beginning: "If you sell your audience you won't sell your seats . . ." After the publication of *The Oaken Heart* he wrote to her, "Well, well, so you're still alive. I'm reading your book."

Her one "straight" work, *The Galantrys,* was written between 1942 and 1944. It was to have been her bid for a place among the "serious" novelists of the age, a generation-to-generation history, largely based on her own family story. Sheer fatigue and the necessity for earning enough money to keep the house going (for I was away in the Western Desert) made her finish it at top speed. The first half has all the promise of a masterpiece, but it tails off sadly into a précis of a larger scheme. She had run the billeting and welfare of the evacuees, kept the emergency supplies of food, worked in the A.R.P.* and was First Aid Commandant for the area in addition to being the underground liaison and resistance agent in case of invasion. Food was stored in the garage, explosives at the far end of the garden.

Before I returned from overseas she had also written *Coroner's Pidgin* (*Pearls before Swine* in the U.S.), the one adventure story in which I had no share, for it was her custom to discuss every move, chapter and even paragraph with me before finishing the draft. With peace and the release of enough paper to print books in quantity she repeated her successes of prewar days and became again what she most loved to be, a hostess with a host of friends. We flew perilously to New York in 1949 to make new contacts and she accomplished one of her cherished ambitions which was to sell to the *Saturday Evening Post*, at that time regarded by many writers as a hall mark of professionalism.

The Tiger in the Smoke is generally considered her best book, but her own favourite was *The Beckoning Lady* and indeed it mirrors something of what a summer party could be like at Tolleshunt D'Arcy. The character of Minnie is near to a self portrait, and of necessity, since it has become my nickname, I find echoes of myself in Tonker.

As a craftswoman she had a dedicated conscience, writing, dictating and rewriting until she had achieved a polish which she considered overbright. She then redictated it at speed to an old friend, Alan Gregory, to bring it back into readable colloquial English. She read most of her contemporaries, admiring Josephine Tey and in particular Agatha Christie whom she considered as owning the liveliest intelligence in the business. She eschewed Dorothy Sayers, though she later became a friend and neighbour, because having come upon her work after both ladies were established, she found that it had too many points in common to make it wise to read her regularly. James Bond she regarded as a consumer-goods figure and Dr. No as being too close a relation to Dr. Fu Manchu. Perhaps the fact that a character in *Black Dudley*, written in 1928, had

* Air Raid Precaution Service.

the file number 0072 coloured her opinion.

But in all things she was open-hearted and even a critic who consistently vilified her work earned no more than tolerant amusement.

No young author whose proofs were sent to her ever lacked a quotable phrase unless he dealt in cruelty, for she was the kindest and gentlest of women. She was deeply religious, developing her own philosophy through the years, although she was not a churchgoer, for she found the strict tenets of orthodox faith too narrow for her personal brand of Christian theology.

Her house, her garden and her friends: these in ascending order were her abiding interests, and I do not think that anyone who knew her could fail to love her or to take pride in having met her. She was gay, generous, affectionate and, I think, as near to being a saint as no matter.

Philip Youngman Carter

TALL STORY

London was having one of her days. Outside, the streets glistened dully with half frozen sludge and the air was thick, dark and apparently contaminated with poison gas. But inside the varnished cabin which overhung the huge circular bar of the Platelayers' Arms, W.2, there was still civilization and comfort. In this nest which possessed a staircase direct to the street, privileged customers drank in all the peaceful privacy of a St. James's Club yet without sacrificing anything of the fug and freedom of the true hostelry. Mrs. Chubb, the licensee, who was a genius in such matters called it 'my little room'.

Charlie Luke, at that time the Divisional Detective Chief Inspector of the district, was sitting on the table, his muscles spoiling the cut of his jacket and his hat pulled down over his eyes. He looked like a gangster, was a tough, and with his live dark face and diamond-shaped eye sockets, he lent a touch of badly needed theatre to the rest of us. We were about half a dozen I suppose, no one of staggering distinction but all friends, resting for half an hour before making the routine after-work effort to totter off home.

Mr. Campion, owlish behind the spectacles for which he had set such a fashion, was chipping Luke gently and

18

affectionately like a man knocking out a favourite pipe. "You put your success as a detective down to your height, Charles?" he was saying. "Really? You astound me. I shouldn't have thought it. Height of brow? Or merely length of leg?"

"Reach, chum." Luke was in fine ferocious form, his eyes snapping and his teeth gleaming in his dark skin. "And I wasn't talking of my success—I could do with a basinful of that—I simply said that it was my height that got me into the C.I.D. I was on the beat—see?"

He adjusted an imaginary helmet strap under his chin and strained his Adam's apple against an imaginary tunic collar. He was away. You could see him fifteen years younger, with pink satin cheeks, loping along, bright, eager, green as lettuce leaves. It was his great gift, as he spoke whole pictures came alive and people one had never heard of seemed to step into the room. Mr. Campion settled back, grinning.

"It was a night just like this, cold and thick as a landlady's kiss and my little beat, which was usually quiet at night except for the rats, had come alive for a change. Our D.I. was expecting a burglary."

He blew out his cheeks, sketched himself a pair of flaring eyebrows and a waterfall moustache with a careless hand and sped on with his narrative, having introduced us to a fussy, worried personality without drawing extra breath.

"Set out!" he said. "Caudblimeah! I thought he was expecting to be a father until seven in the evening when the cars turned out! My sergeant took pity on me in the end and gave it me in clear. News had come through on the grapevine that Slacks Washington, who was one of the slicker practitioners, had run out of money and had been taking sights round a little bookmaker's office in Ebury Court. From information received—and you know what that means . . ." he favoured us with a wide-eyed leer which was somehow wholly feminine and conjured up a traitress of a very definite kind . . . "they'd learned that tonight was the night. The bookie kept his cash in a safe which wouldn't keep out pussy and he was careless. He relied on the position of the office."

There was a square whisky bottle on the mantelshelf—a

19

dummy, as many generations of Ma Chubb's clients had discovered through the years; Luke leant forward without rising and, stretching out a long arm, took it up with which to demonstrate.

"This is just about the shape of Ebury Court," he remarked, placing the bottle on its side. "There's a narrow tunnelled entrance off the Commercial Road, two perfectly blank thirty-foot walls made of soot-blackened brick, smarmed with posters, and, at the end, here at the bottom of the bottle, is a little nest of offices. A small printery on the ground floor, the bookie above and a commercial art studio above that . . . nothing to attract anybody. All deserted at night."

He grinned at us. "They could have cut short the whole exercise by just putting me in the passageway," he said cheerfully. "Naturally. But our D.I. wasn't wasting anything. Slacks was two and one-sixth yards of ill repute at that time. He was tall and thin and dangerous, he used a gun, he was dirty and he stole." He measured two yards in the air as a woman does with outstretched arm and held his nose for a moment. "A *bad* crook," he said. "So it was decided to take him with the stuff on him just to make a nice clean open-and-shut case which no smarty legal-eagle could muck up. It was also to be an object lesson to a collection of new young gentlemen from the C.I.D. (at that time of day, half the stuff they were recruiting spoke so refined their superior officers couldn't understand a word they were saying) and old Superintendant Yeo from the Yard was to be present himself just to hand out the congratulations." He laughed joyfully. "Talk about a police-net!" he said. "The trouble was to prevent it looking like a football crowd caught in the rain. I was the only man allowed to show myself. I was to keep my usual times and 'behave normal' and I was just bright enough to know that didn't mean stopping in a doorway for a fag.

"Off we went. There were police in the area, police on the tiles, police disguised as disappointed lovers waiting for their girls, police disguised as drunks singing in the gutter, police disguised as postmen, police disguised as police going home." He crossed his eyes and his fingers and made an idiot face. "It was quite a do," he said. "It was a wonder to me Slacks pushed past 'em all. There was no one else about. There never were many people around at that time of night, but the rain and the fog seemed to have cleared the district. By midnight I'd given up hope, but at a quarter to one he showed up. He got off a bus on the corner, leaving the man who was tailing him to ride on as arranged, and came striding down the pavement with his raincoat flapping and his long legs making shadows on the pavement under the street lamp. I recognized him at once from the pictures I'd been shown. He saw me and said, 'Good night, officer!' as he passed. He was so much at ease that it was me that gave the guilty start. I made a police-like noise and strolled on—you know." The D.D.C.I. rubbed his cheek and miraculously we saw him as he must have been then, skin like pink satin and the kitten-blue still in his eyes.

"Slacks went into the trap," he went on. "Walked straight into the Court like a man in a hurry, which was the only way; the dark mouth of the tunnel through the houses swallowed him up and after that you could have heard a cat cough.

"It had been arranged that the arrest should be made as he came out of Ebury Court. The idea was that since he was known to be dangerous the actual cop should be covered at all points. It was to be a demonstration, as I said. The whole thing was to be done like the book, neat, swift and with the minimum danger to all present. Since I'd done my little bit, I walked back when I reached the boundary and crossed the road to see the performance.

"There it was, set out like a stage set. There was a man on either side of the entrance waiting to step forward and pin him. There was a car twenty paces up the road and another one thirty paces down, stationary but with engines running. Opposite, there was a borrowed G.P.O. van with two fake postmen in attendance, and all round—hidden, they hoped, in the dusk and weather—there were the privileged audience. We waited. We waited. We waited some more. People began to get windy. There had been time for Slacks to open twenty safes and count the money as well. I could feel our D.I. shaking although he was forty yards away. I know what he felt like. But I was puzzled myself because I knew there was no other way out and the roofs were manned. I found myself wondering if the chap could have broken his leg or something, knocked himself out, perhaps, with the bookie's Scotch. And then quite suddenly, between thought and thought as it were, with no one quite ready in spite of everything, a revolver shot rang out clearly from inside the Court. There was a yelp like the cry of a lost soul (whatever that's like) and someone came staggering out into the street.

"I saw him and I recognized him and I had the shock of my life. The men on the tunnel caught him and he collapsed in their arms and died there, poor chap, at that moment, with a bullet through his windpipe.

"I was one of the first to get there, although there was soon a big enough crowd round the three of them.

"The D.I. charged up spluttering"—Luke blew the imaginary waterfall moustache in and out until we saw it for ourselves—"he kept the watch on the archway intact, though; he was no fool, the Old Man. He turned to me. 'Who the so-and-so is this, constable?' he demanded, as suspiciously as if he thought it was all mine. 'Know him?'

"I said, 'Yessir!' smartly, and I told him. It was a little runt called Church—some relation to the proverbial mouse, I think—he was a crank who spent all his spare time flyposting for some society he was interested in. I always remember those little posters of his, they were printed in emerald on yellow and he stuck them wherever he could on the hoardings, quite illegally. They said: 'YOU'VE GOT A RIGHT TO IT', and then, in some very small type: *Society of Humanity. Meeting Tuesday. Somewhereorother Hall.*' That was all. The most innocent little chap alive. I went to one of the meetings once, but it emerged that the only thing I'd got a right to was the speaker's views and they didn't get me far. Church was daft, that was all. A poor daft little bloke. He must have been hiding in the Court for hours—thinking all the ding-dong was for him, I suppose.

"We could see what had happened. He'd surprised Slacks and got the full benefit. Strewth I was riled!" Even at this distance in time the D.D.C.I.'s diamond-shaped eyes grew narrow at the recollection. "I was all for charging in like a hero and getting the next bullet," he said with a lightning change of mood. "Mercifully I had no enemies among my superiors at that time and I was restrained. We ll waited there till morning. Finally, after sufficient conferences to start a Peace, old D.I. Everett himself went in God bless him he was a brave old boy. He had a bullet-proof shirt on, so his tummy was safe but the etiquette of the time required him to rely on the natural armour plating of his own skull should Slacks have aimed high. He had four of his own boys behind him but I got there next, there being no great competition.

"We found Slacks sitting on a packing-case outside the printery, smoking and admiring the view. He was quite affable, all things considered."

Luke paused and eyed Campion.

"You ought to have been there," he said. "It was like one of your tame pidgins. The crib was cracked, the cash was gone, Church's little paste-pot and Escapist Literature were lying in the yard, but Slacks hadn't a bob on him and nor had he a gun.

"Everett's men took the whole place apart. It was the first time I'd ever seen a full-dress C.I.D. search and it opened my eyes. They took up the drains, although anyone could see they hadn't been disturbed for twenty years, they took the offices apart, they tapped the stones and the walls and they emptied the paste-pot—so it wasn't what you're thinking—and meanwhile Slacks sat placidly in a nice warm room overlooking the river and swore he couldn't think what they were all talking about and hadn't heard a shot or even handled a gun whatevernext.

"No one told me to go off duty so I stayed around. When they were all exhausted and the place looked like the scoured inside of a well-kept saucepan, the C.I.D. boys were called off. The old D.I. was nearly out of his mind. He was standing alone in the middle of the court with the sun shining down through the air-shaft between the building and glinting on his old bald head. The bookie and the printers and the commercial artists were all besieging the entrance behind us and he knew that sooner or later he'd have to let them in and lose the proof for ever.

"Since there was no one else there he spoke to me.

" 'Where did he put it, constable?' he said. 'Where in the name of Gog and Magog did he put that gun—the gun and wad of money as big as a brick?'

"I cleared my throat—I was a bit husky when speaking
23

to D.I.s in those days. 'He's a tall man, sir,' I said.

"He turned and looked at me and I remember I took my cape off and stretched up my hand—my reach was eight inches longer than his own. 'Church was a little man, sir,' I said and I pointed to one of the 'YOU'VE GOT A RIGHT TO IT' posters, which was a good two feet higher than the rest, slapped on in the very midst of an out-of-date Cinema Masterpiece which covered half a wall. He opened his mouth and said a word which was new to me—Hindustani it was. He was an elderly man. He went over and reached up. He wasn't tall enough but I waited for orders and saw the look on his face when he gave them."

Luke sighed and on his dark face there was a gleam of remembered triumph. "It was there," he said. "In a little hole made by the erosion of a couple of bricks. The bill posters always papered over it, but within a day or so the paper always rotted. Slacks, looking round wildly after the shot, must have guessed that he was trapped. He saw the hole, shoved the loot and the gun out of sight, and then spotted the paste-pot and the bills.

"I remember the D.I. holding the stuff in his handkerchief. He was grinning all over his face, like this"—Luke's smile was wonderful to see. " 'You think I'm going to take the credit for this, my boy, don't you?' he said. I said, 'Yessir,' and he laughed. 'How right you are,' he said. 'Learnt anything?' I said: 'Yessir, always take the paper off the wall, sir.' That made him laugh. 'You'll do,' he said. 'You'd better report to me.' So that's how I joined the C.I.D."

Mr. Campion was laughing.

"Brilliant observation," he remarked. "And—er—if I may say so, wonderful restraint."

Luke chuckled, and appealed to the rest of us.

"He always spots the second degree," he said. "Yes, of course you're right, chum! I saw it at once as soon as I stepped into the yard. That hole in the wall was where I kept my sandwiches. It was just high enough to be private. All the same I had to wait my moment—'Honour where honour is going to be duly appreciated'."

THREE IS A LUCKY NUMBER

At five o'clock on a September afternoon Ronald Frederick Torbay was making preparations for his third murder. He was being very wary, forcing himself to go slowly because he was perfectly sane and was well aware of the dangers of carelessness.

A career of homicide got more chancy as one went on. That piece of information had impressed him as being true as soon as he had read it in a magazine article way back before his first marriage. Also, he realized, success was liable to go to a man's head, so he kept a tight hold on himself. He was certain he was infinitely more clever than most human beings but he did not dwell on the fact and as soon as he felt the old thrill at the sense of his power welling up inside him, he quelled it firmly.

For an instant he paused, leaning on the rim of the wash-basin, and regarded himself thoughtfully in the shaving glass of the bathroom in the new villa he had hired so recently.

The face which looked at him was thin, middle-aged and pallid. Sparse dark hair receded from its high narrow forehead and the well-shaped eyes were blue and prominent. Only the mouth was really unusual. That narrow slit, quite straight, was almost lipless and, unconsciously, he persuaded it to relax into a half smile. Even Ronald Torbay did not like his own mouth.

A sound in the kitchen below disturbed him and he straightened his back hastily. If Edyth had finished her ironing she would be coming up to take her long discussed bubble-bath before he had prepared it for her and that would never do. He waited, holding his breath, but it was all right: she was going out of the back door. He reached the window just in time to see her disappearing round the side of the house into the small square yard which was so exactly like all the other square yards in the long suburban street. He knew that she was going to hang the newly pressed linen on the line to air and although the manoeuvre gave him the time he needed, still it irritated him.

Of the three homely middle-aged women whom so far he had persuaded first to marry him and then to will him their modest possessions, Edyth was proving easily the most annoying. If he had told her once not to spend so much time in the yard he had done it a dozen times in their six weeks of marriage. He hated her being out of doors alone. She was shy and reserved but now that new people had moved in next door there was the danger of some over-friendly woman starting up an acquaintance with her and that was the last thing to be tolerated at this juncture.

Each of his former wives had been shy. He had been very careful to choose the right type and felt he owed much of his success to it. Mary, the first of them, had met her fatal 'accident' almost unnoticed in the bungalow on the housing estate very like the present one he had chosen but in the north instead of the south of England. At the time it had been a growing place, the coroner had been hurried, the police sympathetic but busy and the neighbours scarcely curious except that one of them, a junior reporter on a local paper, had written a flowery paragraph about the nearness of tragedy in the midst of joy, published a wedding day snapshot and had entitled the article with typical northern understatement 'Honeymoon Mishap'.

Dorothy's brief excursion into his life and abrupt exit from it and her own, had given him a little more bother but not much. She had deceived him when she had told him she was quite alone in the world and the interfering brother

26

who had turned up after the funeral to ask awkward questions about her small fortune might have been a nuisance if Ronald had not been very firm with him. There had been a brief court case which Ronald had won handsomely and the insurance had paid up without a murmur.

All that was four years ago. Now, with a new name, a newly invented background and a fresh area in which to operate, he felt remarkably safe.

From the moment he had first seen Edyth, sitting alone at a little table under the window in a seaside hotel dining-room, he had known that she was to be his next subject. He always thought of his wives as 'subjects'. It lent his designs upon them a certain pseudo-scientific atmosphere which he found satisfying.

Edyth had sat there looking stiff and neat and a trifle severe but there had been a secret timidity in her face, an unsatisfied, half-frightened expression in her short-sighted eyes and once, when the waiter said something pleasant to her, she had flushed nervously and had been embarrassed by it. She was also wearing a genuine diamond brooch. Ronald had observed that from right across the room. He had an eye for stones.

That evening in the lounge he had spoken to her, had weathered the initial snub, tried again and, finally, had got her to talk. After that the acquaintance had progressed just as he had expected. His methods were old-fashioned and heavily romantic and within a week she was hopelessly infatuated.

From Ronald's point of view her history was even better than he could have hoped. After teaching in a girls' boarding school for the whole of her twenties she had been summoned home to look after her recluse of a father whose long illness had monopolized her life. Now at forty-three she was alone, comparatively well off and as much at sea as a ship without a rudder.

Ronald was careful not to let her toes touch the ground. He devoted his entire attention to her and exactly five weeks from the day on which they first met, he married her at the registry office of the town where they were both strangers. The same afternoon they each made wills in the other's favour and moved into the villa which he had been

27

able to hire cheaply because the holiday season was at an end.

It had been the pleasantest conquest he had ever made. Mary had been moody and hysterical, Dorothy grudging and suspicious but Edyth had revealed an unexpected streak of gaiety and, but for her stupidity in not realizing that a man would hardly fall romantically in love with her at first sight, was a sensible person. Any other man, Ronald reflected smugly, might have made the fatal mistake of feeling sorry for her, but he was 'above' all that, he told himself, and he began to make plans for what he described in his own mind rather grimly as 'her future'.

Two things signed her death warrant earlier than had been his original intention. One was her obstinate reticence over her monetary affairs and the other was her embarrassing interest in his job.

On the marriage certificate Ronald had described himself as a salesman and the story he was telling was that he was a junior partner in a firm of cosmetic manufacturers who were giving him a very generous leave of absence. Edyth accepted the statement without question, but almost at once she had begun to plan a visit to the office and the factory, and was always talking about the new clothes she must buy so as not to 'disgrace him'. At the same time she kept all her business papers locked in an old writing-case and steadfastly refused to discuss them however cautiously he raised the subject. Ronald had given up feeling angry with her and decided to act.

He turned from the window, carefully removed his jacket and began to run the bath. His heart was pounding, he noticed, frowning. He wished it would not. He needed to keep very calm.

The bathroom was the one room they had repainted. Ronald had done it himself soon after they had arrived and had put up the little shelf over the bath to hold a jar of bathsalts he had bought and a small electric heater of the old-fashioned two-element type, which was cheap but white like the walls and not too noticeable. He leant forward now and switched it on and stood looking at it until the two bars of glowing warmth appeared. Then he turned away and went out on to the landing, leaving it alight.

The fuse box which controlled all the electricity in the house was concealed in the bottom of the linen cupboard at the top of the stairs. Ronald opened the door carefully and using his handkerchief so that his fingerprints should leave no trace pulled up the main switch. Back in the bathroom the heater's glow died away; the bars were almost black again by the time he returned. He eyed the slender cabinet approvingly and then, still using the handkerchief, he lifted it bodily from the shelf and lowered it carefully into the water, arranging it so that it lay at an angle over the waste plug, close to the foot where it took up practically no room at all. The white flex ran up over the porcelain side of the bath, along the skirting board, under the door and into wall socket, just outside on the landing.

When he had first installed the heater Edyth had demurred at this somewhat slipshod arrangement, but when he had explained that the local Council was stupid and fussy about fitting wall sockets in bathrooms since water was said to be a conductor she had compromised by letting him run the flex under the lino where it was not so noticeable.

At the moment the heater was perfectly visible in the bath. It certainly looked as if it had fallen into its odd position accidentally but no one in his senses could have stepped into the water without seeing it. Ronald paused, his eyes dark, his ugly mouth narrower than ever. The beautiful simplicity of the main plan, so certain, so swiftly fatal and above all, so safe as far as he himself was concerned gave him a thrill of pleasure as it always did. He turned off the bath and waited, listening. Edyth was coming back. He could hear her moving something on the concrete way outside the back door below and he leant over to where his jacket hung and took a plastic sachet from its inside breast pocket. He was re-reading the directions on the back of it when a slight sound made him turn his head and he saw, to his horror, the woman herself not five feet away. Her neat head had appeared suddenly just above the flat roof of the scullery, outside the bathroom window. She was clearing the dead leaves from the guttering and must, he guessed, be standing on the tall flight of steps which were kept just inside the back door.

It was typical of the man that he did not panic. Still holding the sachet lightly he stepped between her and the bath and spoke mildly.

"What on earth are you doing there, darling?"

Edyth started so violently at the sound of his voice that she almost fell off the steps and a flush of apprehension appeared on her thin cheeks.

"Oh, how you startled me! I thought I'd just do this little job before I came up to change. If it rains the gutter floods all over the back step."

"Very thoughtful of you, my dear." He spoke with that slightly acid amusement with which he had found he could best destroy her slender vein of self assurance. "But not terribly clever when you knew I'd come up to prepare your beauty bath for you. Or was it?"

The slight intonation on the word 'beauty' was not lost on her. He saw her swallow.

"Perhaps it wasn't," she said without looking at him. "It's very good of you to take all this trouble, Ronald."

"Not at all," he said with a just amount of masculine off-hand insensitivity. "I'm taking you out tonight and want you to look as nice as—er—possible. Hurry up, there's a good girl. The foam doesn't last indefinitely and like all these very high-class beauty treatments the ingredients are expensive. Undress in the bedroom, put on your gown and come straight along."

"Very well, dear." She began to descend at once while he turned to the bath and shook the contents of the sachet into the water. The crystals, which were peach coloured and smelled strongly of roses, floated on the tide and then, as he suddenly turned the pressure of water full on, began to dissolve into thousands of irridescent bubbles. A momentary fear that their camouflage would not prove to be sufficient assailed him, and he stooped to beat the water with his hand, but he need not have worried. The cloud grew and grew into a fragrant feathery mass which not only obscured the bottom of the bath and all it contained, but mounted the porcelain sides, smothering the white flex and overflowing on to the wall panels and the bath-mat. It was perfect.

He pulled on his jacket and opened the door.

"Edyth! Hurry, dearest!" The words were on the tip of

30

his tongue but her arrival forestalled them. She came shrinking in, her blue dressing-gown strained round her thin body, her hair thrust into an unbecoming bathing cap.

"Oh, Ronald!" she said, staring at the display aghast. "Won't it make an awful mess? Goodness! All over the floor!"

Her hesitation infuriated him.

"That won't matter," he said savagely. "You get in while the virtue of the foam is still there. Hurry. Meanwhile I'll go and change, myself. I'll give you ten minutes. Get straight in and lie down. It'll take some of the sallowness out of that skin of yours."

He went out and paused, listening. She locked the door as he had known she would. The habit of a lifetime does not suddenly change with marriage. He heard the bolt slide home and forced himself to walk slowly down the passage. He gave her sixty seconds. Thirty to take off her things and thirty to hesitate on the brink of the rosy mass.

"How is it?" he shouted from the linen cupboard doorway.

She did not answer at once and the sweat broke out on his forehead. Then he heard her.

"I don't know yet. I'm only just in. It smells lovely."

He did not wait for the final word, his hand wrapped in his handkerchief had found the main switch again.

"One, two . . . three," he said with horrible prosaicness and pulled it down.

From the wall socket behind him there was a single spluttering flare as the fuse went and then silence.

All round Ronald it was so quiet that he could hear the pulses in his own body, the faraway tick of a clock at the bottom of the stairs, the dreary buzzing of a fly imprisoned against the window glass and, from the garden next door, the drone of a mower as the heavy, fresh-faced man who had moved there, performed his weekly chore shaving the little green lawn. But from the bathroom there was no sound at all.

After a while he crept back along the passage and tapped at the door.

"Edyth?"

No. There was no response, no sound, nothing.

"Edyth?" he said again.

31

The silence was complete and, after a minute he straightened his back and let out a deep sighing breath.

Almost at once he was keyed up again in preparing for the second phase. As he knew well, this next was tricky period. The discovery of the body had got to be made but not too soon. He had made that mistake about Dorothy's 'accident' and had actually been asked by the local inspector why he had taken alarm so soon, but he had kept his head and the dangerous moment had flickered past. This time he had made up his mind to make it half an hour before he began to hammer loudly at the door, then to shout for a neighbour and finally to force the lock. He had planned to stroll out to buy an evening paper in the interim, shouting his intention to do so to Edyth from the front step for any passer-by to hear, but as he walked back along the landing he knew there was something else he was going to do first.

Edyth's leather writing-case in which she kept all her private papers was in the bottom of her soft-topped canvas hatbox. She had really believed he had not known of its existence, he reflected bitterly. It was locked, as he had discovered when he had at last located it, and he had not prized the catch for fear of putting her on her guard, but now there was nothing to stop him.

He went softly into the bedroom and opened the wardrobe door. The case was exactly where he had last seen it, plump and promising, and his hands closed over it gratefully. The catch was a little more difficult than he had expected but he got it open at last and the orderly contents of the leather box came into view. At first sight it was almost satisfactory, far better than he had anticipated. There were bundles of savings certificates, one or two thick envelopes whose red seals suggested the offices of lawyers and, on top, ready for the taking, one of those familiar blue books which the Post Office issues to its savings bank clients.

He opened it with shaking fingers and fluttered through the pages. Two thousand. The sum made him whistle. Two thousand eight hundred and fifty. She must have paid in a decent dividend there. Two thousand nine hundred. Then a drop as she had drawn out a hundred pounds for her trousseau. Two thousand eight hundred. He thought that

32

was the final entry but on turning the page saw that there was yet one other recorded transaction. It was less than a week old. He remembered the book coming back through the mail and how clever she had thought she had been in smuggling the envelope out of sight. He glanced at the written words and figures idly at first but then as his heart jolted in sudden panic stared at them, his eyes prominent and glazed. She had taken almost all of it out. There it was in black and white: *September 4th Withdrawal Two thousand seven hundred and ninety-eight pounds.*

His first thought was that the money must still be there, in hundred-pound notes perhaps in one of the envelopes. He tore through them hastily, forgetting all caution in his anxiety. Papers, letters, certificates fell on the floor in confusion.

The envelope, addressed to himself, pulled him up short. It was new and freshly blotted, the name inscribed in Edyth's own unexpectedly firm hand, Ronald Torbay, Esqre.

He wrenched it open and smoothed the single sheet of bond paper within. The date, he noted in amazement, was only two days old.

'Dear Ronald,

If you ever get this I am afraid it will prove a dreadful shock to you. For a long time I have been hoping that it might not be necessary to write it but now your behaviour has forced me to face some very unpleasant possibilities.

I am afraid, Ronald, that in some ways you are very old-fashioned. Had it not occurred to you that any homely middle-aged woman who has been swept into hasty marriage to a stranger, must, unless she is a perfect idiot, be just a little suspicious and touchy on the subject of *baths*?

Your predecessor James Joseph Smith and his Brides are not entirely forgotten, you know.

Frankly, I did not want to suspect you. For a long time I thought I was in love with you, but when you persuaded me to make my will on our wedding day I could not help wondering, and then as soon as you started fussing about the bathroom in this house I thought I had better do
33

something about it rather quickly. I am old-fashioned too, so I went to the police.

Have you noticed that the people who have moved in to the house next door have never tried to speak to you? We thought it best that I should merely talk to the woman over the garden wall, and it is she who has shewn me the two cuttings from old provincial newspapers each about women who met with fatal accidents in bubble-baths soon after their marriages. In each case there was a press snapshot of the husband taken at the funeral. They are not very clear but as soon as I saw them I realized that it was my duty to agree to the course suggested to me by the inspector who has been looking for a man answering that description for three years, ever since the two photographs were brought to his notice by your poor second wife's brother.

What I am trying to say is this: if you should ever lose me, Ronald, out of the bathroom I mean, you will find that I have gone out over the roof and am sitting in my dressing-gown in the kitchen next door. I was a fool to marry you but not quite such a fool as you assumed. Women may be silly but they are not stupid as they used to be. We are picking up the idea, Ronald.

Yours, Edyth

P.S. On re-reading this note I see that in my nervous-ness I have forgotten to mention that the new people next door are not a married couple but Detective Constable Batsford of the C.I.D. and his assistant, Policewoman Richards. The police assure me that there cannot be sufficient evidence to convict you if you are not permitted to attempt the crime again. That is why I am forcing myself to be brave and to play my part, for I am very sorry for those other poor wives of yours, Ronald. They must have found you as fascinating as I did.'

With his slit mouth twisted into an abominable 'O', Ronald Torbay raised haggard eyes from the letter.

The house was still quiet and even the whine of the mower in the next door garden had ceased. In the hush he heard a sudden clatter as the back door burst open and heavy footsteps raced through the hall and up the stairs towards him.

34

THE VILLA *MARIE CELESTE*

The newspapers were calling the McGill house in Chestnut Grove 'the villa *Marie Celeste*' before Chief Inspector Charles Luke noticed the similarity between the two mysteries, and that so shook him that he telephoned Albert Campion and asked him to come over.

They met in the Sun, a discreet pub in the suburban High Street, and stood talking in the small bar-parlour which was deserted at that time of day just after opening in the evening.

"The two stories *are* alike," Luke said, picking up his drink. He was at the height of his career then, a dark, muscular cockney, high cheek-boned and packed with energy and as usual he talked nineteen to the dozen, forcing home his points with characteristic gestures of his long hands. "I read the rehash of the *Marie Celeste* in the *Courier* this morning and it took me to the fair. Except that she was a ship and twenty-nine Chestnut Grove is a semi-detached suburban house, the two desertion stories are virtually the same, even to the half-eaten breakfast left on the table in each case. It's uncanny, Campion."

The quiet, fair man in the horn rims stood listening affably as was his habit. As usual he looked vague and probably ineffectual: in the shadier corners of Europe it was said of him that no one ever took him seriously until just about two hours too late. At the moment he appeared faintly amused. The thumping force of Luke's enthusiasm always tickled him.

"You think you know what has happened to the McGill couple, then?" he ventured.

"The hell I do!" The policeman opened his small black eyes to their widest extent. "I tell you it's the same tale as the classic mystery of the *Marie Celeste*. They've gone like a stain under a bleach. One minute they were having breakfast together, like every other married couple for miles and the next they were gone, sunk without trace."

Mr. Campion hesitated. He looked a trifle embarrassed. "As I recall the story of the *Marie Celeste* it had the simple charm of the utterly incredible," he said at last. "Let's see, she was a brig brought into Gib by a prize crew of innocent sailor-men, who had a wonderful tale to tell. According to them she was sighted in mid-ocean with all her sails set, her decks clean, her lockers tidy but not a soul on board. The details were fascinating. There were three cups of tea on the captain's table still warm to the touch, in his cabin. There was a cat asleep in the galley and a chicken ready for stewing in a pot on the stove." He sighed gently. "Quite beautiful," he said, "but witnesses also swore that with no one at the wheel she was still dead on course and that seemed a little much to the court of inquiry, who after kicking it about as long as they could, finally made the absolute minimum award."

Luke glanced at him sharply.

"That wasn't the *Courier*'s angle last night," he said. "They called it the 'world's favourite unsolved mystery'."

"So they did!" Mr. Campion was laughing. "Because nobody wants a prosaic explanation of fraud and greed. The mystery of the *Marie Celeste* is just the prime example of the story which really is a bit too good to spoil, don't you think?"

"I don't know. It's not an idea which occurred to me," Luke sounded slightly irritated. "I was merely quoting the main outlines of the two tales: eighteen seventy-two and the *Marie Celeste* is a bit before my time. On the other hand, twenty-nine Chestnut Grove is definitely my business and you can take it from me no witness is being allowed to

36

use his imagination in this inquiry. Just give your mind to the details, Campion. . . ." He set his tumbler down on the bar and began ticking off each item on his fingers.

"Consider the couple," he said. "They sound normal enough. Peter McGill was twenty-eight and his wife Maureen a year younger. They'd been married three years and got on well together. For the first two years they had to board with his mother while they were waiting for a house. That didn't work out too well so they rented a couple of rooms from Maureen's married sister. That lasted for six months and they got the offer of this house in Chestnut Grove."

"Any money troubles?" Mr. Campion inquired.

"No." The Chief clearly thought the fact remarkable. "Peter seems to be the one lad in the family who had nothing to grumble about. His firm—they're locksmiths in Aldgate; he's in the office—are very pleased with him. His reputation is that he keeps within his income and he's recently had a raise. I saw the senior partner this morning and he's genuinely worried, poor old boy. He liked the young man and had nothing but praise for him."

"What about the girl?"

"She's another good type. Steady, reliable, kept on at her job as a typist until a few months ago when her husband decided she should retire to enjoy the new house and maybe raise a family. She certainly did her housework. The place is like a new pin now and they've been gone six days."

For the first time Mr. Campion's eyes darkened with interest.

"Forgive me," he said, "but the police seem to have come into this disappearance very quickly. Surely six days is no time for a couple to be missing. What are you looking for, Charles? A body?"

Luke shrugged. "Not officially," he said, "but one doesn't have to have a nasty mind to wonder. We came into the inquiry quickly because the alarm was given quickly. The circumstnces were extraordinary and the family got the wind up. That's the explanation of that." He paused and stood for a moment hesitating. "Come along and have a look," he said, and his restless personality was a live thing in the confined space. "We'll come back and have the other

37

half of this drink after you've seen the set-up—I've got something really recherché here. I want you in on it."

Mr. Campion, as obliging as ever, followed him out into the network of trim little streets lined with bandbox villas each set in a nest of flower garden. Luke was still talking.

"It's just down the end here and along to the right," he said, nodding towards the end of the avenue. "I'll give you the outline as we go. On the twelfth of June last Bertram Heskith, a somewhat overbright specimen who is the husband of Maureen's elder sister—the one they lodged with two doors down the road before number twenty-nine became available—dropped round to see them as he usually did just before eight in the morning. He came in at the back door which was standing open and found a half-eaten breakfast for two on the table in the smart new kitchen. No one was about so he pulled up a chair and sat down to wait." Luke's long hands were busy as he talked and Mr. Campion could almost see the bright little room with the built-in furniture and the pot of flowers on the window ledge.

"Bertram is a toy salesman and one of a large family," Luke went on. "He's out of a job at the moment but is not despondent. He's a talkative man, a fraction too big for his clothes now and he likes his noggin but he's sharp enough. He'd have noticed at once if there had been anything at all unusual to see. As it was he poured himself a cup of tea out of the pot under the cosy and sat there waiting, reading the newspaper which he found lying open on the floor by Peter McGill's chair. Finally it occurred to him that the house was very quiet and he put his head round the door and shouted up the stairs. When he got no reply he went up and found the bed unmade, the bathroom still warm and wet with steam and Maureen's everyday hat and coat lying on a chair with her familiar brown handbag upon it. Bertram came down, examined the rest of the house and went on out into the garden. Maureen had been doing the laundry before breakfast. There was linen, almost dry, on the line and a basket lying on the green under it but that was all. The little rectangle of land was quite empty."

As his deep voice ceased he gave Campion a sidelong glance.

"And that my lad is that," he said. "Neither Peter nor
38

Maureen have been seen since. When they didn't show up Bertram consulted the rest of the family and after waiting for two days they went to the police."

"Really?" Mr. Campion was fascinated despite himself. "Is that all you've got?"

"Not quite, but the rest is hardly helpful," Luke sounded almost gratified. "Wherever they are they're not in the house or garden. If they walked out they did it without being seen which is more of a feat than you'd expect because they had interested relatives and friends all round them and the only things that anyone is sure they took with them are a couple of clean linen sheets. 'Fine winding sheets' one lady called them."

Mr. Campion's brows rose behind his big spectacles.

"That's a delicate touch," he said. "I take it there is no suggestion of foul play? It's always possible, of course."

"Foul play is becoming positively common in London, I don't know what the old town is up to," Luke said gloomily, "but this set-up sounds healthy and happy enough. The McGills seem to have been pleasant normal young people and yet there are one or two little items which make you wonder. As far as we can find out Peter was not on his usual train to the city that morning but we have one witness, a third cousin of his, who says she followed him up the street from his house to the corner just as she often did on weekday mornings. At the top she went one way and she assumed that he went the other as usual but no one else seems to have seen him and she's probably mistaken. Well now, here we are. Stand here for a minute."

He paused on the pavement of a narrow residential street, shady with plane trees and lined with pairs of pleasant little houses, stone-dashed and bay-windowed, in a style which is now a little out of fashion.

"The next gate along here belongs to the Heskiths'," he went on, lowering his voice a tone or so. "We'll walk rather quickly past there because we don't want any more help from Bertram at the moment. He's a good enough chap but he sees himself as the watchdog of his sister-in-law's property and the way he follows me round makes me self-conscious. His house is number twenty-five—the odd numbers are on this side—twenty-nine is two doors along. Now number thirty-one which is actually adjoined to

39

twenty-nine on the other side is closed. The old lady who owns it is in hospital; but in thirty-three there live two sisters, who are aunts of Peter's. They moved there soon after the young couple. One is a widow." Luke sketched a portly juglike silhouette with his hands, "And the other is a spinster who looks like two yards of pump-water. Both are very interested in their nephew and his wife but whereas the widow is prepared to take a more or less benevolent view of her young relations, the spinster, Miss Dove, is apt to be critical. She told me Maureen didn't know how to lay out the money and I think that from time to time she'd had a few words with the girl on the subject. I heard about the 'fine linen sheets' from her. Apparently she'd told Maureen off about buying anything so expensive but the young bride had saved up for them and she'd got them." He sighed. "Women are like that," he said. "They get a yen for something and they want it and that's all there is to it. Miss Dove says she watched Maureen hanging them out on the line early in the morning of the day she vanished. There's one upstairs window in her house from which she can just see part of the garden at twenty-nine if she stands on a chair and clings to the sash." He grinned. "She happened to be doing just that at about half past six on the day the McGills disappeared and she insists she saw them hanging there. She recognized them by the crochet on the top edge. They're certainly not in the house now. Miss Dove hints delicately that I should search Bertram's home for them."

Mr. Campion's pale eyes had narrowed and his mouth was smiling.

"It's a peach of a story," he murmured. "A sort of circumstantial history of the utterly impossible. The whole thing just can't have happened. How very odd, Charles. Did anyone else see Maureen that morning? Could she have walked out of the front door and come up the street with the linen over her arm unnoticed? I am not asking would she but could she?"

"No." The Chief made no bones about it. "Even had she wanted to, which is unlikely, it's virtually impossible. There are the cousins opposite, you see. They live in the house with the red geraniums over there directly in front of number twenty-nine. They are some sort of distant relatives of Peter's. A father, mother, five marriageable daughters—

it was one of them who says she followed Peter up the road that morning. Also there's an old Irish granny who sits up in bed in the window of the front room all day. She's not very reliable—for instance she can't remember if Peter came out of the house at his usual time that day—but she would have noticed if Maureen had done so. No one saw Maureen that morning except Miss Dove, who, as I told you, watched her hanging linen on the line. The paper comes early; the milkman heard her washing machine from the scullery door when he left his bottles but he did not see her."

"What about the postman?"

"He's no help. He's a new man on the round and can't even remember if he called at twenty-nine. It's a long street and, as he says, the houses are all alike. He gets to twenty-nine about seven-twenty-five and seldom meets anybody at that door. He wouldn't know the McGills if he saw them, anyhow. Come on in, Campion, take a look round and see what you think."

Mr. Campion followed his friend down the road and up a narrow garden path to where a uniformed man stood on guard before the front door. He was aware of a flutter behind the curtains in the house opposite as they appeared and a tall thin woman with a determinedly blank expression walked down the path of the next house but one and bowed to Luke meaningly as she paused at her gate for an instant before going back.

"Miss Dove," said Luke unnecessarily, as he opened the door. Number twenty-nine had few surprises for Mr. Campion. It was almost exactly as he had imagined it. The furniture in the hall and front room was new and sparse, leaving plenty of room for future acquisitions but the kitchen-dining-room was well lived in and conveyed a distinct personality. Someone without much money, who had yet liked nice things, had lived there. He or she, and he suspected it was a she, had been generous, too, despite her economies, if the 'charitable' calendars and the packets of gipsy pegs bought at the door were any guide. The breakfast-table had been left as Bertram Heskith had found it and his cup was still there beside a third plate.

The thin man wandered through the house without comment, Luke at his heels. The scene was just as stated.

41

There was no sign of hurried flight, no evidence of packing, no hint of violence. The dwelling was not so much untidy as in the process of being used. There was a pair of man's pyjamas on the stool in the bathroom and a towel hung over the basin to dry. The woman's handbag on the coat on a chair in the bedroom contained the usual miscellany, and two pounds three shillings, some coppers and a set of keys. Mr. Campion looked at everything, the clothes hanging neatly in the cupboard, the dead flowers still in the vases but the only item which appeared to hold his attention was the wedding group which he found in a silver frame on the dressing-table. He stood before it for a long time, apparently fascinated, yet it was not a remarkable picture. As is occasionally the case in such photographs the two central figures were the least dominant characters in the entire group of vigorous, laughing guests. Maureen timid and gentle, with a slender figure and big dark eyes, looked positively scared of her own bridesmaids while Peter, although solid and with a determined chin, had a panic-stricken look about him which contrasted with the cheerful assured grin of the best man.

"That's Heskith," said Luke. "You can see the sort of chap he is—not one of nature's great outstanding success types but not the man to go imagining things. When he says he felt the two were there that morning, perfectly normal and happy as usual, I believe him."

"No Miss Dove here?" said Campion still looking at the group.

"No. That's her sister though deputizing for the bride's mother. And that's the girl from opposite, the one who thinks she saw Peter go up the road." Luke put a forefinger over the face of the third bridesmaid. "There's another sister here and the rest are cousins. I understand the pic doesn't do the bride justice. Everybody says she was a good-natured pretty girl. . . ." He corrected himself. "Is, I mean."

"The bridegroom looks a reasonable type to me," murmured Mr. Campion. "A little apprehensive, perhaps."

"I wonder." Luke spoke thoughtfully. "The Heskiths had another photo of him and perhaps it's more marked in that, but don't you think there's a sort of ruthlessness in that face, Campion? It's not quite recklessness, more like

42

decision. I knew a sergeant in the war with a face like that. He was mild enough in the ordinary way but once something shook him he acted fast and pulled no punches whatever. Well, that's neither here nor there. Come and inspect the linen line, and then, Heaven help you, you'll know just about as much as I do."

He led the way out to the back and stood for a moment on the concrete path which ran under the kitchen window separating the house from the small rectangle of shorn grass which was all there was of a garden.

A high rose hedge, carefully trained on rustic fencing, separated it from the neighbours on the right; at the bottom there was a garden shed and a few fruit trees and, on the left, greenery in the neglected garden of the old lady who was in hospital had grown up high so that a green wall screened the lawn from all but the prying eyes of Miss Dove, who, even at that moment, Mr. Campion suspected, was standing on a chair and clinging to a sash to peer at them.

Luke indicated the empty line slung across the green. "I had the linen brought in," he said. "The Heskiths were worrying and there seemed no earthly point in leaving it out to rot."

"What's in the shed?"

"A spade and fork and a hand-mower," said the Chief promptly. "Come and look. The floor is beaten earth and if it's been disturbed in thirty years I'll eat my ticket. I suppose we'll have to fetch it up in the end but we'll be wasting our time."

Mr. Campion went over and glanced into the tarred wooden hut. It was tidy and dusty and the floor was dry and hard. Outside a dilapidated pair of steps leaned against the six-foot brick wall which marked the boundary.

Mr. Campion tried them gingerly. They held, but not as it were with any real assurance, and he climbed up to look over the wall to the narrow path which separated it from the tarred fence of the rear garden of a house in the next street.

"That's an odd right of way," Luke said. "It leads down between the two residential roads. These suburban places are not very matey, you know. Half the time one street doesn't know the next. Chestnut Grove is classier than

Philpott Avenue which runs parallel with it."

Mr. Campion descended, dusting his hands. He was grinning and his eyes were dancing.

"I wonder if anybody there noticed her," he said. "She must have been carrying the sheets, you know."

The chief turned round slowly and stared at him.

"You're not suggesting that she simply walked down here over the wall and out! In the clothes she'd been washing in? It's crazy. Why should she? Did her husband go with her?"

"No. I think he went down Chestnut Grove as usual, doubled back down this path as soon as he came to the other end of it near the station, picked up his wife and went off with her through Philpott Avenue to the bus stop. They'd only got to get to the Broadway to find a cab, you see."

Luke's dark face still wore an expression of complete incredulity.

"But for Pete's sake *why*?" he demanded. "Why clear out in the middle of breakfast on a wash-day morning? Why take the sheets? Young couples can do the most unlikely things but there are limits. They didn't take their savings bank books you know. There's not much in them but they're still there in the writing desk in the front room. What are you getting at, Campion?"

The thin man walked slowly back on to the patch of grass.

"I expect the sheets were dry and she'd folded them into the basket before breakfast," he began slowly. "As she ran out of the house they were lying there and she couldn't resist taking them with her. The husband must have been irritated with her when he saw her with them but people are like that. When they're running from a fire they save the oddest things."

"But she wasn't running from a fire."

"Wasn't she!" Mr. Campion laughed. "There were several devouring flames all round them just then I should have thought. Listen, Charles. If the postman called he reached the house at seven-twenty-five. I think he did call and with an ordinary plain business envelope which was too commonplace for him to remember. It would be the

44

plainest of plain envelopes. Well, who was due at seven-thirty?"

"Bert Heskith. I told you."

"Exactly. So there were five minutes in which to escape. Five minutes for a determined, resourceful man like Peter McGill to act promptly. His wife was generous and easy going, remember, and so, thanks to that decision which you yourself noticed in his face, he rose to the occasion. He had only five minutes, Charles, to escape all those powerful personalities with their jolly, avid faces, whom we saw in the wedding group. They were all living remarkably close to him, ringing him round as it were, so that it was a ticklish business to elude them. He went the front way so that the kindly watchful eye would see him as usual and not be alarmed. There wasn't time to take anything at all and it was only because Maureen flying through the back garden to escape the back way saw the sheets in the basket and couldn't resist her treasures that they salvaged them. She wasn't quite so ruthless as Peter. She had to take something from the old life however glistening were the prospects for—" He broke off abruptly. Chief Inspector Luke, with dawning comprehension in his eyes, was already half-way to the gate on the way to the nearest police telephone box.

Mr. Campion was in his own sitting-room in Bottle Street, Piccadilly, later that evening when Luke called. He came in jauntily, his black eyes dancing with amusement.

"It wasn't the Irish Sweep but the Football Pools," he said. "I got the details out of the promoters. They've been wondering what to do ever since the story broke. They're in touch with the McGills, of course, but Peter had taken every precaution to ensure secrecy and is insisting on his rights. He must have known his wife's tender heart and have made up his mind what he'd do if ever a really big win came off. The moment he got the letter telling him of his luck he put the plan into practice." He paused and shook his head admiringly. "I hand it to him," he said. "Seventy-five thousand pounds is like a nice fat chicken, plenty and more for two but only a taste for the whole of a very big family."

"What will you do?"

"Us? The police? Oh, officially we're baffled. We shall

45

retire gracefully. It's not our business." He sat down and raised the glass his host handed to him.

"Here's to the mystery of the Villa *Marie Celeste*," he said. "I had a blind spot for it. It foxed me completely. Good luck to them, though. You know, Campion, you had a point when you said that the really insoluble mystery is the one which no one can bring himself to spoil. What put you on to it?"

"I suspect the charm of relatives who call at seven-thirty in the morning," said Mr. Campion simply.

THE PSYCHOLOGIST

Did you ever see a man set light to money? Real money: using it as a spill to light a cigarette, just to show off? I have. And that's why, when you used the word 'psychologist' just now, a little fish leapt in my stomach and my throat felt suddenly tight. Perhaps you feel I'm too squeamish. I wonder.

I was born in this street. When I was a girl I went to school just round the corner and later on, after I'd served my apprenticeships in the big dress houses here and in France, I took over the lease of this old house and turned it into the smart little gown shop you see now. It was when I came back to do that I saw the change in Louise.

When we went to school together she was something of a beauty with streaming yellow hair and the cockney child's ferocious knowing grin. All we kids used to tease her because she was better looking than we were. The street was just the same then as it is now. Adelaide Street, Soho. Shabby and untidy and yet romantic, with every other doorway in its straggling length leading to a restaurant of some sort. You can eat in every language of the world here. Some places are as expensive as the Ritz and others are as cheap as Louise's papa's Le Coq Au Vin with its one dining-room and its single palm in the white-washed tub outside.

Louise had an infant sister and a father who could hardly speak English but who looked at one with proud foreign eyes from under arched brows. I was hardly aware that she had a mother until a day when that grey woman emerged from the cellar under the restaurant to put her foot down and Louise, instead of coming with me into the enchantment of the workshops, had to go down into the kitchens of the Coq.

For a long time we used to exchange birthday cards since neither of us were writers exactly and then even that contact dropped, but I never forgot her and when I came back to the street I was glad to see the name 'Frosne' still under the sign of the Le Coq Au Vin. The place looked much brighter than I remembered it and appeared to be doing fair business. Certainly it no longer suffered so much by comparison with the expensive Glass Mountain which Adelbert kept opposite. There is no restaurant bearing that name in this street now, nor is there a *restaurateur* called Adelbert, but diners-out of a few years ago may remember him if not for his food at least for his conceit and the two rolls of white fat which were his eyelids.

I went in to see Louise as soon as I had a moment to spare. It was a shock, for I hardly recognized her, but she knew me at once and came out from behind the cash desk to give me a welcome which was pathetic. It was like seeing thin ice cracking all over her face as if by taking her unawares I'd torn aside a barrier.

I heard all the news in the first ten minutes. Both the old people were dead. The mother had gone first, but the father had not died until some years later and, meantime, Louise had carried everything including his vagaries on her shoulders, or that was what I gathered. She did not complain. Things were a bit easier now. Violetta, the little sister, had a young man who was proving his worth by working there for a pittance, learning the business.

It was a success story of a sort, but I thought that Louise had paid pretty dearly for it. She was a year younger than I was, but she looked as if life had already burned out over her, leaving her hard and polished like a bone in the sun. The gold had gone out of her hair and even the thick lashes looked bleached and tow coloured. There was something else there, too: something hunted which I did not understand at all.

I soon fell into the habit of going in to have supper with her once a week and at these little meals she used to talk. It was evident that she never opened her lips on any personal matter to anyone else, but for some reason she trusted me. Even so, it took me months to find out what was the matter with her. When it came out, it was obvious.

The Coq Au Vin had a debt hanging over it. In Mama Frosne's time the family had never owed a penny, but in the few years between her death and his own, Papa Frosne had somehow contrived not only to borrow the best part of four thousand pounds from Adelbert of the Glass Mountain but to lose every halfpenny of it in half a dozen senile little schemes.

Louise was paying it back in five-hundred-pound instalments. As she first told me about it I happened to glance into her eyes and I saw there one sort of hell. It has always seemed to me that there are people who can stand debt in the same way that some men can stand drink. It may undermine their constitutions, but it does not make them openly shabby. Yet, to others, debt does something unspeakable. The Devil was certainly having his money's worth out of Louise.

I did not argue with her, of course. It was not my place. I sat there registering sympathy until she surprised me by saying, suddenly:

"It's not so much the work and the worry, nor even the skimping I really hate so much. It's the awful set-out when I have to pay him. I dread that."

"You're too sensitive," I told her. "Once the money's in the bank you can put the cheque in the envelope for once, can't you?"

She glanced at me with an odd expression in her eyes; they were almost lead coloured between the bleached lashes.

"You don't know Adelbert," she said. "He's a queer bit of work. I have to pay him in cash and he likes to make a regular little performance of it. He comes here by appointment, has a drink and likes to have Violetta as a witness by way of audience. If I don't show him I'm a bit upset he goes on talking until I do. Calls himself a psychologist; says he knows everything I'm thinking."

"That's not what I'd call him," I said. I was disgusted. I hate that sort of thing.

Louise hesitated. "I have known him burn most of the money for effect," she admitted. "There, in front of me."

I felt my eyebrows rising up into my hair. "Get away!" I exclaimed. "The man's not right in the head."

She sighed, and I looked at her sharply.

"Why, he's twenty years older than you are, Louise," I began. "Surely there wasn't ever anything between you? You know . . . like *that*?"

"No. No, there wasn't, Ellie, honestly." I believed her: she was quite frank about it and as puzzled as I was. "He did speak to Papa once about me when I was a kid. Asked for me formally, you know, as they still did round here at that time. I never heard what the old man said, but he never minced words, did he? All I can remember is that I was kept downstairs out of sight for a bit, and after that Mama treated me as if I'd been up to something, but I hadn't even spoken to the man—he wasn't a person a young girl *would* notice, was he? That was years ago, though. I suppose Adelbert could have remembered it all that time, but it's not reasonable, is it?"

"That's the one thing it certainly isn't!" I told her. "Next time I'll be the witness."

"Adelbert would enjoy that," she said, grimly. "I don't know that I won't hold you to it. You ought to see him!"

We let the subject drop, but I couldn't get it out of my mind. I could see them both from behind the curtains in my shop window and it seemed that whenever I looked out there was the tight-lipped silent woman, scraping every farthing and there was the fat man watching her from his doorway across the street, secret satisfaction on his sallow face.

In the end it got on my nerves and when that happens I have to talk, I can't help it.

There was no one in the street I dared to gossip to, but I did mention the tale to a customer. She was a woman called Mrs. Marten whom I'd particularly liked ever since she'd come in to inquire after the first model I ever put in my shop window. I made most of her clothes and she had

50

recommended me to one or two ladies in the district where she lived, which was up at Hampstead, nice and far away from Soho. I was fitting her one day when she happened to say something about men and the things they'll stoop to if their pride's been hurt and before I'd realized what I was doing I'd come out with the little story Louise had told me. I didn't mention names, of course, but I may have conveyed that it was all taking place in this street. Mrs. Marten was a nice gentle little thing with a sweet face, and she was shocked.

"But how awful," she kept saying, "how perfectly awful. To burn it in front of her after she's worked so hard for it. He must be quite insane. Dangerous."

"Oh, well," I said, hastily, "it's his money by the time he does that and I don't suppose he destroys much of it. Only enough to upset my friend." I was sorry I'd spoken. I hadn't expected her to be quite so horrified. "It just shows you how other people live." I finished and hoped she'd drop the subject. She didn't, however. The idea seemed to fascinate her even more than it had me. I couldn't get her to leave it alone and she chattered about it all through the fitting. Then, just as she was putting on her hat to leave, she suddenly said; "Miss Kaye, I've just thought. My brother-in-law is Assistant Commissioner at Scotland Yard. He might be able to think of some way of stopping that fearful man torturing that poor little woman you told me about. Shall I mention it to him?"

"Oh, no! Pray don't!" I exclaimed. "She'd never forgive me. There's nothing the police could do to help her. I do hope you'll forgive me for saying so, Madam, but I do hope you won't do anything of the sort."

She seemed rather hurt, but she gave me her word. I had no faith in it, naturally. Once a woman has considered talking about a thing it's as good as out. I was quite upset for a day or two because the last thing I wanted was to get involved, but nothing happened and I'd just started to breath again, so to speak, when I had to go down to Vaughan's, the big wholesale trimming house, at the back of Regent Street. I was coming out with my parcels when a man came up to me. I knew he was a dick; he was the type, with a very short haircut, a brown raincoat and that look of being in a settled job and yet not in anything particular. He

51

asked me to come along to his office and I couldn't refuse. I realized he'd been tailing me until I was somewhere right away from Adelaide Street where someone would have noticed him at once.

He took me to his boss who was another definite policeman. Quite a nice old boy in his way, on nobody's side but his own, as is the way with coppers, but I got the impression that he was square on the level, which is more than some people are. He introduced himself as Detective Inspector Cumberland, made me sit down and sent out for a cup of tea for me. Then he asked me about Louise.

I got into a panic because when you're in business in Adelaide Street you're in business and the last thing you can afford is to get into trouble with your neighbours. I denied everything, of course, said I hardly knew the woman.

Cumberland wouldn't have that. I must say he knew how to handle me. He kept me going over and over my own affairs until I was thankful to speak about anything else. In the end I gave way because, after all, nobody was doing anything criminal as far as I could see. I told him all I knew, letting him draw it out bit by bit and when I'd finished he laughed at me, peering at me with little bright eyes under brows which were as thick as a bit of silver fox fur.

"Well," he said, "there's nothing so terrible in all that, is there?"

"No," I said, sulkily. He made me feel a fool.

He sighed and leant back in his chair.

"You run away and forget this little interview," he told me. "But just so that you don't start imagining things let me point out something to you. The police are in business, too, in a way. In their own business, that is, and when an officer in my position gets an inquiry from higher up he's got to investigate it, hasn't he? He may think the crime of destroying currency, 'defacing the coin of the realm' we call it, is not very serious compared with some of the things he's got to deal with, but all the same if he's asked about it he's got to make some sort of move and make some sort of report. Then it can all be . . . er . . . filed and forgotten, can't it?"

"Yes," I agreed, very relieved. "Yes, I suppose it can."

52

They showed me out and that seemed to be the end of it. I'd had my lesson though, and I never opened my lips again on the subject to anybody. It quite put me off Louise and for a time I avoided her. I made excuses and didn't go and eat with her. However, I could still see her through the window sitting at the cash desk and I could still see Adelbert peering at her from his doorway.

For a month or two everything went on quietly. Then I heard that Violetta's boy had got tired of the restaurant business and had taken a job up north. He had given the girl the chance of marrying and going with him and they'd gone almost without saying goodbye. I was sorry for Louise; I had to go and see her. She took it very well and was pretty lucky really, for she got a new waiter almost at once and her number one girl in the kitchen stood by her and they managed. She was very much alone though, and so I drifted back into the habit of going in there for a meal once a week. I paid, of course, but she used to come and have hers with me.

I kept her off the subject of Adelbert, but one day near the Midsummer's quarter day she referred to him outright and asked me straight if I remembered I'd promised to be witness on the next pay day. Since Violetta had gone she'd mentioned me to Adelbert, she said, and he'd seemed pleased.

Well, I couldn't get out of it without hurting her feelings and since nothing seemed to turn on it I agreed. I don't pretend I wasn't curious: it was a love affair without any love at all, as far as I could see.

The time for payment was fixed for half an hour after closing time on Midsummer's Day and when I slipped down the street to the corner the blinds of the Coq were closed and the door was shut. The new waiter was taking a breath of air on the basement steps and let me in through the kitchens. I went up the dark service stairs and found the two of them sitting there waiting for me.

The dining-room was dark except for a single shaded bulb over the alcove table where they sat and I had a good look at them as I came down the room. They made an extraordinary pair.

I don't know if you've ever seen one of those fat little Chinese gods whom people keep on their mantelshelves to bring them luck? They are all supposed to be laughing, but some only pretend and the folds of their china faces are stiff and merciless for all the upward lines. Adelbert reminded me of one of those. He always wore a black dinner jacket for work, but it was very thin and very loose. It came into my mind that when he took it off it must have hung like a gown. He was sitting swathed in it, looking squat and flabby against the white panelling of the wall.

Louise, on the other hand, in her black dress and tight woollen cardigan, was as spare and hard as a withered branch. Just for an instant I realized how mad she must make him. There was nothing yielding or shrinking about her. She wasn't giving any more than she was forced, not an inch. I never saw anything so unbending in my life. She stood up to him all the time.

There was a bottle of Dubonnet on the table and they each had a small glass. When I appeared Louise poured one for me.

The whole performance was very formal. Although they'd both lived in London all their lives the French blood in both was very apparent. They each shook hands with me and Adelbert kicked the chair out for me if he only made a pretence of rising.

Louise had the big bank envelope in her black bag which she nursed as if it was a pet, and as soon as I'd taken a sip of my drink she produced it and pushed it across the table to the man.

"Five hundred," she said. "The receipt slip is in there, made out. Perhaps you'd sign it, please."

There was not a word out of place, you see, but you could have cut the atmosphere with a knife. She hated him and he was getting his due and nothing else.

He sat looking at her for a moment with a steady, fishy gaze, waiting for something, just a flicker of regret or resentment, I suppose; but he got nothing and presently he took the envelope between his sausage fingers and thumbed it open. The five crisp packages fell out on the white tablecloth. I looked at them with interest as one does a money. It wasn't a fortune, of course, but to people like myself and Louise who have to earn every penny the hard way it was a tidy sum representing hours and hours of hard graft, scheming and self privation. I didn't like the way the

54

man's fingers played over it and the sneaking spark of sympathy I'd begun to feel for him died abruptly. I knew then that if he'd had his way and married her when she was little more than a child all those years ago he would have treated her abominably. He was a cruel so-and-so; it took him that way.

I glanced at Louise and saw she was unmoved. She just sat there, her hands folded, waiting for her receipt.

Adelbert began to count the money. I've always admired the way tellers in banks handle notes, but the way Adelbert did it opened my eyes. He went through them like a gambler goes through a pack of cards, as if each individual item is alive and part of his hand. He loved the stuff, you could see it.

"All correct," he said, at last, and put the bundles in his inside pocket. Then he signed the receipt and handed it to her. She took it and put it in her bag. I assumed that it was the end of it and wondered what the fuss was about. I raised my glass to Louise who acknowledged it and was getting up, but Adelbert stopped me.

"Wait," he said. "We must have a cigarette and perhaps another little glass—if Louise can afford it."

He smiled, but she didn't. She poured him another glass and sat there stolidly waiting for him to drink it. He was in no hurry. Presently, he took the money out again and laid a fat hand over it as he passed his case round. I took a cigarette, Louise didn't. There was one of those metal match stands on the table and he bent forward to take and strike one, I moved too, for him to give me a light, but he laughed and drew back.

"This gives it a better flavour," he said, and peeling off one note from the top wad he lit it and offered me the flame. I had seen what was coming so I didn't show any surprise. If Louise could keep a poker face so could I. I watched it burn out though, and when he took another to light his own my eyes were on it.

That having failed, he started to talk. He spoke quite normally about the restaurant business and how hard times were and what a lot of work it meant getting up at dawn to get to the market with the chef. And then how customers liked to keep one up late at night, talking and dawdling as if there was never going to be a tomorrow. It was all directed at Louise, rubbing it in, holding her nose down to exactly what he was doing. She remained perfectly impassive, her eyes dark like lead, her mouth hard.

When that failed he got more personal. He said he remembered us both when we were girls and how work and worry had changed us. I was nettled, but it did not upset me much for it soon became quite obvious that he could not remember me at all. With Louise it was different, he remembered her all right, with something added.

"Your hair was like gold," he said, "and your eyes were blue as glass and you had a little soft wide mouth which was so gay. Where is it now, eh? Here." He patted the money, the old brute. "All here, Louise. I am a psychologist, I see these things. And what is it worth to me? Northing. Exactly nothing."

He was turning me cold. I stared at him fascinated and saw him suddenly take up a whole package of money and fluff it out until it looked like a lettuce. Louise neither blinked nor moved. She sat looking at him as if he was nothing, a passer-by in the street. No one at all. I'd turned my head to glance at her and missed seeing him strike the match so that when he lit the crisp leaves it took me off guard.

"Look out!" I said, involuntarily. "Mind what you're doing. Don't be a fool!"

He laughed like a wicked child, triumphant and delighted. "What about you, Louise, what do you say?"

She continued to look bored and they sat there silent, facing one another squarely. Meantime, of course, the money was blazing. No one seemed to notice it but me.

I was odd man out, the whole thing was nothing to do with me, perhaps that is why it was my control that snapped. There was no reason why it shouldn't, I mean.

Anyhow, I knocked the cash out of his hand. With a sudden movement I sent the whole hundred flying out of his grasp. All over the place it went, the floor, the table, everywhere. The room was alight with blazing notes.

He went after them like a lunatic, you wouldn't have thought a man so fat could move so fast.

It was the one which laddered my stocking which gave the game away. A spark burned the nylon and as I felt it go I looked down and then snatched the singed note, holding

56

it up into the light. We all saw the flaw in it at the same moment. The ink had run and there was a great streak through the middle like the veining in a marble slab.

There was a long silence and the first sound came not from us but from the service door. It opened and the new waiter, looking quite different now that he'd changed his coat for one with a dick's badge on it, came down the room followed by Inspector Cumberland.

They went up to Adelbert and the younger, heavier man put a hand on his shoulder. Cumberland ignored everything but the money. He stamped out the smouldering flames and gathered up the remains and the four untouched wads on the table. Then he smiled briefly.

"Got you, Adelbert. With it on you. We've been wondering who was passing slush in this street and when it came to our ears that someone was burning cash we thought we ought to look into it."

I was still only half comprehending and I held out the pound we'd been staring at.

"There's something wrong with this one," I said stupidly.

He took it from me and grunted.

"There's something pretty wrong with all these. Miss Frosne's money is safe in his pocket where you saw him put it. These are some of the gang's failures. Every maker of counterfeit has them; as a rule they never leave the printing-room. This one in particular is a shocker. I wonder he risked that even for burning. You didn't like wasting it, I suppose, Adelbert. What a careful soul you are."

"How did you find out?" Louise looked from them to me. She was still dazed, but suspicious.

Cumberland saved me:

"We're psychologists, too, Madam, we policemen," he said, laughing. "In our way."

LITTLE MISS KNOW-ALL

Mr. Albert Campion was drifting unobtrusively down the corridor towards Chief Inspector Luke's room at the Central Office when he first saw Melanie and he thought then that any young woman who could look quite so smugly pleased with herself was courting disillusionment.

At that time he was fully occupied with his own affairs but he noticed her particularly because of her smile. A clerk in uniform was showing her out of the building and she was trotting a little ahead of him, her spiked heels squeaking on the stone and her round hips rolling in her tight skirt. Campion supposed she was about twenty-five. She looked curved, petite and purposeful and appeared to be struggling to keep her expression strictly noncommittal but just as she came up with the lean and elegant man, whose pale eyes were so misleadingly blank behind his horn-rimmed spectacles, her inner satisfaction bubbled over. The small mouth in her greedy little face widened suddenly and a grin of pure triumph appeared and vanished. Mr. Campion glanced after her involuntarily and when he turned back he saw that Chief Inspector Charles Luke himself had appeared in his doorway and that he too was watching his departing visitor.

The Chief's dark face cleared as he caught sight of

Campion and his welcome was cordial. The two were old friends and had worked together on many occasions and although Luke who was a giant of a man was inclined to dwarf the thinner, fairer, Campion, he never made the mistake of underestimating the intelligence which lay behind the other man's gentle exterior. It was Mr. Campion who mentioned the girl as they went into the office together.

"A satisfied client, no doubt?" he suggested innocently.

Luke's face grew slowly savage. "I call her 'little Miss Know-All'," he said bitterly. "You recognize her, of course."

"Ought I to have done?" Mr. Campion looked puzzled. "The face is vaguely familiar but I can't place it. She makes me think of rabbit for some reason."

"Rabbit!" Luke's laugh was hollow. "You're on the track but a few thousand pounds out. That's the fur coat girl, Melanie the Mink. Did you see her on telly?"

"Ah!" The appropriate card in Mr. Campion's mental filing system popped up before him. "She won the main prize in the commercial quiz, the modern version of Kim's game, what do they call it now?"

"*Line of Vision*," Luke said. "The players wander round a whole curiosity shop of unlikely objects for four minutes and are then blindfolded and put into sound-proof booths. The winner is the one who can list the most items accurately from memory. One week's winner takes on a new team next session."

Campion nodded. "I remember it now," he said. "The standard became amazingly high. She won, did she? Her observation must be phenomenal."

"She's too clever by half!" Luke spoke bluntly. "She's now set out to beat the police and as far as I can see she's in danger of doing it. Frankly, Campion, I don't quite see where to go from here."

Mr. Campion bowed to the inevitable. He knew his old friend when he spoke like this. He sat down in the visitor's chair and composed himself to listen while Luke strode up and down the rug talking like a dynamo.

"Her name's Melanie Miller, she works behind the Inquiries desk in Cuppage's stores and until she won the Quiz no one had heard of her," he said. "But she went

59

through session after session beating team after team and finally she won the big prize which was a remarkable coat presented by a federation of the fur trade boys. It was an advertising stunt. The fur was crushed sapphire mink fully insured for eight thousand pounds, and she also made about four hundred pounds by posing in it for trade photographers." He paused and smiled briefly. "She was expected to turn it in for cash. I gather she was offered four thousand and a coat in beaver lamb in exchange for it. But she isn't that kind of girl. Her coat is insured for eight thousand pounds and she has a literal mind."

Mr. Campion appeared interested.

"She wanted to wear it, I suppose?"

"She couldn't wear it." Luke objected irritably. "No one could wear it without stopping the traffic. It was an embarrassment on a bus and a liability in a café and as soon as they saw it the neighbours in Lilac Mansions, Plum Street, North-East where she lives with her mum started an agitation. They contended that its presence in the buildings constituted an invitation to burglary. If it was that which gave her the idea, I don't know."

Mr. Campion looked up in the midst of lighting a cigarette. "I remember now; I read it. She's had it pinched, hasn't she? Dear me, quite providential! How do you come to be involved, Charles? I should have thought you were a bit eminent for larceny."

"But not for adverse publicity," said Luke grimly. "Nor do I care to see my chaps made monkeys of. Look here, Campion, we're confronted with a tale which would make a child suspicious. The story is like a conjurer's cabinet—there's a hole in it somewhere, must be. But we simply cannot find it."

"Does she offer any explanation?"

"Oh, she's got a scapegoat, she's not a fool." Luke jerked his dark head. "I think that is what is making me so spiteful. It's a mean explanation which we might fall for if we decided to be lazy. Little Miss Know-All doesn't care whom she hurts." He sat down on the edge of the desk and stretched his long legs out before him.

"When she won the prize just over a month ago she did a very extraordinary thing," he began. "Taking her coat and her four hundred pounds, she moved into a furnished

60

apartment in a small block of mansion flats called Sweetwater Court, Knightsbridge. It isn't at all what you'd expect but very respectable and very dull. The doors are shut tight at eleven every night and a porter is on duty in the hall all day. She only took the place for a month—her story is that she just wanted to see what it would be like to live 'up West'—but she appears to have chosen the block very carefully. At any rate, she went to an agency and asked them to find out if any tenant of Sweetwater would rent her a short lease of his apartment. They were not hopeful, they told us, but they did as they were asked and succeeded. Melanie paid over the odds but she got what she wanted: an old resident with a flat on the second floor obliged her for four weeks at thirty pounds a week."

Mr. Campion sat up.

"How very curious," he said. "You interest me, Charles. Was there nothing extraordinary about the block? No past history of crime there?"

Luke burst out laughing. "You don't miss much, do you?" he said. "That was the only possible reason I could discover for her picking it. This time last year there was an abortive attempt at daylight robbery there and the story made the papers. The girl's memory is extraordinary and she may have recalled it. Otherwise the place has a clean sheet. The tenants have been there for years and so has the porter. Yet the morning after the evening on which Melanie was seen to move in, coat and all, she struggled to the telephone to report that she had been drugged and robbed. A dirty glass on her table contained traces of chloral. Nothing but the mink had gone but that certainly had vanished."

Mr. Campion leaned back in his chair and blinked.

"How nice and tidy," he murmured primly.

"Wasn't it? It sounds as if we ought to have seen through that tale without any difficulty. That's what we each thought until we came into it. Unfortunately the story appears to be water-tight." Luke raised a long hand with the fingers outstretched and ticked off his points as he made them. "The coat was seen to enter the flat. The woman had no key to the main door—she had left the one the tenant had left her, with the agent 'by-mistake-on-purpose'. The coat could not have been destroyed without

61

trace or otherwise disposed of in the flat. It could not have been passed out of a window because there are only three and they are all of a patent type which permit ventilation without opening. It has been proved that these have not been opened for years. Finally the blessed coat could not have been stuffed up a chimney because there are no chimneys nor put under the floorboards because in pure exasperation I've had 'em up."

The thin man avoided any hint of sympathy. "You said something about a scapegoat," he ventured.

Luke scowled. "That's the unforgivable bit . . . I'm not all that stirred by the losses of insurance companies but some things get under my skin. When Miss Know-All took over the apartment on a Tuesday evening she paused at the porter's box—partly, no doubt, to let him get an eyeful of the crushed sapphire mink, but ostensibly to tell him that she expected a Mrs. Pegg to call in with some laundry and to ask him to send her straight up."

Mr. Campion's eyebrows rose behind his spectacles.

"How old world!"

"That's what the porter thought. He's an intelligent chap, an ex-sergeant called Bravington. He's had the job for years and, as he said, he was surprised because old women with comfortable London names don't come trotting round with the washing in these days. Now you have to do it yourself in a machine which looks as if it ought to stand on a pier and show you what the butler saw."

"Yet she arrived, I suppose?" Mr. Campion was very interested. "Basket and all, no doubt."

"Basket and all," Luke agreed. "It's a pleasure to work with you, chum. She arrived but, unless I'm losing my grip, she wasn't an accomplice. I've taken her pretty well to pieces, poor old thing, and I think she's genuine. See how you feel." He slid off the desk to cross the room to an inner door. "I've just been having a session with the two of them face to face," he explained. "Perhaps I'm round the bend but I think this one is innocent."

He went out to return a moment later with a withered scrap of a woman whose shabby, man's overcoat was buttoned across an overall as gay as a flowerborder. She wore an infant's knitted cap of pink wool and, to Mr.

Campion's incredulous astonishment, still carried a shallow basket complete with a piece of faded chintz tied over its mouth. The moment she spoke, however, she convinced him that if she was an anachronism she was certainly no phoney.

"You're looking at me barsket,"," she said huskily, her old eyes peering into his own. "I brought it, see, to show the gentleman it wouldn't hold no fur coat. It couldn't *take* it—wouldn't go *in*. I see the coat in 'er drorin-room when I called. Lying there on the studiho couch voluptuous it was, like it was alive. It was big, you know, big as an animal."

"Just a minute, Ma." Luke dropped a hand on her shoulder while he spoke to his friend. "Mrs. Pegg here used to be a cleaner at Cuppage's stores and Melanie Miller knew her there. Then early this year Mr. Pegg, her husband, had a little—uh—trouble which resulted in the shop dismissing her. . . ."

"'E went inside for burgalary, dear." Mrs. Pegg lowered her voice confidingly, making Mr. Campion feel honoured by true friendship. "It 'appens to 'im from time to time although a better man never lived, I'll say that. But the manager at the store 'ad to put me orf. I was a good worker, 'e said, but he dursent let me 'ave the key, see? Then some of the girls said it was a shame and they give me what work they could. That's why when Miss Importance says, 'Oo, could you oblige me by bringin' my sheets round to my noo flat ternight?' Well, I did. To 'elp 'er, see? After all, while Pegg's restin' I've got to live."

"Of course." Luke sounded as if he had known her all his life as indeed he had, in type. "She brought the washing round to Sweetwater Court, Campion, and was admitted to the flat. There she had a drink. . . ."

"Only one!" Mrs. Pegg put in quickly. "She 'ad it ready for me when I come in. 'Oo, Mrs. P.,' she says. 'I'm just 'aving a nightcap, will you 'ave one?' Then she poured it out and I drank it while she took the barsket into the bedroom."

"She left her own drink unfinished on the table while she did this, I think you said?" Luke put in.

"That's right, duck. But I didn't put nothink in it. I wouldn't be so wicked for one thing and I 'adn't got nothink to put for another. Anythink the police found she •

63

put there for them to find. When she come back she said 'Cheers', knocked the drink back and gave me my money. I come away then and the downstairs doors was locked, so the porter 'ad to open up for me. I wasn't carryin' no sapphire mink, boys." As her husky voice ceased, she stood looking up at them, a bright-eyed bundle as feckless and tousled as the London sparrow she resembled. "Ow *could* I?" she demanded.

Mr. Campion rose with sudden decision. His smile was an echo of Luke's own. "How indeed?" he murmured. "Charles, it appears to be up to us to prove that point. Perhaps you and I could have a word with porter Bravington?"

The commissionaire's cubby-hole in the hallway of Sweetwater Court was built in the panelling, its open hatch giving directly on to the front door. As soon as he saw it, and met the man who kept it, Mr. Campion began to share Luke's bewilderment. Bravington was not the type to let much get past him. His first words confirmed the impression.

"I saw and spoke to the woman Pegg when she left the building that night and she had nothing in her basket which could have been more bulky than a handkerchief. I noticed particularly. Ever since the trouble here last year I've been very careful when dealing with strangers," he announced, standing stiffly before them in his neat blue uniform, his grey head shorn to the bone in the closest of haircuts. "This block of residences is very well kept, the landlord is most particular and the upset we had then shook us both properly. I always keep that picture there to remind me." He stepped back from the entrance to his little room to show them a collection of trophies on the tiny shelf over the heater. Amongst several others there was a framed photograph cut from a newspaper. Mr. Campion adjusted his glasses and regarded it with polite interest. It showed nothing but a leather-bound canvas travelling bag resting on an upholstered bench which he recognized as the one in the hall outside.

"Er . . . quite," he said at last.

Mr. Bravington regarded him severely.

"It was that bag what saved my sight," he said earnestly. "It was about nine o'clock one morning about this time last

64

year when two young thugs, overgrown louts they were, pushed in here and demanded my keys. One of them took out a bottle of ammonia—to throw in my face, you see?—when Mr. Jenner, one of our residents, happened to come down the stairs and see him. Mr. Jenner was too far away to reach the youngster but, quick as a flash, he pitched the bag he was carrying straight at the brute and knocked the bottle out of his hand."

"And that's the bag?" Mr. Campion looked at the cutting again. "I see the initials—H.J."

"That's the bag, sir. Mr. Horace Jenner's bag. He always takes it with him when he goes travelling for his business every Wednesday. He comes back on Fridays; he's in the art trade. He's been here for twenty years same as I have and his wife is most particular. They've got a beautiful flat. She keeps it like a bandbox. If I take anything up there for her she gets me to change my shoes in the vestibule so I don't mark the floors. You'll notice they're very particular people."

"I do. Why did the newspaper men photograph the bag and not Mr. Jenner?"

"Because 'e was above it, sir. 'The bag saved the porter not me', he told them, laughing."

"Heartily, no doubt,' murmured Mr. Campion, absently. "I see. What about the other residents?"

"We've been into that with out customary thoroughness, I'm afraid." The Chief Inspector spoke with a mixture of pride and regret. "There are very few of them, they're all on the wrong side of forty-five and have each been living here for ten years or more. The whole of the top floor is occupied by a bed-ridden invalid and his two old sisters. A couple of businessmen, Mr. Merton and Mr. Long, both in the tea trade, live with their families in the two apartments below. On the floor beneath them is the flat the girl took, with Mr. Jenner and his houseproud wife across the hall and below that, on the first stage, there is the town residence of the old Earl of Granchester which is closed until his lordship returns from South Africa. Each flat was examined on the morning of the robbery. The coat wasn't in the building."

Mr. Campion nodded absently. He knew Luke well enough to be certain that every obvious step had already been taken and that any possibility of an accomplice having been disguised as an early morning deliveryman or postman had been fully explored as a matter of routine.

"Three people and three people only went out of the building that Wednesday morning before Melanie Miller gave the alarm," the Chief Inspector went on. "We've reduced that point to a complete certainty. Mr. Merton and Mr. Long left for Mincing Lane together as they usually did and Mr. Jenner came down alone to catch his train a few minutes after them. Actually, he told us, he was late that particular day and had to wait at Euston Station for a second train but that had no significance." He paused and spread out his hands. "It's crazy," he said. "Either the coat vanished into air or Melanie is right and somehow Mrs. Pegg secreted it in her basket and managed to dispose of it afterwards—I don't know which version I find more unlikely. How do you feel, Campion?"

Mr. Campion sighed.

"If your little Miss Know-All has moved back to Lilac Maisonettes and Mum, I think we should drop in on them, don't you know," he murmured. "I see how it was done but I should like to check with the estate office of their buildings." He grinned suddenly. "That triumphant smile will fade when she is persuaded to hand over the cloakroom ticket, I fancy."

"Cloakroom. . . ? What are you talking about?" Luke's tone was startled and his stare blank. Mr. Campion took his arm.

"Where else *can* the coat be, Charles?" he said gently.

"By the way, Bravington, how many bags was Mr. Jenner carrying that morning, did you notice?"

The porter hesitated. "I can't say, sir," he said at last. "Sometimes he takes a second one. I'm not sure if he had two that morning—but if you'll forgive me for saying so, I can't credit what you're suggestin'. Mr. Jenner wouldn't lend himself to such a thing. He couldn't have even met the young woman and even if he had, he'd have to have a very strong reason before he helped anybody to *that* extent—particularly with Mrs. Jenner about."

Mr. Campion nodded, his eyes serious.

"A very strong reason—yes, indeed," he agreed. "Well,

66

now, Charles. If you're still hunting mink, it's Lilac Maisonettes and don't spare the horses."

Half an hour later Melanie the Mink and her mother, a vast woman in an apron who confirmed all one's worst fears for her daughter's future development, confronted the Chief Inspector and his companion across the kitchen table of their home in Plum Street, North-East. Luke was holding out his hand. "The cloakroom ticket, please," he insisted. "Who has it? You or your mother?"

"Me?" Mrs. Miller snatched up the cookery book, apparently to defend herself. "Why, I never left home all that day! And I've got witnesses to prove it."

"I daresay you have," Luke sounded grim. "I'll have the ticket from you all the same, if you please. That's where it is, is it?" He leaned forward and took a slip of paper, folded to make a marker, which protruded from the book's greasy pages. As the woman watched him he unfolded it upon the table.

"*Euston Station. Left Luggage Office,*" he said softly and turned to Campion. "And that's the neatest trick of the week," he announced frankly. "What put you on to it?"

The distressing formalities were over, Melanie was on her way to the station, and Campion and Luke were driving back to Central London together when the man in the horn-rims explained.

"It merely turned out to be an exercise in deduction on the elementary or classic pattern, don't you think?" he said modestly. "One follows the rules in these cases and the answer arrives on the penny-in-the-slot principle. When a problem appears to be insoluble because it is contained in a box, one is enjoined to hunt for the sliding panel, starting with any little peculiarity which strikes one as unusual."

Luke grinned. "You can cut the lecture," he said good naturedly. "I couldn't see anything unusual. That's what foxed me. What was it that made you think twice?"

"The woman who forced the porter to change his shoes in the vestibule," said Mr. Campion promptly. "The unusual thing about a woman like that is the fact that the husband puts up with her. As soon as I considered that point I realized that Mr. Jenner *didn't* live with his houseproud wife all the time. His habit was to spend two

67

and half days every week somewhere else. Not unnaturally, I asked myself if it were possible that he spent these days in some humbler but happier establishment where the furnishings were not taken so seriously. In Lilac Maisonettes, perhaps. I then looked at the newspaper picture of his bag and I thought that to a very observant eye like Miss Know-All's it was a distinctive sort of item, its travel stains were defined. The initials H.J. too are not uncommon."

Luke began to laugh.

"I get it," he said. "As soon as we called at the estate office and discovered that there was a traveller living in the next block to the Millers called Herbert Johns—who was away most of the time but who always came home for Wednesdays and Thursdays—I saw it at once. Melanie read about the attempted robbery in the paper and recognized the bag, I suppose. She *would*. Nosey and remembering, that's Melanie."

"Not attractive traits," agreed Mr. Campion. "To do her justice, though, I don't suppose she thought of using the information until she won the mink and was thinking how to beat the insurance people. Then she sought out Jenner and applied the acid."

"Before she took the flat?"

"Oh, no!" Campion looked scandalized. "Jenner wasn't in it until the very last moment. I'm sure of that. She shocked him into it. That's how she got him to play. I think you'll find, Charles, that when Mr. Jenner said goodbye to his fussy wife and stepped out of his front door that Wednesday morning, he walked unexpectedly into the arms of a young woman whom he recognized with horror as a neighbour in his other life. I think all the woman did was to hand him a canvas travelling bag, remarkably like the one he was carrying, and say softly but doubtlessly very clearly: *'Put this in the cloakroom at Euston for me, Mr. Johns. You can drop the ticket through the letter box at mother's when you go home to Lilac Mansions tonight.'*"

"Phew!" Luke shook his head. "That must have been a facer. He fell for it, poor chap. The request did not appear criminal, of course. All the same he shouldn't have done it. It was asking for trouble."

Mr. Campion cocked an eye at him.

"He might have asked for even more trouble if he had retreated into his apartment with Melanie after him," he murmured.

Luke's eyes widened. "You've got something there!" he said heartily. "She might not have changed her shoes in the vestibule, might she? That wouldn't do!"

ONE MORNING
THEY'LL HANG HIM

It was typical of Detective Inspector Kenny, at that time
D.D.I. of the L. Division, that, having forced himself to ask
a favour, he should set about it with the worst grace
possible. When at last he took the plunge, he heaved his
fourteen stone off Mr. Campion's fireside couch and set
down his empty glass with a clatter.

"I don't know if I needed that at three o'clock in the
afternoon," he said ungratefully, his small eyes baleful,
"but I've been up since two this morning dealing with
women, tears, simple stupidity and this perishing rain." He
rubbed his broad face, and presented it scarlet and
exasperated at Mr. Campion's back. "If there's one thing
that makes me savage it's futility!" he said.

Mr. Albert Campion, who had been staring idly out of
the window watching the rain on the roofs, did not glance
round. He was still the lean, somewhat ineffectual-looking
man whose appearance had deceived so many astute
offenders in the last twenty years. His fair hair had
bleached into whiteness and a few lines had appeared
round the pale eyes which were still, as always, covered by

large horn-rimmed spectacles, but otherwise he looked much as Kenny first remembered him—"Friendly and a little simple—the old snake!"

"So there's futility in Barraclough Road too, is there?" Campion's light voice sounded polite rather than curious.

Kenny drew a sharp breath of annoyance.

"The Commissioner has phoned you? He suggested I should look you up. It's not a great matter—just one of those stupid little snags which has some perfectly obvious explanation. Once it's settled, the whole case is open and shut. As it is, we can't keep the man at the station indefinitely."

Mr. Campion picked up the early edition of the evening paper from his desk.

"This is all I know," he said holding it out, "Mr. Oates didn't phone. There you are, in the Stop Press, *Rich Widow in Barraclough Road West. Nephew at police station helping investigation.* What's the difficulty? His help is not altogether wholehearted perhaps?"

"Ruddy young fool," he said, and sat down abruptly. "I tell you, Mr. Campion, this thing is in the bag. It is just one of those ordinary, rather depressing little stories which most murder cases are. There's practically no mystery, no chase—nothing but a wretched little tragedy. As soon as you've spotted what I've missed, I shall charge this chap and he'll go before the magistrates and be committed for trial. His counsel will plead insanity and the jury won't have it. The judge will sentence him, he'll appeal, their Lordships will dismiss it. The Home Secretary will sign the warrant and one morning they'll take him out and they'll hang him." He sighed. "All for nothing," he said. "All for nothing at all. It'll probably be raining just like it is now," he added inconsequentially.

Mr. Campion's eyes grew puzzled. He knew Kenny for a conscientious officer, and, some said, a hard man. This philosophic strain was unlike him.

"Taken a fancy to him?" he inquired.

"Who? I certainly haven't." The Inspector was grim. "I've got no sympathy for youngsters who shoot up their relatives however selfish the old besoms may be. No, he's killed her and he must take what's coming to him, but it's hard on—well, on some people. Me, for one." He took out

71

a large old-fashioned notebook and folded it carefully in half. "I stick to one of these," he remarked virtuously, "none of your backs of envelopes for me. My record is kept as neatly as when I was first on the beat, and it can be handed across the court whenever a know-all counsel asks to see it." He paused. "I sound like an advertisement, don't I? Well, Mr. Campion, since I'm here, just give your mind to this, if you will. I don't suppose it'll present any difficulty to you."

"One never knows," murmured Mr. Campion idiotically. "Start with the victim."

Kenny returned to his notebook.

"Mrs. Mary Alice Cibber, aged about seventy or maybe a bit less. She had heart trouble which made her look frail, and, of course, I didn't see her until she was dead. She had a nice house in Barraclough Road, a good deal too big for her, left her by her husband who died ten years ago. Since then she's been alone except for another old party who calls herself a companion. *She* looks older still, poor old girl, but you can see she's been kept well under"—he put his thumb down expressively—"by Mrs. C. who appears to have been a dictator in her small way. She was the sort of woman who lived for two chairs and a salad bowl."

"I beg your pardon?"

"Antiques." He was mildly contemptuous. "The house is crammed with them, all three floors and the attic, everything kept as if it was brand new. The old companion says she loved it more than anything on earth. Of course she hadn't much else *to* love, not a relation in the world except the nephew—"

"Whose future you see so clearly?"

"The man who shot her," the Inspector agreed. "He's a big nervy lad, name of Woodruff, did very well in his army service. Short-term commission. Saw a lot of action in Cyprus—quite a bit of a hero—but got himself pretty badly injured when a bridge blew up with him on it—or something of the sort, my informant didn't know exactly—and he seems to have become what the boys call 'bomb happy'. It used to be shell shock in my day. As far as I can gather, he always has been quick tempered, but this sent him over the edge. He sounds to me as if he wasn't sane for a while. That may help in his defense, of course."

"Yes." Mr. Campion sounded depressed. "Where's he been since then?"

"On a farm mostly. He was training to be an architect as a student but the motherly old army knew what was best for him and when he came out of the hospital they bunged him down to Dorset. He's just got away. Some home town chum got him a job in an architect's office under the old pal's act and he was all set to take it up." He paused and his narrow mouth, which was not entirely insensitive, twisted bitterly. "Ought to have started Monday," he said.

"Oh dear," murmured Mr. Campion inadequately. "Why did he shoot his aunt? Pure bad temper?"

Kenny shook his head.

"He had a reason. I mean one can see why he was angry. He hadn't anywhere to live, you see. As you know London is crowded, and rents are fantastic. He and his wife are paying through the nose for a cupboard of a bed-sitting-room off the Edgeware Road."

"His wife?" The lean man in the horn-rims was interested. "Where did she come from? You're keeping her very quiet."

To Campion's surprise the Inspector did not speak at once. Instead he grunted, and there was regret, and surprise at it, in his little smile. "I believe I would if I could," he said sincerely. "He found her on the farm. They've been married six weeks. I don't know if you've ever seen love, Mr. Campion? It's very rare—the kind I mean." He put out his hands deprecatingly. "It seems to crop up—when it does—among the most unexpected people, and when you do see it, well, it's very impressive." He succeeded in looking thoroughly ashamed of himself. "I shouldn't call myself a sentimental man," he said.

"No." Campion was reassuring. "You got his army history from her, I suppose?"

"I had to, but we're confirming it. He's as shut as a watch—or a hand grenade. 'Yes' and 'No' and 'I did not shoot her'—that's about all his contribution amounted to, and he's had a few hours of expert treatment. The girl is quite different. She's down there too. Won't leave. We put her in the waiting-room finally. She's not difficult—just sits there."

"Does she know anything about it?"

73

"No." Kenny was quite definite. "She's nothing to look at," he went on presently, as if he felt the point should be made. "She's just an ordinary nice little country girl, a bit too thin and a bit too brown, natural hair and inexpert make-up, and yet with this—this blazing radiant steadfastness about her!" He checked himself. "Well, she's fond of him," he amended.

"Believes he's God?" Campion suggested.

Kenny shook his head. "She doesn't care if he isn't," he said sadly. "Well, Mr. Campion, some weeks ago these two approached Mrs. Cibber about letting them have a room or two at the top of the house. That must have been the girl's idea; she's just the type to have old-fashioned notions about blood being thicker than water. She made the boy write. The old lady ignored the question but asked them both to an evening meal last night. The invitation was sent a fortnight ago, as you can see there was no eager bless-you-my-children about it."

"Any reason for the delay?"

"Only that she had to have notice if she was giving a party. The old companion explained that to me. There was the silver to get out and clean, and the best china to be washed, and so on. Oh, there was nothing simple and homely about that household!" He sounded personally affronted. "When they got there, of course there was a blazing row."

"Hard words or flying crockery?"

Kenny hesitated. "In a way, both," he said slowly. "It seems to have been a funny sort of flare-up. I had two accounts of it—one from the girl and one from the companion. I think they are both trying to be truthful but they both seem to have been completely foxed by it. They both agree that Mrs. Cibber began it. She waited until there were three oranges and a hundred-weight of priceless early Worcester dessert service on the table, and then let fly. Her theme seems to have been the impudence of youth in casting its eyes on its inheritance before age was in its grave, and so on and so on. She then made it quite clear that they hadn't a solitary hope of getting what they wanted, and conveyed that she did not care if they slept in the street so long as her priceless furniture was safely

74

housed. There's no doubt about it that she was very aggravating and unfair."

"Unfair?"

"Ungenerous. After all she knew the man quite well. He used to go and stay with her by himself when he was a little boy." Kenny returned to his notes. "Woodruff then lost his temper in his own way which, if the exhibition he gave in the early hours of this morning is typical, is impressive. He goes white instead of red, says practically nothing, but looks as if he's about to 'incandesce', if I make myself plain."

"Entirely." Mr. Campion was deeply interested. This new and human Kenny was an experience. "I take it he then fished out a gun and shot her?"

"Lord, no! If he had, he'd have a chance at least of Broadmoor. No, he just got up and asked her if she had any of his things, because if so he'd take them and not inconvenience her with them any longer. It appears that when he was in the hospital some of his gear had been sent to her, as his next of kin. She said yes, she had, and it was waiting for him in the boot cupboard. The old companion, Miss Smith, was sent trotting out to fetch it and came staggering in with an old officer's hold-all, burst at the sides and filthy. Mrs. Cibber told her nephew to open it and see if she'd robbed him, and he did as he was told. Of course, one of the first things he saw among the shirts and old photographs was a revolver and a clip of ammunition." He paused and shook his head. "Don't ask me how it got there. You know what army hospitals are like. Mrs. Cibber went on taunting the man in her own peculiar way, and he stood there examining the gun and presently loading it, almost absently. You can see the scene?"

Campion could. The pleasant, perhaps slightly over-crowded room was vivid in his mind, and he saw the gentle light on the china and the proud, bitter face of the woman.

"After that," said Kenny, "the tale gets more peculiar, although both accounts agree. It was Mrs. C. who laughed and said, 'I suppose you think I ought to be shot?' Woodruff did not answer but he dropped the gun in his side pocket. Then he picked up the hold-all and said

75

'Goodbye'." He hesitated. "Both statements say that he then said something about the *sun having gone down.* I don't know what that meant, or if both women mistook him. Anyway, there's nothing to it. He had no explanation to offer. Says he doesn't remember saying it. However, after that he suddenly picked up one of his aunt's beloved china fruit bowls and simply dropped it on the floor. It fell on a rug, as it happened, and did not break, but old Mrs. Cibber nearly passed out, the companion screamed, and the girl hurried him off home.

"With the gun?"

"With the gun." Kenny shrugged his heavy shoulders. "As soon as the girl heard that Mrs. Cibber had been shot she jumped up with a tale that he had not taken it. She said she'd sneaked it out of his pocket and put it on the window sill. The lamest story you've ever heard! She's game and she's ready to say absolutely anything, but she won't save him, poor kid. He was seen in the district at midnight."

Mr. Campion put a hand through his sleek hair. "Ah! That rather tears it."

"Oh, it does. There's no question that he did it. It hardly arises. What happened was this. The young folk got back to their bed-sitting-room about ten to nine. Neither of them will admit it, but it's obvious that Woodruff was in one of those boiling but sulky rages which made him unfit for human society. The girl left him alone—I should say she has a gift for handling him—and she says she went to bed while he sat up writing letters. Quite late, she can't or won't say when, he went out to the post. He won't say anything. We may or may not break him down, he's a queer chap. However, we have a witness who saw him somewhere about midnight at the Kilburn end of Barraclough Road. Woodruff stopped him and asked if the last eastbound bus had gone. Neither of them had a watch, but the witness is prepared to swear it was just after midnight—which is important because the shot was fired at two minutes before twelve. We've got that time fixed."

Mr. Campion, who had been taking notes, looked up in mild astonishment.

"You got that witness very promptly," he remarked. "Why did he come forward?"

"He was a plain clothes man off duty," said Kenny.

calmly. "One of the local men who had been out to a re-union dinner. He wasn't tight but he had decided to walk home before his wife saw him. I don't know why he hadn't a watch"—Kenny frowned at this defect—"anyway, he hadn't, or it wasn't going. But he was alert enough to notice Woodruff. He's a distinctive chap, you know. Very tall and dark, and his manner was so nervy and excitable that the man thought it worth reporting."

Campion's teeth appeared in a brief smile.

"In fact, he recognized him at once as a man who looked as though he had done a murder?"

"No." The Inspector remained unruffled. "No, he said he looked like a chap who had just got something off his mind and was pleased with himself."

"I see. And meanwhile the shot was fired at two minutes to twelve."

"That's certain." Kenny brightened and became businesslike. "The man next door heard it and looked at his watch. We've got his statement and the old lady's companion. Everyone else in the street is being questioned. But nothing has come in yet. It was a cold wet night and most people had their windows shut; besides, the room where the murder took place was heavily curtained. So far, these two are the only people who seem to have heard anything at all. The man next door woke up and nudged his wife who had slept through it. But then he may have dozed again, for the next thing he remembers is hearing screams for help. By the time he got to the window, the companion was out in the street in her dressing-gown, wedged in between the lamp post and the pillar box, screeching her little grey head off. The rain was coming down in sheets."

"When exactly was this?"

"Almost immediately after the shot, according to the companion. She had been in bed for some hours and had slept. Her room is on the second floor, at the back. Mrs. Cibber had not come up with her but had settled down at her bureau in the drawing-room, as she often did in the evening. Mrs. C. was still very upset by the scene at the meal and did not want to talk. Miss Smith says she woke up and thought she heard the front door open. She won't swear to this, and at any rate she thought nothing of it, for Mrs. Cibber often slipped out to the box with letters before

77

coming to bed. Exactly how long it was after she woke that she heard the shot she does not know, but it brought her scrambling out of bed. She agrees she might have been a minute or two finding her slippers and a wrapper, but she certainly came down right away. She says she found the street door open letting in the rain, and the drawing-room door, which is next to it, wide open as well, and the lights in there full on." He referred to his notes and began to read out loud. " 'I smelled burning'—she means cordite—'and I glanced across the room to see poor Mrs. Cibber on the floor with a dreadful hole in her forehead. I was too frightened to go near her, so I ran out of the house shouting "Murder! Thieves!" ' "

"That's nice and old-fashioned. Did she see anybody?"

"She says not, and I believe her. She was directly under the only lamp post for fifty yards and it certainly was raining hard."

Mr. Campion appeared satisfied but unhappy. When he spoke his voice was very gentle.

"Do I understand that your case is that Woodruff came back, tapped on the front door, and was admitted by his aunt? After some conversation, which must have taken place in lowered tones since the companion upstairs did not hear it, he shot her and ran away, leaving all the doors open?"

"Substantially, yes. Although he may have shot her as soon as he saw her."

"In that case she'd have been found dead in the hall."

Kenny blinked. "Yes, I suppose she would. Still, they couldn't have talked much."

"Why?"

The Inspector made a gesture of distaste. "This is the bit which gets under my skin," he said. "They could hardly have spoken long—*because she'd forgiven him*. She had written to her solicitor. The finished letter was on her writing-pad ready for the post. She'd written to say she was thinking of making the upper part of her house into a home for her nephew, and asked if there was a clause in her lease to prevent it. She also said that she wanted the work done quickly, as she had taken a fancy to her new niece and hoped in time there might be children. It's pathetic, isn't it?" His eyes were wretched. "That's what I meant by

78

utility. She'd forgiven him, see? She wasn't a mean old harridan, she was just quick tempered. I told you this isn't a mystery tale, this is ordinary sordid life."

Mr. Campion looked away.

"Tragic," he said. "Yes. A horrid thing. What do you want me to do?"

Kenny sighed. "Find the gun," he murmured.

The lean man whistled.

"You'll certainly need that if you are to be sure of a conviction. How did you lose it?"

"He's ditched it somewhere. He didn't get rid of it in Barraclough Road because the houses come right down to the street, and our chaps were searching for it within half an hour. At the end of the road he caught the last bus, which ought to come along at midnight but was a bit late last night, I'm morally certain. These drivers make up time on the straight stretch by the park; it's more than their jobs are worth, so you never get them to admit it. Anyhow, he didn't leave the gun on the bus, and it's not in the house where his room is. It's not in the old lady's house at 81 Barraclough Road because I've been over the house myself." He peered at the taller man hopefully. "Where would you hide a gun in this city at night, if you were all that way from the river? It's not so easy, is it? If it had been anywhere obvious it would have turned up by now."

"He may have given it to someone."

"And risked blackmail?" Kenny laughed. "He's not as dumb as that. You'll have to see him. He says he never had it—but that's only natural. Yet where did he put it, Mr. Campion? It's only a little point but, as you say, it's got to be solved."

Campion grimaced.

"Anywhere, Kenny. Absolutely anywhere. In a drain—"

"They're narrow gratings in Barraclough Road."

"In a sandbin or a water tank—"

"There aren't any in that district."

"He threw it down in the street and someone, who felt he'd rather like to have a gun, picked it up. Your area isn't peopled solely with the law abiding, you know."

Kenny became more serious. "That's the real likelihood," he admitted gloomily. "But all the same, I don't believe he's the type to throw away a gun casually.

79

He's too intelligent, too cautious. He's hidden it. Where? Mr. Oates said you'd know if anyone did."

Campion ignored this blatant flattery. He stood staring absently out of the window for so long that the Inspector was tempted to nudge him, and when at last he spoke, his question did not sound promising.

"How often did he stay with his aunt when he was a child?"

"Quite a bit, I think, but there's no kid's hiding-place there that only he could have known, if that's what you're after." Kenny could hardly conceal his disappointment. "It's not that kind of house. Besides, he hadn't the time. He got back about twenty past twelve: a woman in the house confirms it—she met him on the stairs. He was certainly spark out when we got there at a quarter after four this morning. They were both sleeping like kids when I first saw them. She had one skinny brown arm round his neck. He just woke up in a rage, and she was more astounded than frightened. I swear—"

Mr. Campion had ceased to listen.

"Without the gun the only real evidence you've got is the plain-clothes man's story of meeting him," he said. "And even you admit that the gallant officer was walking for his health after a party. Imagine a good defence lawyer enlarging on that point."

"I have," the Inspector agreed dryly. "That's why I'm here. You must find the gun for us, sir. Can I fetch you a raincoat? Or," he added, a faint smug expression flickering over his broad face, "will you just sit in your armchair and do it from there?"

To his annoyance his elegant host appeared to consider the question.

"No, perhaps I'd better come with you," he said at last. "We'll go to Barraclough Road first, if you don't mind. And if I might make a suggestion, I should send Woodruff and his wife back to their lodgings, suitably escorted, of course. If the young man was going to crack, I think he would have done so by now, and the gun, wherever it is, can hardly be at the police station."

Kenny considered. "He may give himself away and lead us to it." He agreed without enthusiasm. "I'll telephone. Then we'll go anywhere you say, but as I've told you I've been over the Barraclough Road house myself and if there's anything there it's high time I retired."

Mr. Campion merely looked foolish and the Inspector sighed and let him have his way.

He came back from the telephone smiling wryly.

"That's settled," he announced. "He's been behaving like a good soldier interrogated by the enemy, silly young fool. After all, we're only trying to hang him! The girl has been asking for him to be fed, and reporters are crawling up the walls. Our boys won't be sorry to get rid of them for a bit. They'll be looked after. We shan't lose 'em. Now, if you've set your heart on the scene of the crime, Mr. Campion, we'll go."

In the taxi he advanced a little idea.

"I was thinking of that remark he is alleged to have made," he said, not without shame. "You don't think that it could have been 'Your sun had gone down', and that we could construe it as a threat within meaning of the act?"

Campion regarded him owlishly.

"We could, but I don't think we will. That's the most enlightening part of the story, don't you think?"

If Inspector Kenny agreed, he did not say so, and they drove to the top of Barraclough Road in silence. There Campion insisted on stopping at the first house next to the main thoroughfare. The building had traded on its proximity to the shopping centre and had been converted into a dispensing chemist's. Campion was inside for several minutes, leaving Kenny in the cab. When he came out he offered no explanation other than to observe fatuously that they had a 'nice time' and settled back without troubling to look out at the early Victorian stucco three-storey houses which lined the broad road.

A man on duty outside, and a handful of idlers gaping apathetically at the drawn blinds, distinguished 81 Barraclough Road. Kenny rang the bell and the door was opened after a pause by a flurried old lady with a duster in her hand.

"Oh, it's you, Inspector," she said hastily. "I'm afraid you've found me in a muddle. I've been trying to tidy up a little. *She* couldn't have borne the place left dirty after everyone had been trampling over it. Yet I don't mean to say that you weren't all very careful."

81

She led them into a spotless dining-room which glowed with mahogany and limpid silver, and the wan afternoon light showed them her reddened eyes and worn navy blue housedress. She was a timid-looking person not quite so old as Kenny had suggested, with very neat grey hair and a skin which had never known cosmetics. Her expression was closed and secret with long submission, and her shoulder-blades stuck out a little under the cloth of her dress. Her hands still trembled slightly from the shock of the evening before.

Kenny introduced Campion. "We shan't be long, Miss Smith," he said cheerfully. "Just going to have another little look round. We shan't make a mess."

Campion smiled at her reassuringly. "It's difficult to get help these days?" he suggested pleasantly.

"Oh, it is," she said earnestly. "And Mrs. Cibber wouldn't trust just anyone with her treasures. They are so very good." Her eyes filled with tears. "She was so fond of them."

"I daresay she was. That's a beautiful piece, for instance." Campion glanced with expert interest at the serpentine sideboard with its genuine handles and toilet cupboard.

"Beautiful," echoed Miss Smith dutifully. "And the chairs, you see?"

"I do." He eyed the Trafalgar set with the cherry leather seats. "Is this where the quarrel took place?"

She nodded and trembled afresh. "Yes. I—I shall never forget it, never."

"Was Mrs. Cibber often bad tempered?"

The woman hesitated, and her firm small mouth moved without words.

"Was she?"

She shot a swift unhappy glance at him.

"She was quick," she said. "Yes, I think I ought to say she was quick. Now, would you like to see the rest of the house or—?"

Campion glanced at his watch and compared it with the Tompion bracket clock on the mantelpiece.

"I think we've just time," he said, idiotically. "Upstairs first, Inspector."

The next thirty-five minutes reduced Kenny to a state of

jitters rare to him. After watching Campion with breathless interest for the first five, it slowly dawned on him that the expert had forgotten the crime in his delight at discovering a treasure trove. Even Miss Smith, who portrayed a certain proprietorial pride, flagged before Campion's insatiable interest. Once or twice she hinted that perhaps they ought to go down, but he would not hear of it. By the time they had exhausted the third floor and were on the steps to the attic, she became almost firm. There was really nothing there but some early Georgian children's toys, she said.

"But I must see the toys. I've got a 'thing' on toys, Kenny." Campion sounded ecstatic. "Just a minute—"

A vigorous tattoo on the front door interrupted him and Miss Smith, whose nerves were suffering, emitted a little squeak.

"Oh, dear. Somebody at the door. I must go down."

"No, no." Campion was uncharacteristically effusive. "I'll see who it is and come back. I shan't be a moment."

He flung himself downstairs with boyish enthusiasm, Miss Smith behind him, and Kenny, seeing escape at last, following as quickly as the narrow stairs would permit.

They reached the hall just in time to see him closing the door.

"Only the post," he said, holding out a package. "Your library book, Miss Smith."

"Oh, yes," she came forward, hand outstretched. "I was expecting that."

"I rather thought you were." His voice was very soft and suddenly menacing. He held the cardboard box high over his head with one hand, and with the other released the flap which closed it. The soft gleam of metal appeared in the light from the transom, and a service revolver crashed heavily to the parquet floor.

For a minute there was silence. Even Kenny was too thunderstruck to swear.

Then, most dreadfully, she began to scream . . .

A little over an hour later Kenny sat on a Trafalgar chair in a room which still seemed to quiver and shudder with the terrible sound. He was pale and tired-looking. His shirt was torn and there were three livid nail scratches down his face.

"God," he said, breathing hard. "God, can you beat that?"

Mr. Campion sat on the priceless table and rubbed his ear.

"It was a bit more than I bargained for," he murmured. "It didn't occur to me that she'd become violent. I'm afraid they may be having trouble in the car. Sorry, I ought to have thought of it."

The C.I.D. man grunted. "Seems to me you thought of plenty," he muttered. "It came as a shock to me. I don't mind admitting it since I can't very well help it. When did it come to you? From the start?"

"Oh, Lord, no." Campion sounded apologetic. "It was that remark of Woodruff's you quoted about the sun going down. That's what set me on the train of thought. Weren't you ever warned as a kid, Kenny, and by an aunt perhaps, never let the sun go down on your wrath?"

"I've heard it, of course. What do you mean? It was a sort of saying between them?"

"I wondered if it was. They knew each other well when he was a child, and they were both quick-tempered people. It seemed to me that he was reminding her that the sun *had* gone down, and he showed her he could have smashed her precious bowl if he had liked. It would have broken, you know, if he hadn't taken care it shouldn't. I wondered if, like many quick-tempered people, they got sorry just as quickly. Didn't you think it odd, Kenny, that directly after the row they should *both* have settled down to write letters?"

The detective stared at him.

"She wrote to her solicitor," he began slowly. "And he—? Good Lord! You think he wrote to her to say he was sorry?"

"Almost certainly, but we shall never find the letter. That's in the kitchen stove by now. He came back to deliver it, pushed it through the door, and hurried off looking just as your plain-clothes man said, as if he'd got something off his chest. Then he could sleep. The sun had not gone down on his wrath." He slid off the table and stood up. "The vital point is of course that *Mrs. Cibber knew he would*. She sat up waiting for it."

Kenny sucked in his breath.

84

"And Miss Smith knew?"

"Of course she knew. Mrs. Cibber hadn't the kind of temperament which can be kept secret. Miss Smith knew from the moment that Mrs. Cibber received the initial letter that the nephew would get his way in the end *unless she could stop it somehow!* She was the one with the bee in her bonnet about the furniture. I realized that as soon as you said the whole house was kept like a bandbox. No woman with a weak heart can keep a three-storey house like a palace, or compel another to do it, unless the other wants to. Miss Smith was the one with the mania. Who was to get the house if the nephew were to die on active service? Mrs. Cibber must have made some provision."

Kenny rubbed his head with both hands. "I knew!" he exploded. "The lawyer's clerk told me this morning when I rang up to find out if Woodruff was the heir. I was so keen to confirm that point that I discounted the rest. If he died the companion was to have it for her lifetime."

Campion looked relieved.

"I thought so. There you are, you see. She had to get rid of them both—Woodruff and his new wife. With a young and vigorous woman in the house there was a danger of the companion becoming redundant. Don't you think?"

Kenny was fingering his notebook.

"You think she'd planned it for a fortnight?"

"She'd thought of it for a fortnight. She didn't see how to do it until the row occurred last night. When she found the gun on the window sill, where young Mrs. Woodruff left it, and Mrs. Cibber told her that the boy would come back, the plan was obvious." He shivered. "Do you realize that she must have been waiting, probably on the stairs, with the gun in her hand and the book-box addressed to herself in the other, listening for Woodruff's letter to slide under the door? As soon as she heard it, she had to fly down and get it and open the door. Then she had to walk into the drawing-room, shoot the old lady as she turned to see who it was, and put the gun in the book-box. The instant she was sure Mrs. Cibber was dead, she had to run out screaming to her place between the lamp and the pillar box and—post the package!"

Kenny put down his pencil and looked up.

"Now there," he said with honest admiration, "there I

85

hand it to you. How in the world did you get on to that?"

"You suggested it."

"*I* did?" Kenny was pleased in spite of himself. "When?"

"When you kept asking me where one could hide a gun in a London street with no wide gratings and no sandbins. There was only the mail box. I guessed she'd posted it to herself as no one else would have been safe. Even the dead letter office eventually gives up its dead. That's why I was so keen to get her to the top of the house, as far away from the front door as possible." He sighed. "The book-box was misguided genius. The gun was an old Luger, did you notice? Loot. That's why he never had to turn it in. It just fitted in the box. She must have had a thrill when she discovered that."

Kenny shook his head wonderingly. "Well, blow me down!" he said inelegantly. "Funny that *I* put you on to it!"

Mr. Campion was in bed that night when the telephone rang. It was Kenny again.

"I say, Mr. Campion?"

"Yes?"

"Sorry to bother you at this time of night but there's something worrying me. You don't mind, do you?"

"Think nothing of it."

"Well. Everything is all right. Smith has been certified by three medicos. The little girl is very happy comforting her boy, who seems to be upset about his aunt's death. The Commissioner is very pleased. But I can't get off to sleep, Mr. Campion, *how did you know what time the afternoon post is delivered in Barraclough Road?*"

The lean man stifled a yawn.

"Because I went into the chemist's shop on the corner and asked," he said. "Elementary, my dear Kenny."

THE LIEABOUT

I still have the brooch but I can hardly wear it. I thought of throwing it away once, but it is so very pretty. I don't think it is valuable but I have never dared to take it into a jeweller's to find out. It is a very awkward position.

I might have sent it back to the people who owned it, in fact I ought to have done that, but if ever it was traced to me who would believe my story?

It was when we lived in London. We had a small flat in a courtyard leading off High Holborn, right in the city. The courtyard was really only the foot of an airshaft striking down amid enormous office buildings. There were only two doors in it; one belonged to a printing works and the other one was ours.

When you opened our door you found yourself at the foot of a flight of steep stairs, at the top of which were our three rooms and a sort of corridor called a kitchenette-bath.

Our domain had once been the caretaker's premises of the insurance building which was below us and still ran right through to the main street. By the time we went there it had been converted into two shops. These shops were empty when we arrived and remained so for nearly a year, although from time to time gangs of workmen were very busy in them, obliterating, we supposed, still more of the atmosphere of insurance.

There are several odd things about living in the city. One is the quiet of the place at night. When we moved to the country the noises of the night birds were almost too much for us after that deathly peace of the City of London where the offices have closed.

Another curious thing is the surprising intimacy and friendliness of it all. In no village in which I ever lived did I acquire so many acquaintances.

The shops where one could buy the ordinary necessities of life as opposed to an adding machine, a battleship or a two-thousand-guinea emerald ring were all of the small and homely variety and were nearly all of them tucked away in courtyards like our own. The people who owned them were friendly and obliging and told us their family histories at the slightest encouragement.

The news-sellers and the hawkers were other regulars who were anxious to gossip or pass the time of day, and as I walked down the crowded pavement with my shopping basket on my arm I found I had as many people to nod to as if I were in a small town street which had suddenly become overrun with half a million foreigners.

I first met the Lieabout on our own yard. He was sitting there one evening among a pile of packing-cases from the printing works when I went out to play with Addlepate. Addlepate leapt on him, mistaking him for a sack of waste paper in which he delighted. The misapprehension led to a sort of introduction and after a while the Lieabout watched the dog to see that he did not go out into the traffic and commit suicide and I went up to get the man some tea.

He was a frail old person with a beaky face and little bright red eyes like a ferret or one of the old black rats who come out and dance on the cobbles in the small hours.

All lieabouts are necessarily dirty. Genuine tramping can never be a hygienic method of life. But he was horribly so. He looked as though he had just slipped down from his niche among the gargoyles of St. Paul's before the cleaners could get him. He was sooty with London, and his garments, which were varied and of dubious origin, were all the same grey-black colour, and not with dye.

He was glad of the tea, and when I said I had not seen

88

him about before, he explained that he had come up from Cheapside, where he had been spending the summer. He did not ask for money and I did not offer him any, naturally. We parted friends, he to return to his packing-cases in which he was making himself a temporary home and I to my work upstairs.

He lived in the packing-cases for nearly a week and we kept up a nodding acquaintance.

I was out shopping one morning when I saw the brooch. It was on a lower shelf in the window of one of those very big jewellers and silversmiths whose principal trade seems to be in challenge cups and presentation plate. The shop was not quite opposite the entrance to our courtyard but about fifty yards down on the other side of the traffic. I stood for some time looking at the brooch. It consisted of seven large topaz set in oxydized silver and the finished effect was rather like the rose window in Notre Dame.

I was still gazing at it when the Lieabout appeared at my elbow.

"Nice, ain't it?" he said. "Goin' to 'ave it?"

I laughed and indicated my basket, which held one of the Addlepate's Friday bones protruding rather disgustingly from a sea of lettuce.

"Not this week. Food's gone up," I said, and would have passed on, but the ornament had evidently attracted him, too, for he came nearer to look at it and I should have had to brush past him to get into the jostling stream in the middle of the pavement again.

"It's not worfa thousand quid," he observed, after a moment or so of contemplation. "Go in an' arsk 'em. They'll say a tenner, I betcha."

"Very likely," I said. "And what should I do?"

He grinned at me, disclosing a most disreputable assortment of different-sized teeth.

"Same as me, I reckon," he said. "Beat it like one o'clock. 'Day, lady."

I went home and forgot all about the incident and the next day was Saturday.

Up to this point the story was quite ordinary, but once the police came into it the whole thing became a little fantastic.

Saturday morning in the city always has a last day at

boarding school atmosphere. Fewer strangers swoop out of the fat red buses or come boiling up out of the tubes, and those that do appear are definitely in holiday mood. When the big clock of St. Paul's strikes noon the exodus begins, and by a quarter to one the streets look like a theatre after the show is over.

The road outside our courtyard, which all the week had been a sort of nightmare Brooklands, turned suddenly into a great river of dull glass, with only an occasional bus or taxi speeding happily down its wide expanse.

There were people about, of course, but only a dozen or so, and the city policemen in their enormous helmets, which they use as small personal suitcases, I believe, stood out, lonely and important.

It was nearly two o'clock on this particular Saturday afternoon when the police arrived. My husband leant out of the studio window and reported that there were two large bobbies on the step. I went down to open the door. None of our visitors had left a car outside the yard gates for some considerable time, but although my conscience was clear, much clearer than it is now, I felt vaguely uneasy. One policeman may be a friend, but two are the Law.

On the step I found two of the largest, bluest specimens I have ever seen and they were both vastly uncomfortable. They hesitated, eyeing first me and then each other with embarrassment.

I waited awkwardly for them to begin, and presently the larger one spoke.

"I wonder if you'd do me a personal favour, Ma'am?" he said.

It was such an unexpected request that I gaped at him, and he continued:

"I want you to go out into the street and look in the empty shop next door. Don't say nothing to anyone. Just behave perfectly casual, and then come back and tell us what you think you see."

I began to feel a trifle lightheaded, but they were certainly real policemen and, anyway, Addlepate was barking his head off at the top of the stairs.

"All right," I said stupidly. "Aren't you coming?"

The other constable shook his head.

"No, Ma'am. We don't want a crowd to collect. That's our idea. See?"

I went off obediently, and as soon as I turned out of the yard I saw that any hopes my official friends might have cherished concerning the absence of a crowd were doomed to disappointment. Everyone in the street seemed to be converging on the first of the empty shops, and I saw another policeman hurrying down the road towards the excitement.

On the step of the shop stood my friend the Lieabout. He was making a tremendous noise.

"It's a disgrice!" he was shouting. "A bloomin' disgrice! It's bin there five days to my knowledge. Look at it. Look at it!"

I peered in through the plate glass and suddenly saw what he meant. The sight made me feel slightly sick. At the back of the shop was an archway leading into a further salon, which was lit by a skylight. All kinds of decorators' debris was strewn around, but among the whitewash pails, the planks and the trestles, was something covered with an old coat and a lump of sacking. The shape was suggestive. But the thing that made it horrible was the boot. The boot stuck out from beneath the coat so naturally and yet so lifelessly.

"It's a corp!" shrieked the Lieabout, to the crowd which had just reached us. "A corp! Bin there five days. The p'lice won't do nothink. It's a murder, that's wot it is. A murdered corp!"

He turned to me.

"What you waitin' for, lady? Go and tell the rozzers it's a corp."

His voice in my ear recalled me to my senses and I hurried back to my visitors. They were polite but impatient when I gave them my opinion, and it suddenly dawned upon me why I had been singled out for their confidence. A police officer is not allowed to enter private property without authority, nor do the regulations let him ask the owners of such property for permission to enter. But once he is invited in, and has a witness to prove it, he can go wherever his good sense tells him his duty lies.

91

"If you get out of our bedroom window on to the roof at the back of the shop you could look through the skylight," I said. "Would you care to?"

They were upstairs in an instant, and I had barely time to explain to my astonished husband before they were in the bedroom, negotiating the window. I say 'negotiating' because their climb through it required finesse, and a delicacy one would hardly have expected in men of their bulk.

It was one of those awkward old-fashioned sliding casements which permit a space about two and half feet by one and a quarter when opened to their fullest extent.

It took a little time but out they went at last, helmets and all, and my husband with them. They disappeared over the roofs, and I was left to await their return.

However, by this time an entirely unsuspected blood-lust had taken possession of me and, unable to control my impatience where I was, I trotted down into the yard again and out into the street.

To be honest, I did not reach the street. The crowd was packed solid across our entrance, all straining and jostling to peer into the window of the shop next door.

I climbed up on the iron gate which closed the yard at night, and saw over the people's heads a great expanse of empty street to the east, while the west was packed with every vehicle which had passed that way since the Lieabout's sensational find.

It was because I was prevented by the angle of the wall from seeing my two police friends descending into the shop through the skylight that I was an exception from the rest of the crowd, and did not have my attention diverted from the excitement over the way.

I saw the long black car pull up outside the jeweller's shop and I saw the three men spring out of it. It was not until the crash of broken glass reached me, as the brick went through the window, that I realized that anything untoward was afoot.

The rest happened so quickly that I hardly followed it. I had a confused impression of flying figures, something flashing in the autumn sun and then of the black car sliding round like a speedboat in the broad road and flying away with smooth acceleration. In a moment it had gone completely. I could not even see which way it turned at the end of the street. Nothing but the ragged hole in the window, with a scared assistant's face peering through it, remained to show that the raid had occurred.

At that moment the first policeman to get down into the empty shop must have pulled away the coat, revealed the neatly arranged sacks and distemper tins beneath, and kicked the old boot away angrily, for the crowd suddenly became aware of the other sensation, and surged off across the road to gape anew.

It was extraordinarily neat. The whole thing had been done in one of the most important streets without anyone being able to give a clear picture of any of the men involved.

We heard all about the robbery from the tobacconist on the corner.

Ten thousand pounds' worth of valuables had been snatched, he said, including the gold state salt-cellar which an ancient and worshipful company was presenting to a foreign royal bridegroom, and which had been on view there for a few privileged days. A little small stuff went, too, he said; a couple of trays of rings and several oddments.

I never saw the Lieabout again. Foolishly I supposed that, after making such an ass of himself by his false alarm, he did not care to show his face in the neighbourhood and had moved off to another corner of the town.

The parcel came a week later. I found it in the letter box one night when we came in from a show.

It was the topaz brooch. It lay upon a mat of cottonwool, and there was a note with it written in a neat, educated hand. The message was brief and only too enlightening.

"Very many thanks for your valuable assistance," it ran. "Congratulate you. Very gratefully yours."

There was no signature and the package had not been through the post.

So you see the problem: What should Mrs. A. do now?

FACE VALUE

'I little thought,' wrote Sir Theo in unaccustomed longhand, while the great desk spread round him and the silence of the magnificent room was intense. 'I little thought that towards the close of a long, arduous and, I think I may say with modesty, not unuseful career, I should hear myself described, albeit *sotto voce,* by a comparatively senior officer of the Criminal Investigation Department as a Pompous Old Ass.'

He hesitated and his pen made little circles in the air above the faint blue lines in the exercise book which Miss Keddey herself had run out to buy for him.

'Pompous old ass.' He wrote it again without capitals. 'At the age of fifty-three—hardly a dotage, if certain aspects of the last war are any criterion—such an experience must give any sapient' (crossed out) 'farseeing' (crossed out) 'honest' (underlined) 'man furiously to think'.

He sat back in the beautiful chair which he had inherited from Sir Joseph, the first head of the great firm, read what he had written and permitted a dismayed expression to flit over his handsome clean-shaven face. He removed his eyeglass and changed it for the pair of bent pince-nez which he kept for reading contracts, and, since the room was deserted and the door locked, spoke aloud:

94

"No need to be a ruddy fool!" He bent again to write. 'I have only one natural gift—my success had been due entirely to hard work—and I may at times have appeared vain of it. *Nemo mortalium onmibus horis sapit.* But the fact remains, I have noticed and remarked on it time and time again, *I never forget a face.* My family, Miss Keddey—who has been a secretary for twenty years—my colleagues on the Board, my brother justices on the Bench, the officers with whom—despite my great age!—I was privileged to serve in the Southern Command, everybody who knows me, will confirm that, pompous though I may be, this is my undisputed gift. It has shown itself many times. When Robert St. John walked into the Club, after thirty years, wearing a great black beard as long as one's arm, who recognized him before he had satisfied even the wine waiter? And who—? but this is unnecessary. My gift is undisputed and the matter I have to consider here is more complex.

I come now to Nicholas Parish. This young man entered the firm, of which I have the honour to be the Chairman, some few years before the war. I knew his father and did not like him, but it is typical of me that a circumstance of that sort is more likely to predispose me in the favour of a youngster than to detract. Ass though I am, I try to be fair.

Young Parish is not unhandsome, flashy—by my aged standards—and, according to my wife, who met him once in this office, dangerous, whatever that may mean.

From the start he showed force which I admired, an unconventional streak which was all very well since he had the wit to control it, and a genius for pushing a job through to its conclusion—the trait which made me like him. At one time he was in charge of our new Psychological Department.

During the period when I was the 'unfit' amateur colonel in an army department of 'unfit' amateurs, stationed in a sector of the South Coast which, by the grace of God, was never attacked (Ass perhaps, but not Fool, Mr. Superintendent), I found him a most efficient major. It would hardly be true to describe us as wartime comrades, for I am an old hand in the service of this firm and I have no illusions regarding friendships between the head of such a concern and the men who must ever, to their lives' end, remain his subordinates. But we got on very smoothly. I think I may say that. Very smoothly indeed.

After the war we returned to our respective desks. In a short time his desk became a little larger. Mine remained as it is—as a matter of fact, so Sharman of the Bank was telling me (his hobby is irrelevant figures)—the largest, save one, in the world.

Our association, Parish's and mine, was never social. Theobald Park is in the country and when my wife makes what small effort she can to entertain in these times, the names of the junior members of my staff are not added to her secretary's list. However, we lunched together on occasion and, while he introduced me to the amusing if frivolous *Wardrobe*, I have taken him to the Club. In fact, I believe he is on the waiting list so that, should he live a hundred years, poor fellow, his name may well come up before the committee before he dies.

That is how matters stood on the twenty-third of October last, the date which the Superintendent finds of such absorbing and recurrent interest. It was the night of our regimental dinner. I was to speak and I had, I confess, taken Parish's opinion on the draft of the few words I intended to say. He was very helpful; I can see him now with that flicker in his dark eyes as some little joke of mine touched him.

We were the only two senior officers from this firm attending and it seemed natural that we should go together. As I told the Superintendent and that odd, evasive fellow, Campion who came with him on the third occasion, I have no idea who suggested it. My impression is that it was so obvious that it needed no suggestion. Frankly, I cannot envisage Parish suggesting a course of action to me; I am the natural leader in any decision, great or small. The only faintly unusual feature of our excursion was that I offered to pick him up at his home in Morter Street midway between the Club and the Porchester where we were to dine.

The Superintendent, a squat, obstinate man, did his best to get me to say that Parish *asked me* to fetch him, which would have been absurd. The younger man, Campion (some sort of consultant whose vague, pale face I have seen somewhere unexpected, possibly in the bar of the House of Lords), muttered something more sensible about a man not being able to refuse a civility in certain circumstances, but I could not acquiesce. I am, as it were, the captain of the ship, and since I went to Morter Street I must have arranged it. I remember that both Parish and I spoke of the difficulties of parking at night and the inadvisability of taking two cars.

His house is a pleasant, two-storey affair, worth every penny of the rent he must pay for it. It is a cottage in London, snug and yet dignified. I noticed the leaded lights and the frilled muslin curtains particularly—with a pretty woman looking out from between them it might all have been on the stage of the old Gaiety. When Nicholas came running out to tell me we had made a slight mistake in the time and still had twenty minutes, I was only too delighted to step in and take a very good dry sherry with him.

Poor little woman! She rose up out of the flowered couch which all but smothered her and greeted me like an old friend. In the discreet lighting I like, I saw her small face glowing and her eyes shine. Despite the decrepitude which is so evident to the Superintendent, I felt the warmer for her welcome.

She held out both hands to me and said, "Sir Theo! Do you remember me?"

Well, of course I did! And I was happy to tell her so. Since this report is for a special purpose, I may admit that when I felt her hands tremble in mine it gave me a more pleasurable sensation than I have derived from anything of the kind for very many years. I remembered her face, naturally, but not only that. As soon as Parish mentioned Brabbington I was able to tell them when and where I had the pleasure of being introduced to her, at a sports meeting just before I left the army. At that time she was in uniform herself and those heavy costumes do not reveal a woman's shape in the same way as does an expensive rose-silk gown—they are not designed to. She made even more impression on me at this second meeting, while we chatted in her charming room.

I have been questioned again and again about this simple interlude and I have kept nothing back. The

97

younger people were on edge. I admit it and I cannot think it strange or sinister. The first time Sir Joseph visited my wife and me, *we* were on edge.

We drank excellent sherry and talked nonsense, or I did, mainly about Mrs. Parish's charm. When their clock struck the half hour, Nicholas and I left for the dinner together.

Poor little woman! She came to the door with us to kiss her husband. They were smiling brightly at each other and the only thing I remarked which was at all untoward—I only remember it now as I come to write—was that she refused a wrap and swore she was not cold although I noticed, as I bent towards her fair head, that her teeth were chattering.

I last saw her waving to us from the bright green door and after that, until the message from the police was brought in to him at the table some hours afterwards, *Parish did not leave my side.*

I saw the waiter bring him the note and heard his muttered word of excuse but I did not know, of course, what had called him. Speeches were over by that time, and having done my duty, I was dozing by my glass. In wartime I discovered that I am no soldier, in peacetime I find myself doubly convinced.

The shock came when I had got back to the Club, and was just in my room. Johnson came hurrying up to ask me if I would see an officer from Scotland Yard.

That was my first visit from the Superintendent and he told me the news bluntly. At half past nine that evening Mrs. Parish had been found by her sister, who had visited her unexpectedly, lying in her bedroom with her head smashed in and her pretty face obliterated by many savage blows. The maid had been out all the evening, but the sister, it appeared, had a key.

The Superintendent wanted to know, and he spoke with a frankness which set me wondering about the law of slander, if I could give "the husband" as he called poor Parish, "a clean sheet"!

I soon got rid of the man. Parish had never left my side.

Yet, in the morning, before I was up, the man was back again. He appeared with very little ceremony and requested me, somewhat amazingly I thought, to get up and go with him to a mortuary to identify the body. I own I made every effort to avoid the unpleasant experience, but, on the telephone, my solicitor was quite clear if not helpful, and at length I consented.

We drove to a place which I found chill and there I saw what I expected to see—a fairheaded flower of a woman mutilated by unexampled brutality.

The Superintendent—I hardly suppose any two men have ever disliked each other so thoroughly on a brief acquaintance—asked me if I could swear that the woman before me was the woman whom I had met on the evening before. He struck me as insane. At Parish's house I had met Parish's wife, whom I knew. Subsequently her relatives had identified these repellant remains as the poor lady's body. I waited until I got outside and then gave him no more than he deserved; when I got back Miss Keddey put me through to the Commissioner with whom I had a word. That, one would have thought, should have been the end. Not a bit of it! The moment I was available—it was not until the evening—the unchastened Superintendent called again, bringing with him this consultant fellow, Campion.

I do not admit that I took a liking to Albert Campion but there was certainly no offence in him. He behaved like a gentleman and his pale eyes behind his horn-rims were not unintelligent. Silencing his companion, who made me think of some square dog who was following him, he mentioned some gossip which I confess was new to me.

Intimate friends of the Parish's had hinted that the couple did not get on. I was astonished to hear it but I know how difficult it is to judge such matters from a brief visit. Mr. Campion assured me that a solicitor had been consulted in regard to divorce proceedings but that Mrs. Parish had refused to sue. He told me, but it was hearsay, that Parish was reputed to have many liaisons—typists, shopgirls, minor actresses. It was hardly my affair. He told me the two had separate rooms and never dined together. I shook my head; it is extraordinary how other people live.

Finally, since the interview was taking longer than I could afford, I invited them to put their cards on the table. Immediately the Superintendent, springing from the leash, advanced an extraordinary theory which I can only think was his own. He suggested that Parish had been free to murder his wife before I arrived at the house and had successfully convinced me that she was the wife I had met at Brabbington. It was so absurd and so insulting that I told him of my peculiarity—I never forget a face. I added that I was prepared to go into a witness box and swear it. My old friend, Lord Justice Blossom, might, I thought, confirm me in this modest boast.

He left after that and it was as he went out of the door (Miss Keddey is still tremulous) that he permitted himself the ephithet with which I opened this account. Pompous, old and an ass.

As I recovered from my amazement, I saw that this fellow Campion was still there. He has a certain charm.

"Zeal has no grace," he said and made me an adroit little compliment on the clarity of my evidence. Before very long, I forget how it came about, we were chatting of other things and I found that he was a member of the Junior Greys from whom the Club sometimes accepts hospitality at spring-cleaning time.

At length, I noticed he was hesitating, not venturing to bother me, and, as is my way when people are civil, I gave him a lead. He made what he said himself was a very odd request. He asked me to go with him to buy some flowers.

Why I should have gone, merely to please him, must remain the only mystery in this episode.

We entered the brightly lit Mayfair shop, hot and dank and smelling like a funeral, and a young woman came forward to serve us.

Just for an instant I felt a sudden qualm. The likeness was in her movement, the eagerness of her walk, the brightness in her eyes but at once I saw that I was wrong and I blamed the Superintendent for making a normally nerveless man fanciful. This girl had black hair, the blackest I have ever seen in a European, her face was pallid as wax and she kept her eyes downcast. Her clothes were nondescript and her voice was no more than a whisper. Campion spent so much time buying a few violets from her that I suspected him of not knowing his own mind but we came out at last and stood on the damp pavement together, near a street lamp.

He gave me that gentle smile of his which reminds one

that he has not the drive to make a success of his odious profession and said softly: "Of course *she* has a face anyone could forget—even yourself, Sir Theo."

"Who?" said I. "The shopgirl? No, my boy, I shall know her again if ever I see her—which I doubt."

He sighed at that. "So," he said. "In that case I don't suppose you ever will." Then, with a swiftness which surprised me, he pulled out a photograph and showed it to me in the light. It was one of these fuzzy modern prints showing a woman in Service uniform. She was the same type as Mrs. Parish or the girl in the flower-shop for that matter but the photograph was bad and did not flatter her. She was babyish, round—no animation.

I guessed his plan and smiled.

"I remember her when she was like that—at Brabbington," I said. "It's no good your worrying, Campion. I never do. I never forget a face."

I heard his laugh of resignation and we prepared to part. And then he shook me. "Yes," he said gently. "A great natural gift, Sir Theo—but it's not your only one, you know."

The broad nib came to rest and the writer looked up. He was cramped and cold but there was determination in his small judicial mouth. He turned a page once more.

'I have made this record,' he wrote, 'because it was an axiom of my predecessor's that, when confronted by a grave and knotty problem, a man should sit down alone and transcribe his reflections in longhand, not for the edification of posterity, but for the clarification of his own mind.

For some weeks I have been considering whom I should send to fill a recent vacancy, which has occurred with tragic suddenness, in the service of this firm in South America. The needed man should be resourceful, quick to action, as cunning as his enemies and not overburdened with conventional scruples. He would also understand men. If he succeeds he may become a minor dictator. If he does not succeed he may die.

At this moment our Overseas Manager is waiting near his telephone; I have promised to give him my decision tonight.

Shall I send Nicholas Parish?'

Sir Theo closed the exercise book. For a moment or two he sat, chin on hand, half aware that the glow from the coal fire opposite was turning his black coat to crimson and his linen to ermine.

At length he rose, tore the book to quarters and threw them on the coals. As soon as the last charred flake flew upward he smiled briefly, returned to the desk and picked up the telephone.

EVIDENCE IN CAMERA

There are people who might consider Chippy Wager unethical and others who go a great deal further. At the time I am telling you about he was on the *Cormorant*, which is not that paper's real name, but why make enemies if you don't have to? He was, and is, of course, a photographer; one of those boys who shoot through a cop's legs and jump on the boot of the limousine so that you can see the Society bride in tears as she takes her first cold look at the man she's got. They pay those lads plenty, but Chippy had uses for money, mainly liquid, and he made another income on the side by taking photographs privately of practically everything from the Mayor and Corporation to the local beauty queen.

We went down to St. Piers for the fifth murder. I was on the old *Post* at the time, and when I say 'we' went, I mean among others. The Southern Railway put on one excursion train for the Press and another for the police when the body of Mrs. Lily Clark was found.

The story was simple and, if you like that sort of thing, good. Briefly, someone was killing off middle-aged women redheads in seaside towns. There had been a summer of it. In May Mrs. Wild was killed in Whichborne, in June Mrs. Garrard at Turnhill Bay, and by July the murderer had got round to Southwharf and had attended to a Mrs. Jelf. In August he chose a fashionable resort just outside the polo ground at Prinny's Plage, and in September there was this latest affair at St. Piers.

In all five instances the details were astonishingly similar. Each victim was respectable, homely in appearance, in the habit of letting rooms to visitors, and either naturally or artificially auburn-haired. Each woman was found strangled in a secluded place in the open air, with her untouched handbag beside her. Each woman lost some trifling ornament, such as a cheap ear-ring, a gold clasp from a chain bracelet, a locket containing edelweiss, and once, in Mrs. Hollis's case, a small silver button with a regimental crest upon it.

Not once was any trace of the murderer seen either before or after the crime, and by the time the St. Piers news came through, the Press were on the verge of being bored. There was still plenty to write about, but nothing new. The *Cormorant* and its sisters, who had worked themselves up to screaming hysterics in July, were showing signs of exhaustion, and even the heavies, like ourselves and the *World*, were falling back on such items as the slayer's preference for the new moon.

From my own purely personal point of view the thing was becoming a nightmare, and the principal reason for that was Chippy Wager. I had first met him when I travelled down to Whichborne in May. On that occasion there were seventeen of us in a carriage which might have held ten without active inconvenience, and although he was the last to arrive he was in a corner seat with only myself atop of him before the journey was half-way over. I do not know how he did this. My impression is that there was a jolt in a tunnel and that when we came out into the light there he was, slung with cameras, sitting just underneath me.

Chippy is a thin rag of a man with a surprisingly large square head in which, somewhere low down in front, has been inserted the bright predatory face of an evil child. Whenever I think of him, I receive a mental picture of white lashes on red lids and a row of widely-spaced uneven teeth bared in a 'Have you got anything I want?' smile.

His is hardly one of the dressy professions but I have

104

een his *confrères* blench when confronted by some of his ensembles. Peterson, my opposite number on the *World*, insists that the man finds his clothes lying about in hotel bedrooms. When I first saw him he was certainly wearing jodhpurs, carefully tailored for a larger leg, a green cardigan buttoning on the wrong side, and a new cheap sports coat adorned by a single gigantic beer-stain. Every pocket, one frankly marsupial, bulged strangely rather than dangerously and he carried as much gear as a paratrooper.

I remember my conversation with him on that occasion. I had pulled back my sleeve to glance at the time and he prodded me in the back.

"That's a good watch," he said. "Ever had it photographed?"

I said that, strange as it might seem to him, such a notion had never entered my head.

"It's wise," he assured me seriously. "In case you ever had it pinched, see? Gives the busies something to go on. I'll do it for you when we get in. Won't cost you more than half a bar. You're married, of course. Got any kids?"

I told him no, and he seemed hurt.

"Kids make good pictures," he explained. "Kids and dogs. Got a dog?"

Again I had to disappoint him.

"Pity," he said. "What a pal, eh? What a pal. You might pick up one down here. There's a chap only five miles out who breeds Irish wolfhounds. I'll put you on to him and we'll take a spool. Surprise the wife, eh?"

After that the man became an incubus, haunting me as I drank furtively in corners or hunted our murderer with one eye behind me, so to speak, lest I myself should be waylaid. I could, I suppose, have got rid of him with brutality and the fishy eye, but I could not bring myself to do it. He was so fearful, so unmitigatedly awful that he fascinated me; and then, of course, he was so infuriatingly useful. There was a rumour that he was lucky, but that explanation did him less than justice. He was indefatigable, and his curious contacts and side jobs sometimes provided him with most useful breaks, as, for instance, when he nipped down to Whichborne station to oblige a man who wanted a shot of his greyhound and got instead a very fine one of the Yard's Chief Inspector Tizer getting off the train at a time when

105

no one was sure if the local police had appealed to the Yard and, if so, who was going to be sent.

By the time the murderer had got round to St. Piers, Chippy was most anxious that the homicidal nut should be apprehended and the case finished. His reason was personal and typical. I happened to know about it because he had confided it to me one night in a hostelry at Prinny's Plage. I can see him now, pointing to the brewers' almanac which hung on the varnished matchboarding of the bar wall.

"Look, chum," he said, his forefinger tracing out the dates, "next new moon is September sixteen, isn't it? Don't think I'm complaining about that. It'll still be summer then and the seaside suits me. But what about the month after? New moon, October fourteen. I don't want anything awkward to happen then, do I?"

I made a point of never giving him encouragement and I said nothing, knowing perfectly well I should not silence him.

"October fourteen." He was indignant. "The Distillers Livery Company Conference begins on the fourteenth. Fancy missing that. What a tragedy, eh? What a tragedy!"

That was in August. We were all expecting the September murder, though naturally there was no way of telling where it was going to crop up. When the news broke, it was very nearly anticlimax. As Petersen said, there would have been almost more news value in the story if it hadn't occurred. No one was pleased. The livelier dailies had planted men at most of the larger southern watering-places, but no one had thought of St. Piers, cheap and respectable, out on the mudflats of the estuary. We had a local correspondent there, as we had in every town in the country. The last thing he had sent us, according to the book, was an account of a stork which had been seen flying inland one evening in June the previous year. According to his story, the phenomenon had caused wild excitement in the town. It appeared to be that sort of place.

I managed to avoid Chippy going down, but I saw his back disappearing into the railway Tavern as I picked up a taxi at the station. I was glad of the respite, for the newsflash which had come in was so familiar in its wording—'Body of well-matured woman found strangled.

Lonely woodland. Auburn-haired. Chief Inspector Tizer hurrying to scene'—that I felt a wave of pure nausea at the prospect of having to deal with him as well.

St. Piers was much as I had feared. At first it is only the light and the faint smell of iodine which warns the newcomer that the coast is at hand, but towards the front, where the architecture veers towards Victorian Moorish, a faded ocean licks a duncoloured strand and the shops sell coloured buckets and sticks of sweet rock and crested china to take home.

I found our local correspondent, a tobacconist called Cuffley, in his shop on the parade. He was waiting for me on the step, every hair in his moustache electrified with excitement. He had leapt to the job, had been on the spot soon after the body had been discovered, and had even written a short piece which began, as I remember, 'Mad Killer Visits St. Piers At Last. A baleful sun rose early this morning over the municipally maintained woodland behind the Kursaal and must have shone down unheeding for quite a space on the ghastly blue contorted lips of a respected local resident. . . .'

However, he had got the victim's name and address for me and had written it down in block caps, on the back of one of his trade cards: *MRS. LILY CLARK, KNOLE, SEAVIEW AVENUE.* It was the same sort of name and the same sort of address as all the others in the long weary business, and when he told me with delight that he had recognized a relation of the dead woman among his customers, and had gone to the length of having her waiting for me in the little room behind the shop, I knew before I saw her exactly the kind of gal I was going to find. The sameness of all five cases was slightly unnerving. I recognized at once both her horror and the dreadful secret enjoyment she was finding in it. I had seen it often that summer.

Her story, too, was a fifth variation of a tale I had heard four times already. Like her predecessors, Mrs. Clark had been a widow. She had not exactly dyed her hair but she had touched it up. She had not taken in lodgers in the ordinary way, being much too refined. But, yes, on occasions she had obliged. The idea of her going for a walk with a man she did not know! Well, if the situation had

107

not been so tragic the relation would have had to laugh, she would, really.

I asked the question I had grown used to asking. "Was she a nice woman? Did you like her?" I was prepared for the girl's hesitation and the faint uneasiness, the anxiety to speak well of the dead. I remembered comments on the other women. "She had a temper." "You would not call her exactly generous." "She liked her own way." "She could be very nice when she wanted to."

This time Mr. Cuffley's customer, in speaking of Mrs. Clark, said something which seemed to me to sum up them all.

"Oh, she was all for herself," she said grimly and shut her mouth like a vice.

At Sub-Divisional Police Headquarters there was no information of a startling character. Mrs. Clark had met her death at some time before midnight and in the process she had not been robbed. Fifteen pounds in treasury notes had been found in the mock-crocodile handbag which still hung from her arm. The sergeant in charge spoke of the negligence of the criminal in this respect with an amazement which bordered upon indignation. The only blessed thing she had lost, he said regretfully, was a silver tassel which had hung from the old-fashioned silver brooch she wore in her lapel, and, of course, her life.

As in all the earlier crimes, there was absolutely no suspect. There were no visitors staying at Knole, Seaview Avenue, and so far no one had come forward to report having seen the woman out with a stranger. I sent my story off and took a bus to the Kursaal. Half the town appeared to have the same idea, and I joined a stream of consciously casual strollers advancing purposefully up a threadbare path between ragged ill-used trees. The body had been found in a dusty glade where cartons and little scraps of paper grew instead of anemones. The spot needed no signpost. The police had got their screens up and I could see Inspector Tizer's hunched shoulders appearing above one of them.

The sightseers stood around at a police-prescribed distance, and here again nothing was new. In the last few months reams had been written about the avid, open-mouthed defectives who had come to stare at the last couch of each of the victims, and here as far as I could see they all were once more. I felt certain I had seen the dreary man with the fascinated blue eyes and the watchchain full of darts' medals at every road accident, case of illness in the street, or mere surface reconstruction at which I had had the misfortune to be present. The adolescent girl with the weeping baby brother was familiar, too, and as for the plump, middleaged man with the broad smile, I was sure I had seen him, or someone like him, grinning at the scene of every catastrophe in my experience.

I had a word with Tizer, who was not pleased to see me and had nothing to tell me. He is never sanguine and by this time his gloom was painful. I came away feeling as nearly as sorry for him as I was for myself.

The Press was there in force and I walked down the hill with Petersen. We came on Chippy at the turning where the path divides. He was busy, as usual, and he appeared to be taking a photograph of a holiday trio, two plump blondes in tight slacks and brassières, with a flushed lout wriggling between them. There could be only one explanation of the performance and I was gratified if surprised to see he had the grace not to notice me.

"Grafters and buskers on fairgrounds call it mug-faking, I believe," observed Petersen as we turned into the White Lion. "What does he charge them? Half a dollar? It's an interesting comment on the price of whisky." He has an acid little voice.

For the rest of the week the case dragged on. We had our hopes raised by several false alarms. Tizer thought he had a lead and went scampering to St. Leonards with a trail of us behind him, but the chase led nowhere. From our point of view it was all very dull. The weather turned cold, and three of the best hotels ran out of Scotch. I saw Chippy now and again but he did not worry me. He was picking up plenty of work, I gathered, and, if his glazed eyes in the evening were any guide, appeared to find it profitable.

He had a new friend, I was interested to see. So far I have not mentioned Chippy's friends. It is one of his major disadvantages that he always seems to discover a local drinking companion who matches, if not exceeds, the man himself in pure unpresentableness. On this occasion he had chummed up with the fat man I had seen grinning at the

109

scene of the crime, or if it was not he it was someone very like him. I had nothing against the man save that if I had seen but the soles of his feet through a grating or the top of his hat from a bus I should have known unerringly that he was a fellow for whom I should never have the slightest possible use. He had crumbs in the creases of his blue serge waistcoat, his voice was hoarse and coarse and negligible, and the broad vacant grin never left his face.

Chippy went about with him most of the time, and I was grateful for my release. I was agitating the office for my recall on the Saturday and should have left, I think, by Sunday had not I made a sudden startling discovery. Chippy was trying to avoid me, and not only me but every other newspaper man in the town.

At first I could not bring myself to believe it, but having ceased to hide from him I suddenly found I saw very little of him, and then that Sunday morning we met face to face on the steps of the Grand. In the normal way it would have been I who had become wooden faced and evasive and he who pursued me to insist on the morning snifter, but today he slunk from me, and for the first time in my life I thought I saw him discomposed. I even stood looking after him as he shuffled off, his harness clumping round his shanks; but it was not until I was drinking with Petersen and one or two others some fifteen minutes later that the truth occurred to me.

Someone had asked if Chippy had gone since he had not seen him lately, while somebody else observed that he too had noticed a singular freshness in the atmosphere.

Petersen defended him at once with all that charity of his which is far more lethal than straight attack, and I stood quite still looking at the big calendar over the bar.

Of course. I could not think why I had not realized it before. For Chippy, time was growing pretty short.

I was so anxious that Petersen, whom I love like a brother and who knows me nearly as well, should not cotton on to my idea that I wasted several valuable minutes in which I hope was misleading casualness before I drifted off. From that moment I hunted Chippy as he had never hunted me, and it was not too easy an undertaking, since, as I have said, the place was stiff with pressmen and I was more anxious not to raise any general hue and cry.

I hunted carefully and systematically, and for the best part of the day I was fighting a conviction that he had vanished into air. But just before six, when I was growing desperate, I suddenly saw him, still festooned with cameras, stepping ashore from a so-called pleasure steamer which had been chugging a party round the bay for the best part of three hours. The other people looked to me like the same crowd who had tramped up to the wood behind the Kursaal the day after the body was found. The adolescent girl with the baby brother was certainly there, and so was Chippy's buddy of the moment, the fat man with the smile.

From that moment I do not think I lost sight of him or them either. Shadowing them was comparatively simple. The whole party moved, it seemed by instinct, to the nearest hostelry, and from there in due course they moved to the next. So it went on throughout the whole evening, when the lights first came out yellow in the autumn haze, and too, when they shone white against the quickening dark.

I do not know when Chippy first became aware that I was behind him. I think it was on the second trip up the Marine Boulevard, where the bars are so thick that no serious drinking time is lost in transit. I met his eyes once and he hesitated but did not nod. He had a dreadful group round him. The man with the smile was still there, and so was a little seedy man with a cap and a watchchain, and two plump blondes in slacks. I recognized them all and none of them, if I make myself clear.

I could feel Chippy trying to shake me off, and after a while I realized that he was going somewhere in particular, heading somewhere definitely if obliquely, like a wasp to its nest. His red eyes wandered to the clock more and more often, I noticed, and his moves from pub to pub seemed quicker and more frequent.

Then I lost him. The party must have split. At any rate I found myself following one of the blondes and a sailor who I felt was new to me, unless, of course, it was not the same blonde but another just like her. I was in the older and dirtier part of the town, and closing time, I felt with dismay, could not possibly be far off. For some time I searched in a positive panic, diving into every lighted doorway and pushing every swinging door. As far as I remember, I neglected even to drink, and it may be it was that which saved me.

At any rate I came finally to a big, ugly, old-fashioned drinking-house on a corner. It was as large and drab and inviting as a barn, and in the four-ale bar, into which I first put my head, there was no one at all but a little blue-eyed seedy man wearing a flat cap and a watchchain weighted with medals.

He was sitting on a bench close to the counter, drinking a pint with the quiet absorption of one who has been doing just that for the last two hours. I glanced at him sharply but there was no way of telling if he had been the same seedy little man with medals who had been with Chippy's party. It was not that I am unobservant, but such men exist not in hundreds but in thousands in every town in or off the coast, and there was nothing distinctive about this one. Also he was alone.

I turned away and would have passed on down the street, when I noticed that there was a second frontage to the building. I put my head in the first door I came to and saw Chippy's back. He was leaning on the bar, which was small and temporarily unattended, the landlord having moved farther along it to the adjoining room. At first I thought he was alone, but on coming into the room I saw his smiling friend reclining on a narrow bench which ran along the inner wall.

He was still beaming, but the vacancy of his broad face intensified, if one can say such a thing, and I knew he must have ceased to hear anything Chippy was telling him long ago. Chippy was talking. He always talks when he is drunk, not wanderingly or thickly but with a low intensity some people find unnerving. He was in full flight now. Soft incisive words, illustrated by the sharp gestures of one hand, flowed from him in a steady forceful stream. I had to go very close up behind him to hear what he was saying.

"Trapped," he whispered to his friend's oblivion. "Trapped for life by a woman with a sniff and a soul so mean—so *mean*—so *MEAN*. . . ." He turned and looked at me. "Hullo," he said.

I remember I had some idea that in that condition of his I could fool him that I'd been there all the time or was not

112

here at all, I forget which. Anyway, I certainly stood looking at him in surprise without speaking. The thing that surprised me was that he had his old Rolleiflex, the thing he used for close inside work, hanging round his neck with the sight-screens, or whatever they call them, up ready for action.

He returned my stare with friendliness at first, but I saw caution creep across his eyes, tom-cat fashion, and presently he made an effort.

"Goodbye," he said.

The barman saved me answering him by bustling back, wiping the wood and thrusting a tankard at me all in one motion. He rattled the money I gave him in the till and waddled off again, after nodding to Chippy in a secret important way I entirely misunderstood.

"She was mean, was she?" I ventured, mumbling into my beer.

"As hell," Chippy agreed, and his red eyes wandered up to look over my shoulder towards the door. "Come in, son," he said softly.

A pallid youth was hesitating in the doorway and he came forward at once, a long cardboard roll held out before him like a weapon. He was white with excitement, I thought, and I did not suppose it was at the sight of us.

"Dad said you were to have these and he'd see you tomorrow."

I could see by the way Chippy took the parcel that it was important, but he was so casual, or so drunk, that he almost dropped it, and did scatter some of the coins that he gave the boy. He carried them in handfuls in his jacket pocket, apparently.

As soon as the kid had gone, Chippy tore the paper off the roll and I could see it consisted of four or five huge blown-up photographic prints, but he did not open them out, contenting himself with little squints at each corner, and I could see nothing.

The smiling man on the bench moved but did not rise. His eyes were tightly shut but he continued to grin. Chippy looked at him for some time before he suddenly turned to me.

"He's canned," he said. "Canned as a toot. I've been

113

carting him round the whole week to have someone safe to talk to, and now look at him. Never mind. Listen to me. Got imagination?"

"Yes," I assured him flatly.

"You'll need it," he said. "Listen. He was young, a simple ordinary friendly kid like you or I were, and he came to the seaside on his holiday. Years ago, I'm talking about. Only one week's holiday in the year." He paused for the horror to sink in. "One week and she caught him. God, think of it!"

I looked at the smiling man on the bench and I must have been a little whistled myself for I saw no incongruity in the tale.

"He was *ordinary!*" shouted Chippy suddenly. "So ordinary that he might be you or me."

I did not care for that and I spoke sharply.

"His wife caught him, you say?"

"No." He lowered his voice to the intense stage again. "Her mother. The landlady. She worked it. Twisted him." He made a peculiar bending movement with his two hands. "You know, said things. Made suggestions. Forced it. He had to marry the girl. Then he had hell. Couldn't afford it. Got nagged night and day, day and night. Got him down."

He leaned towards me and I was aware of every one of his squat uneven teeth.

"He grew old," he said. "He lost his job. Got another, buying old gold. Used to go round buying old gold for a little firm in the Ditch who kept him skint. It went on for years and years. Years and years. A long time. Then it happened. He began to see her."

"Who?" I demanded. "His wife?"

"No, no." Chippy was irritated. "She'd left him, taken all he had, sold the furniture and scarpered with another poor mug. That was years ago. No, he began to see the mother."

"Good God," I said, "and she was red-haired, I suppose?"

"And mean," he told me solemnly. "Mean as hell."

I was trembling so much I had to put my beer down.

"Look here, Chippy," I began, "why wasn't he spotted? Why didn't *she* spot him?"

He took me by the coat collar.

114

"Imagination," he whispered at me. "Use it. Think. He married the girl thirty years ago, but this year he began to see the mother as she used to be."

Our heads were very close together over the bar and his soft urgent voice poured the story at me.

"He's been travelling round the coast for years buying old gold. Everybody knows him and nobody notices him. Millions of women recognize him when he taps at their doors and very often they sell him little things. But he was ill last winter, had pleurisy, had to go into hospital. Since he's been out he's been different. The past has come back to him. He's been remembering the tragedy of his life." He wiped his mouth and started again.

"In May he saw her. At first she looked like a woman he knew called Wild, but as they were talking her face changed and he recognized her. He knew just what to do. He told her he'd had a bargain he didn't feel like passing on to his firm. Said he'd got a ring cheap and if she'd meet him he'd show it to her and maybe sell it to her for the same money he paid for it. She went, because she'd known him for two or three years coming round to the door, and she didn't tell anybody because she thought she was doing something shady, see?"

"And when he got her alone he killed her?" I whispered.

"Yes." Chippy's voice held an echoed satisfaction. "Paid her out at last. He went off happy as an old king and felt freed and content and satisfied until June, when he went to Turnhill Bay and knocked all unsuspecting at a door in a back street and—*saw her again.*"

I wiped my forehead and stood back from him.

"And at Southwharf, and at Prinny's Plage?" I began huskily.

"That's right. And now St. Piers," said Chippy. "Whenever there's a new moon."

It was at this precise moment that the smiling drunk on the bench opened his eyes and sat straight up abruptly, as drunks do, and then with a spurt set out at a shambling trot for the door. He hit the opening with a couple of inches to spare and was sucked up by the night. I yelled at Chippy and started after him, pausing on the threshold to glance back.

Chippy leant there against the bar, looking at me with

fishlike unintelligence. I could see he was hopeless and the job was mine. I plunged out and saw the smiling man about fifty yards down the street. He was conspicuous because he kept to the middle of the road and was advancing at a perfectly extraordinary trot which had a skip or a gallop in it every two or three yards, as if he were jet-propelled. I was not in sprinting form myself, but I should certainly have caught him and broken my heart if I had not tripped over a grating thirty feet from the pub door.

It was as I was getting up that I looked over my shoulder and saw Chief Inspector Tizer and the local Super, together with a couple of satellites, slipping quietly into the bar I had left. It was just enough to make me stone-cold sober and realize I might have got the story wrong. I slid into the pub behind the police.

Chippy was standing at the bar with Tizer on one side of him and the local man on the other. The five enlarged prints were spread out on the wood, and everyone was so engrossed in them that I came quietly up behind and saw everything over Chippy's own head.

They were five three-quarter-length portraits of the same man. Each man had been taken out of doors in a gaping crowd, and on each print a mid-section was heavily circled with process-white. In each case, within the circle, was a watchchain hung with darts' medals and other small decorations which might easily have been overlooked had not attention thus been called to them. In the first portrait the watchchain carried two medals and a cheap silver ear-ring. In the second, a gold clasp from a chain bracelet had been added. In the third, a small locket. In the fourth, a silver button. And in the fifth there hung beside the rest an ugly little tassel from an old-fashioned brooch.

Tizer, who is one of those men who look as if they have been designed by someone who was used to doing bison, put a fist as big as a ham on Chippy's little shoulder.

"You're trying to tell me you only noticed this yesterday and you had the outstanding luck to find the earlier photographs in your file?" His tone was pretty ugly, I thought, but Chippy shrugged himself free. Like myself, he was sober enough now.

"I am lucky," he said coldly, "and observant." He glanced at the barman, who was fidgeting in the archway where the counter ran through into the other room. "Ready, George?"

"Yes, he's still there, Mr. Wager. I've slipped round and shut the doors on him. He's sitting very quiet, just drinking his beer."

He lifted the flap and the police moved forward in a body. Chippy turned to me.

"Poor little blob," he said. "He's quite happy now, you see, till next new moon."

"When you will be otherwise engaged, I seem to remember," I said acidly.

He glanced at me with a sudden smile and adjusted his camera.

"That's right," he said. "There's sympathy in this business, but no sentiment. Wait just a minute while I get the arrest."

JOKE OVER

"It began with an ordinary 'missing person' notification," Superintendent Luke was saying as he opened an imaginary ledger of enormous size and felt for the pencil which was not behind his ear. "The woman came sweeping in and I took no sort of shine to her. She was smart enough to look at but you felt her skin was stretched over solid brass and that she'd get her own way if it was over your dead body. When I heard it was her boss and not a relative who had vanished into the blue I began to understand her interest for the first time. However, she told her story very clearly. She was crackingly efficient."

Almost absently he was building up one of his visual character impersonations as he talked, tightening his jacket skirts over his hips and thrusting his chin forward with an air which was both provocative and forceful. "The missing man was, she said, a Mr. John Joseph Miller, owner and director of a small firm called Quips Ltd. She gave a very fair *portrait parlé* of him; he was five foot ten, walked with a slight limp for which he wore a special boot, had protruding teeth, grey eyes, gold spectacles and usually wore brown clothes. She herself was the only other member of the concern and her name was Hilda Quidlip. They had an office off Custard Lane and they dealt in novelties for the catering trade—funny noses, bangers, streamers, paper hats and lion powder—that sort of thing."

"Lion powder?" Mr. Campion, his friend and companion for the evening, conveyed that he hated to interrupt but would care to know.

"Powder to keep away lions." Luke took the query in his stride. "Makes you sneeze so much it puts the brutes off. Well, they sold these things and did very well out of them and Miss Quidlip did all the work. She was empowered to sign cheques and make wholesale purchases so there hadn't been too much for Miller to do. He came in when he thought he would as far as I could hear. Then one week he didn't appear at all and so she carried on and the same thing happened the next week and the next. And then she realized he hadn't drawn any cash for some time and after a bit she got the wind up. It wasn't as if there was anything wrong with the business. I touched on that at once, naturally, but no, they were doing fine. Money was rolling in: Miss Quidlip *was* the business, she pointed out, so she knew. I betted she did." He broke off to reach for his glass and stood sipping it, his eyes bright above its clouded rim. "She told me she'd been to the flat where he lived alone—he was a bachelor—and could neither get in nor hear any news of him. She'd telephoned the hospitals and inquired at the morgue and finally she'd gone back to the flat which was on the top of one of those old houses behind Bedford Square and had climbed up the fire escape and got in. What she found there had startled her out of her wits and I must say the way she told it she shook *me*. I got an order and went round with her." He hesitated, searching for words to convey the bewilderment of that moment.

"He wasn't there," he announced at last. "Yet most of him was, if you see what I mean."

"Imperfectly," said Mr. Campion.

"Well, his teeth were there, for one thing." Luke made himself a set of ferociously protruding tusks with his free hand. "And his clothes and his watch and his pocket book and his ring and his boots—one of them surgical in appearance and his keys and his morning paper, dated the last day he went to the office, and his spectacles. They were all there together in and around the big chair on the hearth and they were very strangely arranged." He illustrated his point with astonishing vividness, drawing himself into his clothes and sagging back on his heels. "It was the queerest thing I ever saw. The underclothes were inside the suit, the shirt and collar still buttoned, the tie in the collar: the socks were in the boots which were laced. The ring was on the arm of the chair where the hand would have rested and the wristwatch, buckled, was beside it."

"Dear me," said Mr. Campion blinking. "And the teeth?"

"They were on top of the back of the chair with the spectacles around them and they were both covered with the hat." Luke laughed abruptly. "My report read like a bit of space fiction," he continued. "Or it would have done if I hadn't been darn careful that it didn't. There was no getting away from it. '*Gone to lunch in the fourth dimension*.' I shouldn't have been surprised to have found it pinned up on the door."

"Delightful." Mr. Campion sounded appreciative. "Did the lady get the inference?"

Luke grinned. "It seeped through," he conceded. "At any rate she kept prodding *me* with long red fingernails and saying, 'He's gone! Look! He isn't there!' until I took her both in hand. 'Routine,' I told her just as the lecturer had told me. 'That's what'll give us the answer—if there is one.' And I got down to it." He reseated himself before the fire. "There was quite a bit of work," he said reminiscently. "The more I found out about the chap the less I seemed to know. He didn't seem to have been in the habit of eating out anywhere locally. He hadn't done any cooking at his flat, there was no food or crockery of any description in the place. He'd rented the place just about the same time that he'd started Quips Ltd. which was two years before and the rent was paid quarterly in advance from the office. No one knew of anyone going in to clean for him, no one in the building seemed to know anything about him and even the people below couldn't remember when they had last seen him on the stairs. They also said they never heard him at night and in the daytime they weren't there themselves. He had very little furniture, few clothes and the only personal items seemed to be a few books of a semi-scientific nature and thousands of comic papers."

"Really?"

"Yes. Kid's stuff. Nothing sensational, just funny ha-ha. All very well read. There was nothing much in his wallet by the way except cash, stamps and one or two business letters." Luke leant back in his chair, his dark face alive with remembered interest. "So it was just solid homework," he went on. "I always feel I owe that case something. It taught me the meaning of the verb 'to plod'. I was nine or ten months on it altogether, the work done mostly in between regular jobs. I had no luck. We couldn't find any firm of dental mechanics which would own to the teeth and as I told you it was the same with the boot. Meanwhile the woman nagged us. The business was booming and she had to tell somebody." He pushed a long hand through his hair until it stood upright. "It was a worrying time," he said. "Old Georgie Bull was the C.I.D. Sergeant at that time of day and he didn't make things any smoother. He was the most miserable old cuss who ever breathed. What with one thing and another I was almost off my feed at the end of the time. And then one day I was sitting in my corner of the C.I.D. room in the old St. Mary's Street Station with the blessed boot on the floor in front of me and I suddenly got the urge to try it on. It fitted like a glove and I walked round the room in it. Caudblimeah! I felt like Cinderella!"

He looked slyly at Campion. "It wasn't surgical. It was a stage prop. After that, it was easy. I went round to Paynes the theatrical people who were the only firm who *could* have supplied it and got an address out of them. Twenty minutes later I was in a posh dentist's waiting-room among the reading matter with my parcel and after a bit I was shown into the chamber of horrors. The dentist was standing with his back to me washing his hands as they always are, the blighters, and when he turned round I took him by surprise. I just unwrapped my exhibit and we both stood looking at it.

"There are only two kinds of men who become dentists," he continued. "The ones who love it and ones who get miserable. Think round and you'll see I'm right. This chap I'm talking about was one of the second kind. He had no limp and his teeth turned in, not out, and he didn't wear spectacles.

"No one who knew him as Mr. Miller would have

121

recognized him. He had been in successful practice for years and, quite obviously, he was miserable as sin. I understood as soon as I saw him. He'd been making himself a jolly-joke world to hide in sometimes when things got too gloomy altogether. He let me do all the talking but there was nothing much I could say, of course. There was no charge involved.

"Finally I just put it to him. I said 'Is this your property, sir?' He said, 'Yes. Take it away, there's a good fellow. I—I've done with it—rather. Will that be all right?' I said it was nothing to do with us and it wasn't. He saw me to the door. Just as I went out he paused and looked at me like a wistful kid. 'Don't let her find me,' he said softly. 'She spoilt everything. At first it was such a wonderful escape but I saw it leading irrevocably to a stronger prison than ever. I had to get away from her and I went so *utterly*. I thought I'd made that so clear.' "

Mr. Campion got up.

"What a sad story," he said.

"Not really." Luke was grinning. "When I got back to the station I went up to old George who was sitting looking out of the window scowling like a wet weekend and I edged up to him very close.

"Sarge,' I said softly. 'You've always said you wanted to retire. Would you be interested in a nice flourishing foolproof little business with someone really efficient to run it? It would cheer you up you know; no end.' "

THE LYING-IN-STATE

How the body of the young Emir of Eulistahn came to lie in state in the vaults of the Norfolk Street Safe Deposit is one of London's secrets. The city takes its oversea visitors far more seriously than most of them suspect. Under a blank exterior there lurks an almost fanatical determination to oblige the poor lunatics however absurd their requirements. All it insists upon is the exercise of a modicum of common sense.

On this occasion it was the famous, if slightly ramshackle Alderton's Hotel which did the insisting. The Emir's entourage was composed of his black-bearded uncle, his doctor, two private secretaries and the best part of half a dozen valets and cooks.

His death occurred very suddenly, less than two hours after his arrival in Britain to attend a Royal wedding and the first reaction of his staff was to insist that he must lie in state for two days in the centre of his private drawing-room overlooking the park.

Even this could have been arranged had it not been for the value of the state jewellery with which protocol demanded the corpse should be arrayed.

Actually, Mr. Sydney Robbins who was the manager of

Aldertons had won a minor tussle about this very jewellery before the party arrived in London at all.

He was one of those placid business men who appear to have been knitted rather loosely out of woolly good nature until something arises to threaten interests when they become opaque-eyed and quite incredibly obstinate. Therefore, when the Emir's Second Secretary, who was young, slim and olive-skinned, had first arrived earlier in the month to make the original booking and had mentioned, in an impeccable Oxford accent, the question of adequate protection for the Diamond Shawl, the Pigeon's Egg Rings, the Five Emerald Stars and the Black Pearl, Mr. Robbins put his foot down at once.

He pointed out that the Emir would be only one of five foreign Royalties honouring the hotel and whereas the security arrangements were adequate for most eventualities this occasion was a little out of the ordinary. He then recommended the Norfolk Street Safe Deposit as he always did in similar circumstances.

The Second Secretary protested that His Highness was bringing the jewels to *wear*, first at the Reception and Ball and, next day, at the Abbey, and he mentioned several illustrious sponsors. But he was no match for Mr. Robbins when it came to discreet name dropping and in the end he listened meekly to the merits of the Safe Deposit.

Everything Mr. Robbins said about the place was quite true. It *was* a British Institution, it *was* used by the highest in the land, all personnel *were* appointed on a basis of heredity and safety and discretion were indeed guaranteed. In the midst of a covetous world it lay inviolate a nest of five steel chambers deep in the yellow London clay.

A great deal of legend surrounded its contents. At least two South American dictators were said to prefer it to Switzerland for the safe keeping of certain negotiable items; the secret recipes of two sauces and one world-famous liqueur were certainly there, for their advertisers said so, and connoisseurs were always criticizing the Stanoway family for hiding the rarest of all art treasures in its darkness; three little studies for the 'Mona Lisa', only a few inches square made in sanguine and said to be as fresh and lovely as the day Leonardo drew them. Yet the Stanoways were poor one would have thought. The first

124

ountess had laid waste most of the family fortune before
er lord divorced her in one of the bitterest suits on record
nd the second poor lady, her son who was the heir, and his
oung sister were kept busy exhibiting the mansion at five
aillings a time. But the Leonardos remained out of sight to
dd to the covetous dreams of wealthy collectors.

After listening for half an hour the Emir's Second
ecretary gave way gracefully and negotiations were
urried through. At Norfolk Street the Second Secretary
ired a small casket in his own name in Vault 4 where the
maller containers were kept and as decreed, received its
ey with the number of the box engraved upon it. He then
alked back and forth three times before a panel of
crutineers and had it explained to him that the mere
hysical possession of the key meant nothing. The
epositor must always come himself whenever the box was
pened. The jewels were solemnly handed over and the
hief Custodian assured him that at any time of the day or
ight one of the keepers of Vault 4, who now knew him by
ight, would be waiting for him. These were the unvarying
ules of the establishment.

The Second Secretary, left, but a few weeks later all his
appy arrangements were violently upset.

The blow fell on the eve of the wedding for the sickly
oung Emir arrived at the hotel in a state of collapse and
lied almost at once. He had it seemed, defied his doctors'
dvice and a bad air trip had proved fatal.

It was a great shock, said the black-bearded uncle, but
o doubt the will of Heaven. As for earth and Eulistahn in
articular, custom decreed that the body must lie in state
or a setting and rising of the sun' with the jewels and
egalia. A strong police guard, say twenty chosen men,
ust be arranged at once.

Mr. Robbins was appalled. It was against his whole
hilosophy to disoblige distinguished guests but at such a
noment it was impossible.

It was the Second Secretary who came to his rescue, and
is words burst on the distracted manager with the blessing
f water in a desert.

Instead of taking the jewels to the Emir, why not take
ne Emir to the jewels? Have the lying-in-state in the
aults? Mr. Robbins trembled with relief. It was un-

conventional but reasonable. Ludicrous even but practical.

"Could it be arranged?" murmured the Second Secretary.

"Leave it to me," said Mr. Robbins briefly.

Within an hour the Emir's frail body was taken to the Safe Deposit and carried into Vault 4 by his own people. They laid it revently upon a table moved down from the Chief Custodian's room and the Second Secretary, accompanied by the keeper on duty unlocked the steel box and took out the leather jewel cases. Then, as the official withdrew discreetly to the doorway, the uncle assisted by a doctor and a valet arrayed the body in its traditional glory. From his position the Safe Deposit man saw the gleam of stones. When the ritual was complete everybody retired to the ante-room and the keeper locked the door of the vault. For the rest of the night the four privileged members of the Emir's household took turns two at a time to keep watch from the keeper's bench while the official himself retired to the far end of the apartment where he could see but not overhear.

The Safe Deposit made only one stipulation in the whole business. No publicity. Since the same request was echoed by the Emir's suite and had also been made by Mr Robbins on behalf of the hotel, there was no difficulty about it.

In the dawn next day when Norfolk Street was empty, a motor hearse drew up outside the Safe Deposit, a coffin was carried in and presently brought out again. The Emir's uncle shook hands with the chief Custodian and the Second Secretary paid the dues. Mr. Robbins too was formally thanked and presented with a signed portrait of the late Emir.

The rest of the day was devoted to the wedding and no one in London was permitted to think of anything else. Mr. Robbins forgot about the Emir and indeed, in the flurry of three hundred departures, he had little time to recall him during the following week, but some ten days later when the hotel was its dull discreet self again his eyes rested on the portrait of the young Emir and he wondered who his successor might be.

For all up-to-date information he had long ceased to rely upon the printed word. He had a very good friend on the

126

entral switchboard of the British News Service and on
npulse he dialled her number. As usual she had the
nswer at her fingertips. Cool and efficient her lovely voice
ame back to him with authority.

"Eulistahn? It hasn't existed for some time. Don't you
emember Ernst Bey took over all that corner last year.
¿mir? Oh, no. That title has been extinct for a generation.
¿an I help you?"

Mr. Robbins hung up very slowly and sat still. From a
pot just above the nape of his neck a sliver of ice ran
moothly down his spine. He put out his hand to telephone
ie Safe Deposit but withdrew it cautiously, and from that
noment his life became a nightmare of apprehension. Yet
radually the days passed and no whisper reached him and
fter a while he gave up waking in the night and sweating
lthough the question remained in his mind. Seven months
rept by and still there was no inquiry, no scandal. The
¿mir and his retinue could have been as insubstantial and
neaningless as a dream.

The news that the Earl of Stanoway was permitting the
vorld to see the 'Mona lisa' studies after all and the usual
ontroversy about whether he should be allowed to sell
hem across the Atlantic broke in the spring of the
ollowing year. Naturally there was gossip.

People remembered the story of how the first Countess
it the time of her divorce had taken the drawings and
placed them in the Safe Deposit. 'Enclosed with this letter
s the key of the box,' she had written. 'So don't accuse me
·f robbing you. Whenever you want the drawings, come
ound and apologise and we'll go together and get them
rom the vaults. You see, without me, they just won't let
ou in. It's as simple as that, my dear man. Just apologize
ind then you can go to hell.'

Mr. Robbins heard the gossip and tried hard to put two
ind two together, but with no result until one day, his eye
ighted on a paragraph in one of the more frivolous of the
iews magazines. It was no more than a caption under a
aughing picture of a young brother and sister in fancy
lress, the boy dark, the girl very fragile and both curiously
amiliar to Mr. Robbins.

'Recently much in the news because of the proposed sal of a family treasure, *Viscount Bluebrooke*, son and hei of *The Earl of Stanoway,* and his sister *Lady Sarah* ar both of an age when there is no greater fun than th stage. They are said to be quite ruthless in th furtherance of their hobby and, I am told, even Lor Stanoway was compelled to grow a vast black beard t suit a recent part. The family motto is in old French an can be translated: *"Without Impudence I take M Own"*.'

Mr. Robbins looked at the somewhat fuzzy portrait o the young Emir and then at the girl in the magazine. Afte that he tore them both up into very small pieces.

THE PRO AND THE CON

Mr. Campion, stepping out of the cold sunlight of the Monte Carlo square into the dim warmth of the Casino vestibule, saw a plain good-tempered female face which reminded him for some reason he could not instantly trace of beautiful food.

He glanced at the woman curiously. She was square and respectable and would have been a natural part of the landscape at any country church, fête, but here, among a cosmopolitan crowd on a late afternoon in the height of the Côte D'Azur season, she was as out of place as a real dandelion in a bouquet of wax orchids.

She did not see him and he moved on, completed the usual formalities, and wandered into the Grande Salle. He did not cross to the tables but stood watching for a moment, his long thin figure hidden in the shadow of the columns. It was a scene he knew well but one which never failed to thrill him. Apart from the usual large percentage of tourists and wealthy regular visitors there were the professional gamblers, earnest folk with systems, and, of course, the strange and rather terrible old ladies, avid behind their make-up.

However, it was not at these that Mr. Campion gazed with such benevolent interest. Here and there among the throng he saw a face he recognized. A woman with grey hair and the carriage of a duchess caught his attention and he raised his eyebrows. He had not known that Mrs. Marie Peeler, alias Edna Marie James, alias the Countesse de Richechamps Lisieux, was out of Holloway already.

There were others to interest him also. At one of the *chemin* tables he noticed a large man with very blue eyes and the stamp of the Navy about him sitting beside a very pretty girl and her father. Mr. Campion eyed father and daughter sympathetically and hoped they could afford so expensive an acquaintance.

He had been playing his private game of 'spot the crook' for some minutes before he saw Digby Sellers. The man came lounging across the room, his hands in his pockets, his sharp bright eyes peering inquisitively from beneath carefully lowered lids. Considered dispassionately, Mr. Campion decided, even for a third-rate con man his technique was bad. In spite of his unobtrusive clothes he looked at first glance exactly what he was, a fishy little person, completely untrustworthy. Campion marvelled at his success in an overcrowded profession and glanced round for the other figure who should have accompanied him.

Tubby Bream had been Digby Sellers's partner in crime for so many years that the police of two continents had come to regard them as inseparable. Bream, Mr. Campion knew, was generally considered to have the brains of the act. At the moment he was nowhere to be seen and Campion missed that solid, respectable figure with the unctuous manner and the fatherly smile.

Mr. Campion suddenly succumbed to an urge to observe Mr. Sellers more closely. Moving quietly from his position in the shadow he followed the man out into the vestibule and arrived through the double doors just in time to see him snubbed by the female with the plain sensible face. Campion came upon the scene at the moment when the woman's plump countenance was burning with maidenly resentment and Mr. Sellers was hurrying away abashed.

"I don't know you and I don't want to," the lady observed to his retreating figure.

The voice and the blush recalled her to Mr. Campion's bewildered mind. On their previous meeting, however, the

130

olour in her face had been occasioned by the heat rather than by embarrassment.

"Why, it's Rose, isn't it?" he said.

She turned and stared at him.

"Oh, good afternoon, sir." There was relief in her tone. "It's very foreign here, sir, isn't it?"

"Very," he agreed and hesitated, remembering just in time that while he might find the presence of Margaret Buntingworth's invaluable Suffolk cook alone in the Casino at Monte Carlo unexpected, he could hardly say so without the risk of giving offence.

Rose was disposed to chat.

"Alice is coming for me in five minutes," she remarked confidentially. "I didn't go right inside because you have to pay, but I thought I'd come into the building because then I can say I have when we get home."

Mr. Campion's astonishment increased.

"Alice? That's the housemaid, isn't it?" he said. "Dear me, is she here too?"

"Oh yes, sir. We're all here." Rose spoke placidly. "Me, Alice, the Missus and Miss Jane. We're all staying at the Hotel Mimosita, sir. I'm sure the Missus would be very pleased to see you if you cared to call."

His curiosity thoroughly aroused, Mr. Campion went down to the Hotel Mimosita without more ado.

Margaret Buntingworth met him with open arms in the literal as well as figurative sense of the term. Rising from her basket chair on the terrace, which imperilled both the vermouth-cassis at her plump elbow and the American seated directly behind her, she welcomed him like a mother.

"Oh, my dear boy!" Her words tumbled over one another as they always did. "Oh, Albert! Oh, my dear! Do sit down. Do have a drink. What a fantastic place! How on earth did you get here? Isn't it all too absurd? Come into the lounge. It's cooler, the flies aren't so filthy and there aren't such hordes of people."

The solid American, the only person in sight at this siesta hour, glanced up in mild reproach, but Mr. Campion was whisked away.

Maragret was forty-five, natural blonde, plump, vivacious and essentially a countrywoman. As he glanced at her across the small table in the Mimosita's florid lounge Mr. Campion wondered if she had ever grown up. Her china-blue eyes danced with childlike excitement and the ruffles on her ample bosom were fastened with one of the little coral trinkets which are sold to the tourists all along the coast.

"It's exciting," she said. "I've always wanted to come here but I've never had enough money. Morty and I used to talk about Monte Carlo years ago." She paused and frowned. "I wish Morty were here now," she added as the thought occurred to her. "He'd tell me what to do in an instant. Still, here we are and the bills are paid till the end of the week so I expect it's all right. It's marvellous seeing you."

Mr. Campion blinked. He had always thought the defunct Buntingworth had been christened 'George', but he knew Margaret well enough to realize that she might easily have renamed him in her own mind, or on the other hand equally well be speaking of the hero of the last novel to take her fancy. The reference to some sort of predicament disturbed him, however. Margaret was not the sort of person to be trusted with a predicament.

"What happened?" he inquired. "Come into a fortune?"

"Oh no, not so exciting as that." The blue eyes saddened momentarily before they began to twinkle again. "I've let the house, my dear—let it really well."

Mr. Campion tried not to look bewildered.

"Not Swallows Hall?" he asked involuntarily.

She laughed. "It's the only house I've got, my pet. It's a dear old place but awfully cold in the winter, and of course it is miles from anywhere. It wants doing up too just now. Modernizing, you know. Re-wiring and central heating and that sort of thing. So I was delighted when these people took it. They gave me three hundred down and promised me another three hundred at the end of the week. I jumped at it. Wouldn't you?"

The man in the horn-rimmed spectacles gaped at her.

"Six hundred pounds?" he said faintly. "You've sold the place . . ."

"No, just let it." Margaret was beaming. "Let it for three months at fifty pounds a week. Isn't it good?"

"Unbelievable," said her visitor bluntly. "You ought to
132

be head of the Board of Trade. Any catch in it?"

"Well, I'm wondering." Mrs. Buntingworth's still pretty face was grave. "The rest of the money hasn't turned up yet and it's a week overdue. I wish Morty were here. He'd tell me just the sort of wire to send."

Mr. Campion was still mystified.

"I say," he said, "don't think me unkind, but in your part of Suffolk rents are inclined to be cheap, aren't they?"

"I know." Mrs. Buntingworth was smiling. "That's the lovely part. These people just came out of the blue and put down the money. They insisted that I took a holiday and they said they didn't want any of the servants, and when I was hesitating, wondering where I'd go, they suddenly suggested that I took the suite they had booked and couldn't use. It was rather a wild idea, but Rose and Alice have worked for me for years and years and have never had a decent holiday in their lives, and I suddenly said to myself 'Well, why not?' So here we all are."

"Stop," murmured Mr. Campion who was becoming confused. "Who booked the suite? Who couldn't use it?"

"The people who've taken the house, of course," said Mrs. Buntingworth calmly. "A Mrs. Sacret and her husband. I didn't see him. She and I fixed up everything between us."

There was a long pause before she looked up. Her natural featherbrained expression had given way to unexpected shrewdness.

"I say," she said, "do you think it all sounds a bit fishy? I do now I'm here. Frankly, I've been trying not to think about it. Mrs. Sacret seemed such a nice woman, so rich and friendly. I was fed up. Keeping the place eats up my income and I never have any fun. It was terribly cold, too, and unbelievably dull. So I fell for the scheme and got so excited that I didn't really have time to think things out until I got here. We arrived within a week of her seeing the house. Now I'm beginning to wonder. It seems so funny, doesn't it, anyone wanting to bury themselves at Swallows Hall in the winter? I do wish I had Morty with me."

Mr. Campion endeavoured to be cheerful.

"You've got the three hundred pounds, anyway," he said.

Margaret met his eyes.

"If you ask me, that's the fishiest part about it," she remarked, echoing his own private opinion. "I can't tell you how worried I've been. There's nothing of value in the house, of course, nothing they could steal that would be worth their while, and there can't be anything hidden there, buried treasure or that sort of thing. Albert, you're all mixed up with the police. You ought to be able to help me if anyone can. Supposing these people weren't straight, what could they be up to down at Swallows Hall?"

Mr. Campion was silent. In his mind's eyes he saw again the big rambling Tudor house standing in a belt of trees six miles from the nearest village. He imagined it in winter, cold, draughty and damp. He looked at Margaret blankly.

"Heaven only knows," he said.

Margaret frowned. "I ought not to have let it," she said. "But they would have it. I refused point-blank at first, but I couldn't get rid of them. The woman had just set her heart on it, she said, and her offers got better and better until I just had to take it. What shall I do? I'm so far away."

Mr. Campion grinned at her. "I'm on my way home," he said at last. "I've been on a cruise with some people. I left the yacht at San Remo. I'm catching a morning plane from Nice. I'll reconnoitre a bit for you, shall I?"

Mrs. Buntingworth's relief was childlike.

"Oh, my dear," she said, "if only you would! You're so frightfully clever, Albert. Apart from Morty you're the only person I know who can really deal with difficult situations. Do you remember how wonderful you were the night when the roof leaked?"

Mr. Campion modestly ignored the tribute.

"Look here," he said, "about this Mrs. Sacret, what does she look like?"

Margaret considered. "Oh, rather nice," she said. "About my age, small and dark and soignée, with quite a broad forehead."

Her visitor's face grew blank.

"She hadn't a very faint, not unattractive cast in one eye, I suppose?" he inquired quietly.

Mrs. Buntingworth gaped. "How did you know?"

Campion was silent. So Dorothy Dawson, of all people, was at Swallows Hall, he reflected. Dorothy Dawson had passed as Mrs. Tubby Bream before now, and Tubby

134

Bream's partner, Digby Sellers, was keeping an eye on Margaret Buntingworth's maid here in Monte Carlo. It was all rather significant.

Margaret escorted him to the door of the hotel.

"The odd thing is what on earth these Sacret people can be doing at Swallows Hall if they're not honest," she said as they parted. "After all, what can they possibly hope to gain?"

"What indeed?" echoed Mr. Campion and it was with a view to elucidating that very point that he wandered into Scotland Yard on the morning after his return home.

Superintendent Stanislaus Oates welcomed him with heavy humour and underlying affection.

"Sellers and Bream?" he said, leaning back in his hard chair behind his scrupulously tidy desk. "Con men, aren't they? Baker's the man you want. We'll have him in."

He spoke into the house phone and returned to his visitor with a smile.

"You're quite the little busy these days, aren't you?" he observed. "All your pals seem to get into trouble some time or other. Do you pick 'em, or just attract suckers naturally?"

"Neither. I am obliging." Mr. Campion put forward the explanation modestly. "Crooks come to the crook conscious; you know that."

"Ah, but I get paid for it," said the Superintendent. "Hallo, Baker, this is Mr. Campion. He does it for the thrill."

Inspector Baker, who had just entered, was a square, sober-looking young man who regarded Campion severely but was anxious to assist.

"Those two have split, I think," he said, glancing at a typewritten sheet in his hand. "Sellers came back from Canada a fortnight ago and left the country three days later. Bream has been in London for the last six months living in a flat in Maida Vale. The Dawson woman was with them. We kept an eye on them in the usual way, of course, and one of our men thought there was something brewing a month or so ago. But the punter got wise and nothing transpired. Now they've disappeared and I'm afraid we've lost them. If you ask me, they were getting anxious. Bream likes his comforts and usually needs a bit

135

of capital behind him for his little flutters. Funds were rather low, I should think."

Mr. Campion contributed his own small store of information concerning the partnership and the two Yard men listened to him attentively.

"A lonely house?" inquired the Superintendent at last. "Lonely and biggish?"

"It's certainly lonely and fairly big, but not attractive in winter." Mr. Campion spoke feelingly.

"Still, it's been a good home in its time?" suggested Inspector Baker. "Worth a bit some years ago?"

Campion was still mystified.

"Yes," he admitted. "Property out there has gone right down, of course, but in its heyday it might have fetched fifteen or twenty thousand pounds. Still, I don't see—"

The Inspector met the eyes of his superior officer.

"Sounds like 'the old home' again," he said.

"It does, doesn't it?" Oates was thoughtful. "Sellers!" he ejaculated suddenly. "That's it. Sellers met the sucker on the boat coming home from Canada, of course. He, Bream, and the woman must have been going to team up in Monte for the season, but when he arrived home he had this scheme all set, having picked it up on the boat. Bream and Dorothy dealt with Mrs. Buntingworth and bundled her off to the suite they'd already booked, not being certain of getting her right out of the way by any other method. Sellers followed her to watch things that end, because, of course, he couldn't appear at the house, while Bream and Dorothy are down there now, I suppose, in the thick of it."

Mr. Campion leant back in the visitor's chair and stretched his long thin legs in front of him.

"This is all very interesting," he said mildly, "but I don't follow it. What exactly do you mean by 'the old home'?"

"Good heavens, something he doesn't know at last," said the Superintendent, his lugubrious face brightening. "You tell him, Baker. I like to see him learn."

The Inspector fixed his visitor with a chilly eye.

"Well, you see, Mr. Campion," he began, "every now and again a man who has made good overseas returns to this country with the intention of purchasing his old home at all costs. Sometimes he's foolish enough to talk about it on the boat and a clever crook can get details out of him.

136

During the voyage the crook can usually size up his man and decide if the game is worth the candle. If it is, he arranges for an accomplice to get hold of the house. Sometimes they go so far as to buy it very cheaply, sometimes they just rent it. Anyway, they get possession, and then, since they've always been careful to pick a really rich man, they run him up over the deal and clear a packet. If they buy the place it's not criminal, of course, but in this case, if they've merely rented it, they'll be letting themselves in for false title deeds and heaven knows what."

Mr. Campion remained silent for some time and the Superintendent laughed.

"He's thinking of the wickedness and ingenuity of man," he said. "It surprises me myself sometimes. You'd better go along to the County Police, my boy. They can't do anything until the fellow actually pays over cash, of course, but either they or we will pick up Bream and Dorothy in the end. Well, well, we aim to please. Anything else you'd like to know?"

"Yes," said Campion slowly. "Yes, there is, rather. You're obviously right, of course, but there is one point I don't see at all. I'll tell you some time. Thank you kindly for the lecture. Most instructive. See you when I get back."

"Oh, Campion—" Oates called him when he reached the door, and when he spoke he was not joking. "Look out for Bream. He's nasty when he's cornered. Got a dirty streak in him."

"My dear fellow"—Campion was grinning,—"there's nothing I'm so careful of as my valuable skin."

Oates grunted. "I'm not so sure," he said. "Still, never say I didn't warn you. So long."

Mr. Campion returned to his flat where he was detained by an unexpected visitor. The following day brought unavoidable delays also, so that it was not until the afternoon of the third day of his return that he turned the nose of hs big four-litre Lagonda into the overgrown drive of Swallows Hall.

The long, low, half-timbered house, which was so prettily rose-entwined in summer, had an untidy and dilapidated aspect in mid-January. The miniature park was desolate, the iron railings flattened in many places and the grass long and yellow through lack of grazing.

As he came slowly up the moss-grown way he fancied he saw a curtain drop back into place across one of the lower windows. His ring, too, was answered with suspicious promptness and he found himself looking down at Dorothy Dawson herself as soon as the door opened.

She had dressed the part, he noticed. Her country tweeds were good but shabby and her make-up was restrained almost to the point of absence. She looked up into his face and he saw her eyes flicker.

It was evident that he was not the person she had expected but there was no way of telling if she had recognized him. Her expression remained polite and questioning.

"Mr. Sacret?" he inquired.

"Yes. Will you come in here? I'll tell my husband."

Her voice was very soft and she led him swiftly into Margaret's shabby drawing-room. Mr. Campion found himself a little surprised. Although she had shown no sign of actual haste the whole incident had passed with most unusual speed, and it occurred to him that he had never before entered any house with such little delay. He glanced at his watch. It was a minute to three.

He heard the quick step on the stones of the hall outside a second before the door swung open with a subdued rattle of *portière* rings and Tubby Bream came hurrying into the room.

His round white face shone smug and benevolent above the neatest of dark suits, and his grey hair, which was longer than is customary, was sleeked down on either side of a centre parting which added considerably to the general lay-reader effect.

In the doorway he paused with theatrical astonishment.

"Why, if it isn't Mr. Campion," he said. "Inquisitive, friendly Mr. Campion. My dear wife said she thought it was you but she couldn't be sure. Well, well, what a pity you should choose just this moment for a call."

He had a thick, not unmelodious voice with a crack in it, and all the time he was speaking, his small bright eyes shot little darting glances about the room, now out of the window, now at his visitor's face. He was a shorter man than Campion but his shoulders were powerful and his neck square.

"It's a pity," he repeated. "Such a very inconvenient time. Let me see now, you're not actually connected with the police, are you, Mr. Campion? Just a dilettante, if I may use the word?"

Mr. Campion shrugged his shoulders.

"I'm an old friend of Mrs. Buntingworth's," he began. "That's the only reason I'm here."

"Oh dear!" Bream's small round eyes widened. "Oh dear, isn't that interesting? Have you known her long, Mr. Campion?"

"Since I was a child."

"Thirty years or more?" Bream was rubbing his fat hands together. "How unfortunate. Really it couldn't be more unfortunate. You're so untrustworthy and there's such a little time. In fact"—he tugged at the chain leading to his fob pocket—"there really isn't any time at all. A minute to the hour, I see. *Put up your hands, Mr. Campion.*"

It was a new trick and one that added considerably, Mr. Campion felt, to his education. The wicked little snub-nosed Colt shot into the pudgy white hand with the speed and smoothness of a conjuring trick while the chain dangled harmlessly.

"You're making a great mistake, Bream," he began but the other interrupted him.

"Put up your hands. It's a question of time. Put up your hands."

There was nothing for it. Mr. Campion raised his arms.

"Turn round, please." The liquid voice with the unexpected harshness in it was complacent. "I'm afraid I can't keep you in the drawing-room. We're expecting an important visitor, you see. He's due at three o'clock. Dorothy, my dear—"

Mr. Campion did not hear Dorothy Dawson come into the room, but with the nose of the Colt pressing dangerously into a spot between his shoulder-blades, he was forced to suffer her to bind his wrists behind him. The strands of soft cord cut viciously into his flesh and he knew at once that it was not the first time she had tied up a captive. He ventured to congratulate her.

"No talking, if you please." Bream was breathing on his neck and the revolver muzzle pressed a little harder. "This

139

way. The cupboard where the baskets are, Dorothy. Such a damp little hole, I'm afraid, Mr. Campion, but you weren't invited, you know. Walk quickly, please."

Campion suffered himself to be driven into the disused butler's pantry across the hall where Margaret kept her gardening baskets. It was damp and smelt of mice.

The moment his foot touched the brick floor the man behind him sprang. The ferocity of the attack was wholly unwarranted and, unable to defend himself, Campion went down like a log in the darkness. He kicked out, only to receive a blow above the ear with the butt end of the gun which knocked him senseless.

When he came to himself a few minutes later his ankles were tied with the same paralysing tightness and there was a wad of paper in his mouth, kept in place by a strangling handkerchief.

"Tubby, he's here."

The woman's whisper reached the young man through the open doorway into the hall and he heard Bream's voice replying.

"Let him in then, my dear. I'll straighten myself. What an inconvenient visit from the silly, silly fellow."

The pantry door closed, the key turned softly in the lock and Campion heard the pattering of feet trotting towards the back of the house. He lay still. The effects of the blow he had received had by no means worn off and he dared not make an attempt to try the full strength of his bonds until he was sure he had all his wits about him.

Meantime there was plenty to interest him. Far off down the hall he heard the front door open. He listened intently but had no need to strain his ears. The newcomer had a voice which entirely defeated its owner's obvious efforts to soften it. His military, not to say parade-ground tones echoed round the old house, setting the glasses ringing.

"Mrs. Sacret? Got my letter? Very obligin' of you. Just home, don't you know. Naturally anxious to see the old place again. Just the same, just the same. Not a stone altered, thank God."

At this point the stranger evidently blew his nose and in spite of the acute discomfort which he suffered Mr. Campion's eyes widened and he pricked up his ears. There is a type of Englishman which cannot be copied. Caricatured, they make an unconvincing spectacle. Mr. Campion wished he could see Mr. Digby Sellers's dupe, for he sounded genuine, and that brought up the one point which had puzzled him ever since he had visited the Superintendent, the same point which had brought him down to Swallows Hall and head first into his present predicament.

Meanwhile, a conducted tour of the house was evidently taking place. The visitor's stentorian tones, punctuated by soft murmurs from the woman and Bream's less frequent unctuous rumbles, sounded at intervals from all over the house. Always the newcomer's theme was the same.

"Hasn't changed; hasn't changed. Used to play in here, don't you know. Happy days . . . youth . . . childhood. Makin' a fool of myself, I'm afraid. But affectin', you know, very affectin'."

In the basket cupboard Mr. Campion wrestled his bonds. His hands and feet were numb and the gag was choking him. The experience was both painful and infuriating. Even his attempts to make a noise were frustrated, for not only was it impossible for him to move but the effects of the blow, coupled with the lack of air, fast made him faint.

Meanwhile the party seemed to have gone into the garden. The visitor's voice, muffled but still audible, percolated through the lath and plaster walls. Campion caught a few disjointed phrases.

"Stayin' at Ipswich a douple of days . . . have to think it over, don't you know . . . lot of money . . . need repairin'. Who had the place before you, do you know? What? God bless my soul!"

There followed a long period of silence, broken only, for Mr. Campion, by exquisitely distasteful scratchings in the panelling near his left ear. He cursed himself mildly and closed his eyes.

His next conscious moment came nearly an hour later when the door was thrust cautiously open and he saw the silhouette of a square head and shoulders against the faint light of the hall.

"I think we might now consider our visitor, Dorothy my dear." Bream's voice was ingratiating and somehow anticipatory. "Well, Mr. Campion, comfortable, I hope?"

He came soft-footed into the room, managing to tread on the edge of Campion's upper arm, driving his heel hard into the flesh. The young man forced himself to remain inert and was rewarded.

"Dorothy"—Bream's voice was sharp—"come here. Bring a light."

"Oh, what's happened? What's happened? You haven't killed him?"

"That would be awkward, my child, wouldn't it? He's such an old friend of the police."

There was a laugh in the fat voice but it was not altogether one of amusement.

"Oh don't—" The woman sounded genuinely frightened. "You're so crazily cruel. There was no need to hit him as you did. If you've killed him—"

"Be quiet, my dear. Help me to get him out of here. He's alive all right."

Together they dragged the young man out into the hall and Bream bent down and tore the gag out of his mouth. The woman brought a glass of water. Mr. Campion drank and thanked her feebly.

At the sound of his voice Bream chuckled.

"That's better, that's better," he said, smoothing his large moist hands down the sides of his coat. "It's all most unfortunate. I don't like to have to inconvenience anyone like this, especially a guest. But it's entirely your own fault, you know, for choosing to come at such a very awkward moment. Believe me, my young friend, if you had called at any other time, any other time at all, it would have been very different. As it is, you've put me in a very uncomfortable position. I really don't see what to do with you. If you were only more dependable."

He broke off with a sigh of regret and stood looking down at his victim, a sad smile on his round white face.

"How are the wrists?" he inquired presently. "Sore? I feared so. Dear dear, this is very awkward. You may have to remain like that for some time. I don't see what else I can do, do you, Dorothy, my dear? Since he's precipitated himself into my—ah—my business affairs, I fear he may have to stay here until the project goes through. You see,

142

Ir. Campion, if I let you go you may so easily spoil all my eautiful work."

Mr. Campion stirred painfully.

"I hope your visitor liked his old home," he said bitterly.

"Oh, he did." The round eyes became shrewd and winkling. "You overheard him, did you? He had a rather ud voice, hadn't he? I was afraid you might. Ah well, that ractically clinches the matter, doesn't it? You must ertainly spend a day or two with us. I see no other way ut."

He was silent for a moment or so, lost in comtemplation f the younger man's discomfort.

"Yes, he liked it very much indeed," he went on at last, till in the bantering affected tone he had adopted hroughout their entire enterview. "I think I can safely say hat he is in love with it. Such a charming man, Mr. Campion. You'd have been touched if you'd seen his eyes ght up at each familiar scene. I was quite affected. I think ve shall have an offer from him in the morning. Oh yes, I o indeed. When I told him I was thinking of cutting down he trees and refacing the house he seemed quite disturbed."

Mr. Campion opened his eyes.

"He didn't attempt to borrow a tenner, I suppose?" he murmured.

Bream raised his eyebrows.

"No," he said. "No, he did not. He was hardly the type. What a pity you couldn't meet."

Mr. Campion began to laugh. The exertion hurt him considerably but he was genuinely amused.

"Bream," he said faintly, "do you see any reason why I hould give you a hand out of your filthy troubles? You lways were pigheaded and now, damn it, you deserve vhat's coming to you."

There was a long silence after he had spoken and he emained very still, his eyes closed. The other man pulled up a chair and sat down on it. He was not exactly shaken out the habitual crook has a suspicious mind.

"Mr. Campion," he began quietly, "why exactly did you come down here?"

"On an errand of mercy." Mr. Campion's voice was aint but resentful. "Like most acts of pure charity it was

143

misunderstood. You can go and hang yourself, Bream, before I help you now!"

"Perhaps you'd care to explain a little more fully?" The soft voice was very gentle. "My wife is in the back of the house now. I mention this because women are squeamish, as you know, and you might think I might hesitate to persuade you to talk a little if she were present."

He began to beat a slow tattoo on Campion's shinbone with the heel of his broad shoe.

"Good God, what do you think I'm here for!" The righteous anger in Campion's voice was convincing. "Do you think I would go scouring the country in an attempt to capture your scurvy little hide? That's a job for the police. I came here in a perfectly friendly spirit. I happen to have a useful piece of information which would save you time and money, and because you happen to be in the house of a friend of mine, and after the showdown I thought you might work off some of your natural resentment on the house itself, I dropped in to give you a brotherly tip. Instead of listening to me, as any sane man would, you started this kind of monkey-trick. Use your head, Bream."

"But, Mr. Campion, you gave me no option." There was the beginning of doubt in the greasy voice and the man on the floor was quick to press his advantage.

"Option be damned," he said cheerfully. "You were so afraid that your bird would drop in and find me that you lost your nerve. If you'd only paused to consider the obvious it might have dawned on you that if I meant to be unfriendly, I had only to run round to the county police, who would have bided their time, waited until you'd done something they could pin on you, and walked in at the psychological moment to nab you in the decent and time-honoured manner."

"But, Mr. Campion, consider. . . ." Bream's voice was unhappy. "Supposing you had dropped in here by chance. . . ."

Campion stirred. "Is this the kind of place anyone would drop into by chance?" he demanded. "Mrs. Buntingworth is in the south of France. I left her there three days ago. When she gave me a description of your wife, I recognized it, and when I called in at the Yard the other morning they were kind enough to explain the game you were playing.
144

and so, because I knew something you didn't, I came trotting down here in a positively brotherly spirit instead of going to the police. Now, believe me, I don't feel brotherly and you can sit here and wait for Nemesis."

"Oh, Mr. Campion." Bream had lost his banter and his voice and manner were no longer carefully matched to his costume. He was still wary but his eyes were anxious. "I'm beginning to be very interested."

"Very likely, but I'm in pain," suggested his victim. "My wrists are raw and I'm feeling spiteful. If you have any sense at all, you'll untie them. After all, you've got the gun; haven't."

The reasonableness of the request seemed to appeal to the crook. He cut the cords carefully and stepped back.

"I think I'll leave your ankles, if you don't mind," he said. "I'm not so agile as I was and I can't trust you at all."

Mr. Campion wriggled into a sitting position and rubbed his bruised wrists. His yellow hair was dishevelled and his pale eyes were hard and angry.

"Now, what do you think you are going to do?" he inquired. "It's a pretty heavy sentence for assault, you know, and quite a set-out for murder."

Bream scowled. "You may be lying," he suggested softly.

"Oh, have a heart, man." Campion sounded exasperated. "Is there any other reasonable explanation for my coming down here at all? Haven't I told you the obvious truth? Haven't I behaved like any other sane man in similar circumstances? You're the fellow who's lost his head and jumped into trouble feet first. However, I'll do you one more courtesy just to prove how well I meant. I told you I had known Mrs. Buntingworth all my life. What I haven't mentioned is that I knew her father and mother, who lived in this house until they died and it had to go up for sale. Mrs. Buntingworth's husband bought it, I believe. Now do you see what I'm driving at?"

Tubby Bream sat forward in his chair, his plump face even more pallid than before.

"Yes, Mr. Campion."

"Margaret Buntingworth was the only child of her parents," Mr. Campion continued, still with the same weary exasperation. "So any noisy, middle-aged gentleman

145

who comes roaring round here, moaning about his o
home, is bogus, my poor friend. He's just anoth
practitioner like yourself, working up to a loan of a d
cheque or whatever piece of fancy work is his particul
specialty. In fact, you've been done. Now are y
grateful?"

Bream's jaw tightened. "But Sellers . . ." he began.

Mr. Campion was derisive. "I saw Sellers in Mor
Carlo," he said, "and believe me he wouldn't deceive
nursemaid. No; your overseas pal saw Sellers on the bo
recognized a weak brother with capital, and played him f
a sucker, trusting to match his wits against yours when t
time came. Better face up to it."

Bream rose to his feet and walked slowly down t
room. He looked a dangerous little customer with h
heavy shoulders and short, powerful arms. It was evide
that he was going over Campion's arguments in his mir
and was finding them unpleasantly convincing.

Suddenly, however, he swung round.

"No, you don't, Campion!" he said sharply.

The young man withdrew his hands from the ank
bonds and looked unwaveringly into the muzzle of the litt
Colt.

"All right," he said, shrugging his shoulders. "B
frankly, I don't see the point of all this. What are you goi
to do, exactly? In view of all the facts, I mean."

"Find out if you're right."

"And when you discover that I am'?"

The man laughed.

"Then I shan't waste my time any longer, of course," h
said. "We shall clear out. Unfortunately, I can't trust yo
to keep your fingers out of my affairs, so naturally you
have to stay behind. It's a cold house, I know, but you'
tough. I should think you'd be alive when they find you."

Mr. Campion looked incredulous.

"But that's suicide on your part," he said. "Scotlan
Yard know I came down here to look for you. They'll g
you if I die, Bream."

The man in the neat dark suit spread out his hands.

"It's a risk I shall have to take," he said. "I may leav
word for a village woman to come and clear up o

Monday. If she's conscientious—well, you'll only have had four days of it."

Campion sat stiffly, staring up at him. His pale eyes looked furious and Bream was amused.

"My dear wife says that there are rats in the outer kitchen," he began. "Of course, they'll cling to you for the warmth. But they're companionable little creatures if they're not hungry."

His voice changed again and for a moment he showed the anger which was consuming him.

"If you're right, I hope they start in on you," he said. "Hullo, the thought's too much for you, is it?"

Mr. Campion's eyes had closed and now he swayed violently and slumped down upon the stones his face pallid and his mouth loose. Bream advanced cautiously to kick the inert body in the ribs. It rolled lifelessly and the man laughed.

Slipping the gun into his pocket he stepped forward and bent down to raise his victim's eyelids. Because of his bulk he had to kneel to do so, and as his body swung down a hand as delicate as any pickpocket's moved quietly and Mr. Campion's long fingers closed gratefully over the little gun.

"Get back. Shout and I'll plug you."

The vigorous voice startled Bream quite as much as the sudden movement, which brought his adversary up on one elbow, the revolver levelled. He darted backwards and Campion grinned dangerously as the startled figure flattened against the panelling of the opposite wall.

"Of course, there's no earthly reason why I shouldn't kill you," he observed affably. "I've got a bona-fide self defence plea. That's where I'm one up on you. Stick your hands up and come away from that bell."

Bream did not hesitate.

"I was getting at you, Mr. Campion," he said huskily. "You brought me a bit of bad news and I dare say it made me angry."

"Well, make up your mind." The man on the floor was aggressively pleased. "Is this your idea of humour or ill temper? Don't move!"

The final admonition was occasioned by a wholly unexpected development. The front door at the other end

147

of the hall was moving furtively. Campion kept his gun turned on Bream.

"Now go over," he whispered. "I'll shoot, remember."

Obediently the crook edged towards the widening door his arm raised. From his place of vantage on the floor Mr. Campion had an excellent view of the ensuing scene. Over the threshold, stepping gingerly to avoid making a sound, came a red-faced, white-haired stranger who stopped in his tracks, not unnaturally, when confronted by the spread-eagle Bream.

"Beg your pardon," he ejaculated, his bright eyes widening and his face burning with embarrassment. "Ought not to have come bargin' in again like this. Very foolish of me." He cleared his throat noisily. "Tell you what happened. Matter of fact was nearly in Ipswich when it came to me I wanted to clinch the deal. Came back, came up to the door, saw it wasn't latched and couldn't resist the impulse to come in like I used to thirty years ago. Good God, man, don't stand lookin' at me like that. What have you got your hands up for?"

"Oh, my hat. The colonial," murmured Mr. Campion wearily.

Bream was quick to seize the advantage.

"Look out!" he shouted and leapt behind the bewildered visitor for the open door.

Campion fired, but avoiding the newcomer the shot went wide and splintered the woodwork of the door frame.

"God bless my soul!" The stranger peered into the shadow of the hall, and suddenly perceived Campion still sitting on the floor. "Firin'?" he demanded. "You can't do that here, man. Get up and fight like a Christian. Oh, I see, tied you up, has he? What are you doin'? Burglin'? Put that gun away."

This matter-of-fact reaction to what must have seemed to say the least of it, a remarkable situation had a profound effect upon the young man. The newcomer was such a perfect specimen of his type that to doubt his integrity seemed comparable with the suspicion that the Nelson monument was built of plaster.

"I say, is this really your old home?" he heard himself saying stupidly.

"Certainly. Best years of my life were spent in this house.

nd I hope to die in it. Don't see what the devil it's got to
o with you, though. Got him, Sacret?"

He spoke a moment too soon. Bream, who had been
reeping up behind Campion from the inner doorway, had
ot quite reached his goal. Campion swung over just as the
an leapt. The gun shot out of his hand and slithered
cross the stones towards the stranger. Bream was after it
stantly but Campion gripped him by the lapel and they
olled over together.

"Pick it up!" he shouted, trying to put authority into his
oice. "Pick it up, for the love of Mike! This chap's
angerous."

The rest of his appeal was choked as Bream's hands
ound his throat. His blunt fingers dug into his neck and he
ound himself weaken.

"Look out, man, you'll kill him!" The stranger's
igorous voice echoed through the room. "Stand up, sir!
've got you covered. What are you doin', damn you? The
eller's tied."

The shocked astonishment in the last phrase had its
ffect. The fingers relaxed their strangle-hold and Bream
taggered to his feet, his puffy face twisted in a
epreciatory grimace.

"I'm afraid I forgot myself," he said. "He frightened me.
'll take the gun, shall I?"

"No!"

Campion's croak was frantic in its appeal and the
tranger stepped back.

"Wait a moment," he said. "Keep your distance, sir.
Untie the feller's legs. Like to have this all made clear, if
ou don't mind."

"Oh, come now, really." Bream had gone back to his old
ngratiating manner. "This is my house, you know."

"Lying," whispered Campion again. "Don't let him have
he gun."

"Not your house, eh?" The newcomer seized the
uggestion with interest. "Hang it, whose house is it? Must
et that straight. Explain yourselves, both of you."

"All in good time." Bream was edging forward. "I'll just
ake the gun first. They—they are such dangerous things.

"The devil you do! Stand back." The old man was
howing remarkable spirit. "This fellow here has made a

149

serious allegation and I'd like it properly refuted. Frankly, Sacret, there were one or two things you said this afternoon which made me wonder. Do you know you pointed out the old walnut on the lower lawn and told me there were fine pears on it last year? At the time I thought it was a slip of the tongue, but now I'm beginnin' to look at it in a different light."

Bream drew back from the revolver.

"This is an outrage," he said feelingly. "Holding up a man in his own house."

The newcomer's bright blue eyes snapped suspiciously.

"Who's house is it?" he demanded, his voice raising. "For the last time, sir, who owns this house?"

"I do, I'm afraid. Is anything wrong?"

The pleasant voice from the doorway behind them startled everybody. Margaret Buntingworth, followed by Jane, Rose and Alice, to say nothing of a taximan with the luggage, trooped into the hall. Margaret was weary, dishevelled and utterly charming, the complete mistress of any situation.

The stranger thrust the gun behind him and stepped back. Bream gaped helplessly and Mr. Campion perforce remained where he was. Margaret caught sight of him and paused in the act of removing her travelling coat.

"Oh, Albert," she said, "how nice of you to be here! I didn't see you at first down there. I got your telegram, my dear, and we packed up and came home just as soon as we could. What on earth are you doing? Your ankles. . . . Dear me, is something going on?"

She turned to face the others, passing over Bream, who evidently meant nothing to her, and came face to face with the stranger. The man stared at her for a moment, grew an even more virulent crimson, and finally uttered a single strangled word.

"Meggie!" he said.

Margaret Buntingworth dropped her coat, her gloves, and the rolled travelling rug which contained the two half litres of eau-de-Cologne she had smuggled so successfully through the customs. Her little scream was an expression of pure delight.

"Morty!" he said. "Oh, Morty, my dear boy, how you startled me!"

150

Mr. Campion bent forward and began to untie his ankles. He looked up at Bream.

"Twenty-four hours," he said meaningly. "And it's a great deal more than you deserve."

The man glanced at him and nodded. His face was blank. Without a look behind he made for the inner door.

As Campion scrambled painfully to a chair Margaret came over to him, dragging the newcomer behind her.

"Isn't this all wonderful?" she said, her eyes dancing. "Morty says you two haven't actually met yet. My dear, this is Morty himself. I haven't seen him for years and years and years. He used to live in a cottage down by the plantation and we used to play together up here when we were kids. He was the cleverest boy in the world. I cried my eyes out when he went away. He always promised to come back and buy the old house for me but, of course, I never believed him. Neither of us wrote, of course. You know how it is. And now here he is! Morty, you haven't changed a bit."

"I've never forgotten you, Meggie." The stranger seemed suddenly overcome with shyness. "Matter of fact I came down here in the hope—in the hope—" He coughed, blew his nose and steered away from a dangerous subject. "Upset me to see that chap in possession," he remarked. "Where is he, by the way? Something' very funny was goin' on here just now, Meggie. We'll have to have an explanation from you, young feller. I'm completely in the dark. Where is that man Sacret?"

"Oh, the Sacrets!" Margaret remembered them with consternation. "I forgot all about them. You put them clean out of my head, Morty. I've let the house. I ought not to be here if everything's all right. What has happened, Albert? Where are the Sacrets, dear?"

Campion ceased to massage his bruised ankles.

"If you listen," he said, "you'll just hear their car going off down the drive. I should forget 'em, if I were you. Something tells me that neither of us will hear of them for some considerable time."

Margaret frowned and gave the subject up as being too difficult.

"Perhaps if we all had some food and something to drink?" she suggested. "Food helps the brain so, don't you

151

think? After we've eaten you two boys must tell me all about it. Morty, can you draw a cork?"

"Comin', me dear." The stranger strode after her, regaining his youth at every step.

Mr. Campion rose stiffly to his feet and practised walking.

Much later that evening the two men sat before the fire in the big shabby drawing-room. Margaret had gone to bed after an orgy of remembrances. Morty glanced round the room affectionately.

"Just as I remember it," he said. "Foolish of me to confuse everybody by callin' it my old home. Had always thought of it that way, you see."

Mr. Campion looked into the fire.

"Thinking of buying it?" he inquired.

The elder man cocked a bright blue eye in his direction.

"Well," he said evasively, "I've found just exactly what I was lookin' for, don't you know."

IS THERE A DOCTOR
IN THE HOUSE?

If Detective-Constable Macfall had been a man with charm about him this story would have been too tragic to relate and as it is, with him, the thickest dunderhead God ever put breath into, it has an element of great sadness.

On what was surely the most unfortunate day in his whole existence he was walking down the narrow city street, pleased and proud of himself as he usually was, for his remarkable gift gave him always a feeling of delighted astonishment that he was so much more powerful than anyone else. He was not exactly thinking about his accomplishments as he strode along for he had possessed it so long that the thing was a common place with him but he was reflecting how splendid it was that he had it and how the police could hardly fail to promote him fairly soon. His gift was indeed a remarkable one and the police doctor, who was of an inquiring mind and did not like wonders, had made him display it again and again without satisfying himself about it. Something must be double-jointed but he said he was darned if he saw what.

The fact was that the slender Detective-Constable Macfall was able by some trick of muscle, leverage, or mysterious power as yet unknown to science, to put any other man, up to twice his own weight, neatly upon his back upon the floor. He did not know how he did it and nor did anybody else. Experts, and the Metropolitan Police of London is a body which is no shorter of those than is any other authority, rose irritably from the C.I.D. room floor and said "Oh, Judo, of course. An interesting throw!" and went off sulkily, talking of something else. Macfall would swell a little and grin and mention that he never drank or smoked either. It had gone through his mind once or twice, in the vague way that one speculates about the outcome of nuclear fission, or the eternal mysteries of life and death, that it was astounding that he was not more popular. But the question did not bother him. Why should it? Who cares if a man likes you or not if you can put him on his back and keep him there?

On the whole Macfall got along very well without popularity and on that fateful day when he was walking along Old Soot Lane, which is one of the few remaining shopping centres in that corner of business London, he was as happy as it is reasonable to suppose a human bulldozer can be.

It was at this point that Mr. Mevagissy, the manager and proprietor of one of those minute jeweller's shops whose size of premises has nothing to do with the size of their prices, popped out of his dusty but elegant doorway and beckoned to Macfall whom he knew slightly.

Innocent and proud as the day he was born the Detective-Constable went across.

Mr. Mevagissy, who was an elderly gnome of a man, neat and prim looking with the mouth of a worrier or a string bag, was in something of a tizzy.

He had nothing to complain of, he said, but it was odd. . . . Didn't the constable think it was odd? The man wasn't in the book, not a sign of him in the medical register. But that was not the affair of Mevagissy and Company, was it? Or was it? A firm couldn't be too careful could it? What did the Detective-Constable *think*?

Macfall, who never thought at all according to the best authorities, appeared completely befogged and Mr. Mevagissy hastened to make himself clear.

A customer had come into his shop that morning, he explained, and had left a large old-fashioned silver salver

have an error corrected in the engraved inscription upon
. It was not a very valuable piece in the jeweller's opinion
nd he mentioned that it was the kind of item which could
e picked up fairly cheaply in any of the silver auctions in
he city any day of the week. The inscription upon it was to
he effect that it was presented to Dr. Phinias P. Roup
M.D., etc, etc, on the occasion of his marriage by his
rateful pupils and the nurses of St. Jude's Hospital,
'rinidad. The customer had explained that he was the Dr.
Roup in question and that he had just noticed that his
econd initial was given as P. and not B. He asked Mr.
Mevagissy to have the triffling matter put right and
rranged to call for it at noon that day week.

Mr. Mevagissy had accepted the small commission
vithout any surprise at all. As he told Macfall the
requency with which the donors of presentation plate
nake errors in their instructions to the engravers had long
eased to astonish him. There was probably some deep
sychological reason for it in his opinion, he said, but he
vouldn't bother Macfall with that. However, later, when he
vas wrapping the salver to send it round to the back-street
ngraver who did that sort of work for him, he noticed that
he design of the piece of lettering was not quite
ymmetrical and that did astonish him for that is not the
ort of mistake engravers ever make.

He examined the blank space very carefully and
liscovered that something had already been erased by
ome other craftsman. When at last, by some jewellerish
nethod best known to himself, he found out what it was, it
roved to be a date, 1888. Far too early to have anything
o do with his customer or even his father before him.

The little mystery nagged him all the morning and,
ecause he was that sort of fussy little man, he put on his
at and stepped down to the library on the corner and
ooked up Roup in the medical register. The name was not
here and indeed, the only trace of it which he could find
nywhere was as the author of a long out-dated treatise on
ropical medicine published at the end of the last century.
Ie came back puzzled but, of course, not alarmed for, as
ie pointed out, the customer had done nothing but entrust
im with a piece of plate. All the same it was a peculiar
ittle incident and he felt bound to report it to somebody.

Seeing Detective-Constable Macfall walking down the road it had come to him that the easiest thing to do would be to mention it. What did Macfall *think*?

It may have been the unfortunate insistence by Mr. Mevagissy on this fatal word, or it may have been merely Macfall's unlucky day but, at any rate, his narrow, deep-set eyes appeared to move a fraction closer together. His expression became wooden and he flushed as at some secret effort.

"This day week at noon, eh?" he said. "He's coming back is he?" Mr. Mevagissy intimated that indeed was so.

"Then don't worry," said Macfall. "And don't mention it to anybody else either. I'll be along myself."

He went off even more pleased with himself than usual and when he returned to the station he did not report the matter.

To those unacquainted with the machinery of the Metropolitan Police this omission may seem, perhaps, to be of a trifling nature but that remarkable body has a rule, which is as hard and fast as those governing say, mathematics, or the laws of supply and demand, which decrees that when an officer receives an intimation from a responsible member of the public that something suspicious may have occurred he shall, forthwith, write it all down and pass it on to the man above him.

It is important to make it clear here that Macfall knew perfectly well what he was doing. Moreover, the omission was the outcome of what was, for him, deep thought. He arrived at Mevagissy's shop on the appointed day soon after the shutters were down. He had worked out a plan and his mind was fully occupied with the difficulty which he foresaw in persuading the jeweller to fall in with it. He wanted to spend the morning behind the silver counter as a temporary assistant so that he could serve the doctor when he arrived. A little to his regret he discovered Mr. Mevagissy not only perfectly willing to let him do anything he liked but also not particularly interested in the matter any more. A new interest was absorbing him. He told Macfall about it hurriedly between frenzied orders to his two regular assistants.

He was expecting a highly important customer, he told

the Detective-Constable, "somebody, quite somebody, indeed."

Macfall gathered that the distinguished visitor was a foreigner, a senior member of the suite of a celebrated Indian Prince, who had arrived at the Lorraine Hotel in a blaze of publicity, earlier in the week. Along with other jewellers of repute, Mevagissy had sent in his trade card and had been delighted to get a telephone message the night before telling him that a royal representative would call to see his choicer stones on the stroke of ten in the morning.

There was such an air of excitement in the place that in spite of himself Macfall was entertained. The minute premises which consisted of two showrooms, one leading out of the other, were positively seething. Macfall was in the outer room which was reserved for silver but he could just see through the small doorway into the inner chamber, which was so protected it was virtually a large safe, and where, as Mr. Mevagissy had just told him, there was one of the most interesting small collections of gems in London.

Punctually at ten the representative arrived and was ushered into the fastness by Mr. Mevagissy and his two bona fide assistants. All Macfall saw of him was a shock of white hair above a very dark neck.

For the rest of the morning a deep and reverent hush spread over the little shop. The visitor was both knowledgeable and thorough and the whole of the more valuable part of Mr. Mevagissy's stock was considered.

No one else who mattered came into the shop. The few customers were met at the doorway and all but hustled out by the junior assistant before he rushed back to rejoin the seance round the table under the bright lights, where the little glasses were busy and the talk was conducted in reverent murmurs.

Macfall himself was almost carried away by the sense of drama which is always present when great deals are in progress but when, on the stroke of twelve, a car pulled up on the kerb and a man sprang out and strode into the shop, he was prepared for him.

The newcomer was a large and powerful person with the
157

sloping shoulders of a prize-fighter but there was nothing hostile in his manner when he walked up to Macfall and made his request. His name was Dr. Roup, he said, and was his salver waiting for him? The Detective-Constable produced it and his eyes were sharp and his muscles ready but there was no sudden movement, no stealthy dive for a weapon. Dr. Roup took the silver dish in both hands, read the inscription with apparent satisfaction and inquired what he owed. While the police officer wrapped the parcel he stood with both fists on the counter fidgeting with his feet like any man in a hurry. Macfall had parted with the parcel and given the man his change with a growing sense of anti-climax before a sudden horrified cry came from the inner room.

"A doctor! Get a doctor!"

As Mr. Mevagissy came scuttling out with what hair he possessed standing on end, the man with the salver under his arm turned in the doorway.

"What's the matter?" he demanded without any great enthusiasm.

"I don't know!" Mevagissy was ringing his hands. "He's foaming. It's horrible." And then, as he recognized the customer, but forgot, in his anguish, all he knew about him, "Oh, Doctor, it's you! Thank God for that. In here, sir. Quickly."

Reluctantly it seemed, the customer came back into the shop, set down his parcel and went into the smaller room. Macfall followed promptly.

The distinguished visitor lay on the floor, his face congested and his eyes tightly closed.

One of Mevagissy's assistants had undone his collar and the other, with commendable presence of mind was shovelling the jewels back into the safe.

The doctor's examination had a professional touch which shook Macfall's confidence but only for an instant. When the pronouncement came he was ready for it.

"This man is seriously ill. There is one chance in a thousand of saving his life. Help me to get him into my car and ring up St. Bede's Hospital, Extension 3, and warn them we'll be there in ten minutes."

Poor Mevagissy was so appalled by the disaster which had overtaken not only his client but his deal, that he might have fallen for the trick completely but the second assistant, who was the one with the brains, pointed out in a startled whisper that the Burma ruby, which was the star of the collection, was still clutched in the sick man's hand. Nothing would open the clenched fingers and the doctor became angry.

"Good heavens, we can't help that," he said. "Don't you understand the man is dying? Look at him. If he's holding something valuable of yours, come with us. Hurry. That's the vital thing now!"

Mr. Mevagissy, an old man with the physique of a weakly hen, looked about him wildly and Macfall stepped forward only just able to keep the grin off his face.

"Let me go, sir," he murmured.

The powerful man who called himself Dr. Roup measured the young man with his eye and found the answer satisfactory. "Very well," he said. "You'll do. Now then, raise the patient very carefully by the shoulders, please. Oh, and somebody bring my salver."

Macfall sighed with deep satisfaction. His moment had come. He picked up the parcel and followed the little procession out of the shop.

At first he had all the luck in the world. He put his remarkable gift to the test and it stood up to it well. He waited until it became clear that wherever the self-styled 'doctor' was driving it was not to the hospital, and then he went through the prescribed police drill for such an emergency with perfect confidence and, indeed, success.

He chose a moment when the road was clear, revealed himself as a police officer, challenged the driver to stop, and then, on receiving unsatisfactory if commendably terse replies, went smartly into action.

He overpowered the two men, relieved them of their guns and their loot, saved the car from destruction and drove his prisoners back to his own station in it with all the speed and efficiency of a good gun dog retrieving a couple of birds.

Only his ineffable smugness prevented several startled officers there from telling him that it was a very creditable performance.

The blow fell on the following morning when he was summoned to the Divisional Detective Chief Inspector's private office. He could hardly walk there he was so pleased with himself and he went stumbling in, lowered his eyes modestly and waited for the bouquet.

A silence which had something of the chill of the grave about it went on so long that it became embarrassing. Macfall looked up and, for the first time, the wraith of a doubt crept unwillingly into his mind.

The D.D.C.I. possessed many of the attributes of an elderly schoolmaster; he never blustered but there was acid in the man. At the moment he was not looking at Macfall but was sitting with his head down, his lazy, heavy-lidded glance fixed on the blotter on which he was making idle drawings.

After a little he began to speak in the dry, precise voice his subordinates knew so well and imitated so accurately.

"Ah, Macfall," said he with the hint of the Dublin accent which only appeared when he was deeply moved. "I don't suppose you've ever heard of a gentleman by the name of Elroy Muspratt? Don't tell me. I can see by the expression on your face—which I'm not even looking at—that the name is Greek to you. Let me tell you about the man. In the first place, he's most intelligent, the most impudent and the most dangerous jewel thief in the continent of Europe; and in the second, he's the man for whom the whole of the Criminal Investigation Department has had its eyes skinned ever since they learned that there was a chance he was coming to this country." Macfall stood looking at his chief blankly and the dry voice continued without pause.

"Unfortunately, the agents abroad lost sight of the fellow and, although all the usual precautions were taken, and the man was known to be audacious, somehow nobody guessed he'd have the calm effrontery to impersonate a famous Indian nobleman and come over with a retinue."

For the first time he raised his eyes which were as bleak as wet paving stones to survey the Detective-Constable.

"The Superintendent in charge at the central office did all he could," he went on. "He arranged that every suspicious item however trivial which was reported by a jeweller should be passed to his desk. He got a great many and his men got a lot of useless work but the one item which would have paid for his attention didn't come in, and so—what do you think happened?"

He leaned forward and pulled a package of blue slips towards him. "Eighteen of them," he continued calmly. "Eighteen jeweller's shops in Greater London robbed of the finest stones in their safes. Each crime happened precisely at noon and each was worked in exactly the same way. Muspratt was still masquerading as the prince when he left the country by private plane at five minutes before one yesterday afternoon. Most of his 'suite' accompanied him. The Flying Squad is looking for the rest now."

He settled back in his chair and regarded the man in front of him steadily.

"A week," he said distinctly. "The police might have had a full week in which to circularize the jewellers—using the normal 'missing articles list', which is sent to them regularly—asking for details of any medical man who had left a piece of plate to be engraved or altered. It really would not have taken anybody long to notice that there was an unusual number of them who were going to collect the same day at the same hour."

"But why?" The startled question escaped Macfall involuntarily. "Why all at the same time?"

The D.D.C.I.'s expression was pained. "Because it was a good simple idea," he said sadly, "and once it had been done in any place in the world which is served by a newspaper everybody who owned a jeweller's shop would be on the lookout for it."

There was a long pause and when the D.D.C.I. spoke again he sounded depressed.

"Macfall," he said. "You'd go further in the *uniformed* branch, my lad. We don't really need your gifts in this department. It's that parlour trick of yours, you know—I should be very careful of it if I were you. It takes the blood from your head I shouldn't wonder."

THE BORDER-LINE CASE

It was so hot in London that night that we slept with the
wide skylight in our city studio open and let the soot-black
fall in on us willingly, so long as they brought with them a
single stirring breath to move the stifling air. Heat hung on
the dark horizons and beneath our particular bowl of sky
the city fidgeted, breathless and uncomfortable.

The early editions of the evening papers carried the story
of the murder. I read it when they came along about three
o'clock on the following afternoon. My mind took in the
details lazily, for my eyelids were sticky and the printed
words seemed remote and unrelated to reality.

It was a straightforward little incident, or so I thought it
and when I had read the guarded half-column I threw the
paper over to Albert Campion, who had drifted in to lunch
and stayed to sit quietly in a corner, blinking behind his
spectacles, existing merely, in the sweltering day.

The newspapers called the murder the 'Coal Court
Shooting Case', and the facts were simple.

At one o'clock in the morning, when Vacation Street
N.E., had been a deserted land of odoriferous heat, a
policeman on the beat had seen a man stumble and fall to
the pavement. The intense discomfort of the night being
uppermost in his mind, he had not unnaturally diagnosed

case of ordinary collapse and, after loosening the stranger's collar, had summoned the ambulance.

When the authorities arrived, however, the man was pronounced to be dead and the body was taken to the mortuary, where it was discovered that death had been due to a bullet wound neatly placed between the shoulder-blades. The bullet had made a small blue hole and, after perforating the left lung, had furrowed the heart itself, finally coming to rest in the body structure of the chest.

Since this was so, and the fact that the police constable had heard no untoward sound, it had been reasonable to believe that the shot had been fired at some little distance from a gun with a silencer.

Mr. Campion was only politely interested. The afternoon certainly was hot and the story, as it then appeared, was hardly original or exciting. He sat on the floor reading it patiently, his long thin legs stretched out in front of him.

"Someone died at any rate," he remarked at last and added after a pause: "Poor chap! Out of the frying-pan . . . Dear me, I suppose it's the locality which predisposes one to think of that. Ever seen Vacation Street, Margery?"

I did not answer him. I was thinking how odd it was that a general irritant like the heat should make the dozens of situations arising all round one in the great city seem suddenly almost personal. I found I was desperately sorry for the man who had been shot, whoever he was.

It was Stanislaus Oates who told us the real story behind the half-column in the evening paper. He came in just after four, looking for Campion. He was a Detective-Inspector in those days and had just begun to develop the habit of chatting over his problems with the pale young man in the horn-rimmed spectacles. Theirs was an odd relationship. It was certainly not a case of the clever amateur and the humble policeman: rather the irritable and pugnacious policeman taking it out on the inoffensive, friendly representative of the general public.

On this occasion Oates was rattled.

"It's a case right down your street," he said briefly to Campion as he sat down. "Seems to be impossible, for one thing."

He explained after a while, having salved his conscience

163

by pointing out that he had no business to discuss the case and excusing himself most illogically on grounds of the heat.

"It's 'low-class' crime," he went on briskly. "Practically gang-shooting. And probably quite interesting to all of you who like romance in your crimes. However, it's got me right down on two counts; the first because the man who shot the fellow who died couldn't possibly have done so and second, because I was wrong about the girl. They're so true to type, these girls, that you can't even rely on the proverbial exception."

He sighed as if the discovery had really grieved him.

We heard the story of Josephine as we sat round in the paralysingly hot studio and, although I never saw the girl then or afterwards, I shall not forget the scene; the three of us listening, breathing rather heavily, while the Inspector talked.

She had been Donovan's girl, so Oates said, and he painted a picture of her for us: slender and flat-chested with black hair and eyes like a Russian madonna's in a transparent face. She wore blouses, he said, with lace on them and gold ornaments, little chains and crosses and fragile brooches whose security was reinforced by gilt safety-pins. She was only twenty, Oates said, and added enigmatically that he would have betted on her, but that it served him right and showed him there was no fool like an old one.

He went on to talk about Donovan, who, it seemed, was thirty-five and had spent ten years of his life in gaol. The Inspector did not seem to think any the less of him for that. The fact seemed to put the man in a definite category in his mind and that was all.

"Robbery with violence and the R.O. boys," he said with a wave of his hand and smiled contentedly as though he had made everything clear. "She was sixteen when he found her and he's given her hell ever since."

While he still held our interest he mentioned Johnny Gilchick. Johnny Gilchick was the man who was dead.

Oates, who was never more sentimental than was strictly reasonable in the circumstances, let himself go about Josephine and Johnny Gilchick. It was love, he said—love sudden, painful and ludicrous; and he admitted that he liked to see it.

164

"I had an aunt once who used to talk about the Real Thing," he explained, "and embarrassingly silly the old lady sounded, but after seeing those two youngsters meet and flame and go on until they were a single fiery entity—youngsters who were pretty ordinary tawdry material without it—I find myself sympathizing with her if not condoning the phrase."

He hesitated and his smooth grey face cracked into a depreciating smile.

"Well, we were both wrong, anyway," he murmured, "my aunt and I. Josephine let her Johnny down just as you'd expect her to and after he had got what was coming to him and was lying in the mortuary he was born to lie in she upped and perjured her immortal soul to swear his murderer an alibi. Not that her testimony is of much value as evidence. That's beside the point. The fact remains that she's certainly done her best. You may think me sentimental, but it depresses me. I thought that girl was genuine and my judgement was out."

Mr. Campion stirred.

"Could we have the details?" he asked politely. "We've only seen the evening paper. It wasn't very helpful."

Oates glared at him balefully.

"Frankly, the facts are exasperating," he said. "There's a little catch in them somewhere. It must be something so simple that I missed it altogether. That's really why I've come to look for you. I thought you might care to come along and take a glance at the place. What about it?"

There was no general movement. It was too hot to stir. Finally the Inspector took up a piece of chalk and sketched a rough diagram on the bare boards of the model's throne.

"This is Vacation Street," he said, edging the chalk along a crack. "It's the best part of a mile long. Up this end, here by the chair, it's nearly all wholesale houses. This sandbin I'm sketching in now marks the boundary of two police divisions. Well, here, ten yards to the left, is the entrance to Coal Court, which is a cul-de-sac composed of two blank backs of warehouse buildings and a café at the far end. The café is open all night. It serves the printers from the two big presses farther down the road. That's its legitimate trade. But it is also a sort of unofficial headquarters for Donovan's mob. Josephine sits at the desk downstairs and keeps an eye on the door. God knows what hours she keeps. She always seems to be there."

He paused and there came into my mind a recollection of the breathless night through which we had all passed, and I could imagine the girl sitting there in the stuffy shop with her thin chest and her great black eyes.

The Inspector was still speaking.

"Now," he said, "there's an upstairs room in the cafe. It's on the second floor. That's where our friend Donovan spent most of his evening. I expect he had a good few friends with him and we shall locate them in all time."

He bent over the diagram.

"Johnny Gilchick died here," he said, drawing a circle about a foot beyond the square which indicated the sandbin. "Although the bobby was right down the road, he saw him pause under the lamp post, stagger and fall. He called the Constable from the other division and they got the ambulance. All that is plain sailing. There's just one difficulty. Where was Donovan when he fired the shot? There were two policemen in the street at the time, remember. At the moment of the actual shooting one of them, the Never Street man, was making a round of a warehouse yard, but the other, the Phyllis Court chap, was there on the spot, not forty yards away, and it was he who actually saw Johnny Gilchick fall, although he heard no shot. Now I tell you, Campion, there's not an ounce of cover in the whole of that street. How did Donovan get out of the café, where did he stand to shoot Johnny neatly through the back, and how did he get back again without being seen? The side walls of the cul-de-sac are solid concrete backs of warehouses, there is no way round from the back of the café, nor could he possibly have gone over the roofs. The warehouses tower over the café like liners over a tug. Had he come out down the road one or other of the bobbies must have been certain to have seen him. How did he do it?"

"Perhaps Donovan didn't do it," I ventured and received a pitying glance for my temerity.

"That's the one fact," said the Inspector heavily. "That's the one thing I do know. I know Donovan. He's one of the few English mob boys who carry guns. He served five years with the gangs in New York and has the misfortune to take his liquor in bouts. After each bout he has a period of black depression, during which he may do anything. Johnny Gilchick used to be one of Donovan's mob and when Johnny fell for the girl he turned in the gang, which was adding insult to injury where Donovan was concerned."

He paused and smiled.

"Donovan was bound to get Johnny in the end," he said. "It was never anything but a question of time. The whole mob expected it. The neighbourhood was waiting for it. Donovan had said openly that the next time Johnny dropped into the café would be his final appearance there. Johnny called last night, was ordered out of the place by the terrified girl, and finally walked out of the cul-de-sac. He turned the corner and strolled down the road. Then he was shot by Donovan. There's no way round it, Campion. The doctors say that death was as near instantaneous as may be. Johnny Gilchick could not have walked three paces with the bullet in his back. As for the gun, that was pretty obviously Donovan's too. We haven't actually picked it up yet, but we know he had one of the type we are after. It's a clear case, a straightforward case, if only we knew where Donovan stood when he fired the shot."

Mr. Campion looked up. His eyes were thoughtful behind his spectacles.

"The girl gave Donovan an alibi?" he inquired.

Oates shrugged his shoulders. "Rather," he said. "She was passionate about it. He was there the whole time, every minute of the time, never left the upper room once in the whole evening. I could kill her and she would not alter her story; she'd take her dying oath on it and so on. It didn't mean anything either way. Still, I was sorry to see her doing it, with her boy friend barely cold. She was sucking up to the mob, of course; probably had excellent reasons for doing so. Yet, as I say, I was sorry to hear her volunteering the alibi before she was asked."

"Ah! She volunteered it, did she?" Campion was interested.

Oates nodded and his small eyes widened expressively.

"Forced it on us. Came roaring round to the police station with it. Threw it off her chest as if she were doing something fine. I'm not usually squeamish about that sort of thing, but it gave me a distinct sense of distaste, I don't

167

mind telling you. Frankly, I gave her a piece of my mind. Told her to go and look at the body, for one thing."

"Not kind of you," observed Mr. Campion mildly. "And what did she do?"

"Oh, blubbered herself sick, like the rest of 'em." Oates was still disgruntled. "Still, that's not of interest. What girls like Josephine do or don't do doesn't really matter. She was saving her own skin. If she hadn't been so enthusiastic about it I'd have forgiven her. It's Donovan who is important. Where was Donovan when he fired?"

The shrill chatter of the telephone answered him and he glanced at me apologetically.

"I'm afraid that's mine," he said. "You don't mind, do you? I left the number with the Sergeant."

He took off the receiver and as he bent his head to listen his face changed. We watched him with an interest it was far too hot to dissemble.

"Oh," he said flatly, after a long pause. "Really? Well, it doesn't matter either way, does it? . . . Still, what did she do it for? . . . What? . . . I suppose so . . . Yes? . . . Really?"

He seemed suddenly astounded as his informant at the other end of the wire evidently came out with a second piece of information more important than the first.

"You can't be certain . . . you are? . . . What?"

The faraway voice explained busily. We could hear its steady drone. Inspector Oates's exasperation grew.

"Oh, all right, all right," he said at last. "I'm crackers . . . we're all crackers . . . have it your own damned way."

With which vulgar outburst he rang off.

"Alibi sustained?" inquired Mr. Campion.

"Yes." The Inspector grunted out the word. "A couple of printers who were in the downstairs room swear he did not go through the shop all the evening. They're sound fellows. Make good witnesses. Yet Donovan shot Johnny. I'm certain of it. He shot him clean through the concrete angle of a piano warehouse as far as I can see." He turned to Campion almost angrily. "Explain that, can you?"

Mr. Campion coughed. He seemed a little embarrassed.

"I say, you know," he ventured, "there are just two things that occur to me."

"Then out with them, son." The Inspector lit a cigarette and wiped his face. "Out with them. I'm not proud."

Mr. Campion coughed again. "Well, the—er—heat, for me thing, don't you know," he said with profound uneasiness. "The heat, and one of your concrete walls."

The Inspector swore a little and apologized.

"If anyone could forget this heat he's welcome," he said. "What's the matter with the wall, too?"

Mr. Campion bent over the diagram on the boards of the throne. He was very apologetic.

"Here is the angle of the warehouse," he said, "and here is the sandbin. Here to the left is the lamp post where Johnny Gilchick was found. Farther on to the left is the P.C. from Never Street examining a courtyard and temporarily off the scene, while to the right, on the other side of the entrance to Coal Court, is another constable, P.C. someone-or-other, of Phyllis Court. One is apt to—er—think of the problem as though it were contained in four solid walls, two concrete walls, two policemen."

He hesitated and glanced timidly at the Inspector.

"When is a policeman not a concrete wall, Oates? In—er—well, in just such heat . . . do you think, or don't you?"

Oates was staring at him, his eyes narrowed.

"Damn it!" he said explosively. "Damn it, Campion, I believe you're right. I knew it was something so simple that it was staring me in the face."

They stood together looking down at the diagram. Oates stopped to put a chalk cross at the entrance to the cul-de-sac.

"It was *that* lamp post," he said. "Give me that telephone. Wait till I get hold of that fellow."

While he was carrying on an excited conversation we demanded an explanation from Mr. Campion and he gave it to us at last, mild and apologetic as usual.

"Well, you see," he said, "there's the sandbin. The sandbin marks the boundary of two police divisions. Policeman A. very hot and tired, sees a man collapse from the heat under a lamp post on his territory. The man is a little fellow and it occurs to Policeman A that it would be a simple matter to move him to the next lamp post on the other side of the sandbin, where he would automatically become the responsibility of Policeman B, who is even now approaching. Policeman A achieves the change and is

169

bending over the prostrate figure when his colleague come
up. Since he knows nothing of the bullet wound, th
entrance to the cul-de-sac, with its clear view to the caf
second-floor room, has no significance in his mind. Today
when its full importance must have dawned upon him, b
evidently thinks it best to hold his tongue."

Oates came back from the phone triumphant.

"The first bobby went on leave this morning," he sai
"He was an old hand. He must have spotted the chap w
dead, took it for granted it was the heat, and didn't want t
be held up here by the inquest. Funny I didn't see that i
the beginning."

We were all silent for some moments.

"Then—the girl?" I began at last.

The Inspector frowned and made a little grimace o
regret.

"A pity about the girl," he said. "Of course it w
probably an accident. Our man who saw it happen said h
couldn't be sure."

I stared at him and he explained, albeit a little hurriedl

"Didn't I tell you? When my sergeant phoned about th
alibi he told me. As Josephine crossed the road afte
visiting the mortuary this morning she stepped under a b
. . . Oh yes, instantly."

He shook his head. He seemed uncomfortable.

"She thought she was making a gesture when she cam
down to the station, don't you see? The mob must hav
told her to swear that no one had been in the upstair
room; that must have been their first story until they sa
how the luck lay. So when she came beetling down to
she must have thought she was risking her life to give h
Johnny's murderer away, while instead of that she wa
simply giving the fellow an alibi . . . Funny the way thin
happen, isn't it?"

He glanced at Campion affectionately.

"It's because you don't get your mind cluttered up wi
the human element that you see these things so quickly,
he said. "You see everything in terms of A and B. It mak
all the difference."

Mr. Campion, the most gentle of men, made n
comment at all.

170

THEY NEVER GET CAUGHT

Millie dear, this does explain itself, doesn't it?—Henry'
Mr. Henry Brownrigg signed his name on the back of the
little blue bill with a flourish. Then he set the scrap of
paper carefully in the exact centre of the imperfectly
scoured developing bath, and, leaving the offending utensil
on the kitchen table for his wife to find when she came in,
he stalked back to the shop, feeling that he had
administered the rebuke surely and at the same time
gracefully.

In fifteen years Mr. Brownrigg felt that he had mastered
the art of teaching his wife her job. Not that he had taught
her. That, Mr. Brownrigg felt, with a woman of Millie's
staggering obtuseness was past praying for. But how, after
long practice, he could deliver the snub or administer the
punishing word in a way which would penetrate her placid
dullness.

Within half an hour she had returned from shopping
and before lunch was set upon the table, he knew the bath
would be back in the dark-room, bright and pristine as
when it was new, and nothing more would be said about it.
Millie would be a little more ineffectually anxious to please
at lunch, perhaps, but that was all.

Mr. Brownrigg passed behind the counter and flicked a

speck of dust off the dummy cartons of face-creams. It w
twelve five and a half. In four and a half minutes Phy
Bell would leave her office farther down the High Stre
and in seven and a half minutes she would come in throu
that narrow, sunlit doorway to the cool, drug-scented sho

On that patch of floor where the sunlight lay blue a
yellow, since it had found its way in through the enormo
glass vases in the window which were the emblem of I
trade, she would stand and look at him, her eyes limpid a
her small mouth pursed and adorable.

The chemist took up one of the ebony-backed han
mirrors exposed on the counter for sale and glanced
himself in it. He was not altogether a prepossessin
person. Never a tall man, at forty-two his wide, stocl
figure showed a definite tendency to become fleshy, b
there was strength and virility in his thick shoulders, wh
his clean-shaven face and broad neck were short and bu
like and his lips were full.

Phyllis liked his eyes. They held her, she said, and mc
of the other young women who bought their cosmetics
the corner shop and chatted with Mr. Brownrigg across tl
counter might have been inclined to agree with her.

Over-dark, round, hot eyes had Mr. Brownrigg; not at a
the sort of eyes for a little, plump, middle-aged chemi
with a placid wife like Millie.

But Mr. Brownrigg did not contemplate his own eyes. H
smoothed his hair, wiped his lips, and then, realizing th
Phyllis was almost due, he disappeared behind tl
dispensing desk. It was as well, he always thought, not
appear too eager.

He was watching the door, though, when she came i
He saw the flicker of her green skirt as she hesitated on tl
step and saw her half-eager, half-apprehensive expressio
as she glanced towards the counter.

He was glad she had not come in when a customer w
there. Phyllis was different from any of the others who
little histories stretched back through the past fourtee
years. When Phyllis was in the shop Mr. Brownrigg four
he was liable to make mistakes, liable to drop things ar
fluff the change.

He came out from his obscurity eager in spite of himsel
and drew the little golden-haired girl sharply towards hi

172

over that part of the counter which was lowest and which he purposely kept uncluttered.

He kissed her and the sudden force of the movement betrayed him utterly. He heard her quick intake of breath before she released herself and stepped back.

"You—you shouldn't," she said, nervously tugging her hat back into position.

She was barely twenty, small and young looking for her years, with yellow hair and a pleasant, quiet style. Her blue eyes were frightened and a little disgusted now, as though she found herself caught up in an emotion which her instincts considered not quite nice.

Henry Brownrigg recognized the expression. He had seen it before in other eyes, but whereas on past occasions he had been able to be tolerantly amused and therefore comforting and glibly reassuring, in Phyllis it irritated and almost frightened him.

"Why not?" he demanded sharply, too sharply he knew immediately, and blood rushed into his face.

Phyllis took a deep breath.

"I came to tell you," she said jerkily, like a child saying its piece, "I've been thinking things over. I can't go on with all this. You're married. I want to be married some day. I—I shan't come in again."

"You haven't been talking to someone?" he demanded, suddenly cold.

"About you? Good heavens, no!"

Her vehemence was convincing, and because of that he shut his mind to its uncomplimentary inference and experienced only relief.

"You love me," said Henry Brownrigg. "I love you and you love me. You know that."

He spoke without intentional histrionics, but adopted a curious monotone which, some actors have discovered, is one of the most convincing methods of conveying deep sincerity.

Phyllis nodded miserably and then seemed oddly embarrassed. Wistfully her eyes wandered to the sunlit street and back again.

"Goodbye," she said huskily and fled.

He saw her speeding past the window, almost running. For some time Henry Brownrigg remained looking down at the patch of blue sunlight where she had stood. Finally he raised his eyes and smiled with conscious wryness. She would come back. Tomorrow, or in a week, or in ten days perhaps, she would come back. But the obstacle the insurmountable obstacle would arise again, in time it would defeat him and he would lose her.

Phyllis was different from the others. He would lose her. Unless the obstacle were removed.

Henry Brownrigg frowned.

There were other considerations too. The old, mottled ledger told those only too clearly.

If the obstacle were removed it would automatically wipe away those difficulties also, for was there not the insurance, and that small income Millie's father had left so securely tied, as though the old man had divined his daughter would grow up a fool?

Mr. Brownrigg's eyes rested upon the little drawer under the counter marked: 'Prescriptions: private.' It was locked and not even young Perry, his errand boy and general assistant, who poked his nose into most things, guessed that under the pile of slips within was a packet of letters scrawled in Phyllis's childish hand.

He turned away abruptly. His breath was hard to draw and he was trembling. The time had come.

Some months previously Henry Brownrigg had decided that he must become a widower before the end of the year, but the interview of the morning had convinced him that he must hurry.

At this moment Millie, her face still pink with shame at the recollection of the affair of the ill-washed bath, put her head round the inner door.

"Lunch is on the table, Henry," she said, and added with that stupidity which had annoyed him ever since it had ceased to please him by making him feel superior: "Well, you look serious. Oh, Henry, you haven't made a mistake and given somebody a wrong bottle?"

"No, my dear Millie," said her husband, surveying her coldly and speaking with heavy sarcasm. "That is the peculiar sort of idiot mistake I have yet to make. I haven't reached my wife's level yet."

And as he followed her uncomplaining figure to the little
174

room behind the shop a word echoed rhythmically in the back of his mind and kept time with the beating of his heart. "Hurry! Hurry! Hurry!!

"Henry dear," said Millie Brownrigg, turning a troubled face towards her husband, "why Crupiner? He's so expensive and so old."

She was standing in front of the dressing-table in the big front bedroom above the shop, brushing her brown, grey-streaked hair before she combed it into position.

Henry Brownrigg, lying awake in his bed on the far side of the room, did not answer her.

Millie went on talking. She was used to Henry's silence. Henry was so clever. Most of his time was spent in thought.

"I've heard all sorts of odd things about Crupiner," she remarked. "They say he's so old he forgets. Why shouldn't we go to the young National Health doctor? Mother swears by him."

"Unfortunately for your mother she has your intelligence, without a man to look after her, poor woman," said Henry Brownrigg.

Millie made no comment.

"Crupiner," continued Henry Brownrigg, "may not be much good as a general practitioner, but there is one subject on which he is a master. I want him to see you. I want to get you well, old dear."

Millie's gentle, expressionless face flushed and her blue eyes looked moist and foolish in the mirror. Henry could see her reflection in the glass and he turned away. There were moments when, by her obvious gratitude for a kind word from him, Millie made him feel a certain distaste for his project. He wished to God she would go away and leave him his last few moments in bed to think of Phyllis in peace.

"You know, Henry," said Mrs. Brownrigg suddenly, "I don't feel ill. Those things you're giving me are doing me good, I'm sure. I don't feel nearly so tired at the end of the day now. Can't you treat me yourself?"

The man in the bed stiffened. Any compunction he may have felt vanished and he became wary.

"Of course they're doing you good," he said with the
175

satisfaction of knowing that he was telling the truth up to a point, or at least of knowing that he was doing nothing reprehensible—yet.

"I don't believe in patent medicines as a rule, but Fender's Pills are good. They're a well-known formula, and they certainly do pick one up. But I just want to make sure that you're organically sound. I don't like you getting breathless when you hurry, and the colour of your lips isn't good, you know."

Plump, foolish Millie looked in the mirror and nervously ran her forefinger over her mouth.

Like many women of her age she had lost much of her colour, and there certainly was a faint, very faint, blue streak round the edge of her lips.

The chemist was heavily reassuring.

"Nothing to worry about, I'm sure, but I think we'll go down and see Crupiner this evening," he said, and added adroitly: "We want to be on the safe side, don't we?"

Millie nodded, her mouth trembling.

"Yes, dear," she said, and paused, adding afterwards in that insufferable way of hers: "I suppose so."

When she had gone downstairs to attend to breakfast Henry Brownrigg rose with his own last phrase still on his lips. He repeated it thoughtfully.

"The safe side." That was right. The safe side. No ghastly hash of it for Henry Brownrigg.

Only fools made a hash of things. Only fools got caught. This was almost too easy. Millie was so simple-minded, so utterly unsuspecting.

By the end of the day Mr. Brownrigg was nervy. The boy Perry had reported, innocently enough, that he had seen young Hill in his new car going down Acacia Road at something over sixty, and had added casually that he had had the Bell girl with him. The youngest one. Phyllis. Did Mr. Brownrigg remember her? She was rather pretty.

For a moment Henry Brownrigg was in terror lest the boy had discovered his secret and was wounding him maliciously. But having convinced himself that this was not so, the fact and the sting remained.

Young Hill was handsome and a bachelor. Phyllis was young and impressionable. The chemist imagined them pulling up in some shady copse outside the town holding hands, perhaps even kissing, and the heart which could remain steady while Millie's stupid eyes met his anxiously as she spoke of her illness turned over painfully in Henry Brownrigg's side at the thought of that embrace.

"Hurry!" The word formed itself again in the back of his mind. Hurry . . . hurry.

Millie was breathless when they arrived at Crupiner's old-fashioned house. Henry had been self-absorbed and had walked very fast.

Crupiner saw them immediately. He was a vast, dusty old man. Privately Millie thought she would like to take a good stiff broom to him, and the picture conjured in her mind was so ridiculous that she giggled nervously and Henry had to shake his head at her warningly.

She flushed painfully, and the old, stupid expression settled down over her face again.

Henry explained her symptoms to the doctor and Millie looked surprised and gratified at the anxiety he betrayed. Henry had evidently noticed her little wearinesses much more often than she had supposed.

When he had finished his recital of her small ills, none of them alarming in themselves but piling up in total to a rather terrifying sum of evidence, Dr. Crupiner turned his eyes, which were small and greasy, with red veins in their whites, on to Millie, and his old lips, which were mottled like Henry's ledger, moved for a fraction of a second before his voice came, wheezy and sepulchral.

"Well, Madam," he said, "your husband here seems worried about you. Let's have a look at you."

Millie trembled. She was getting breathless again from sheer apprehension. Once or twice lately it had occurred to her that the Fender's pills made her feel breathless, even while they bucked her up in other ways, but she had not liked to mention this to Henry.

Dr. Crupiner came close to her, breathing heavily through his nose in an effort of concentration. He thrust a stubby, unsteady finger into her eye socket, dragging down the skin so that he could peer short-sightedly at her eyeball. He thumped her half-heartedly on the back and felt the palms of her hands.

Mr. Brownrigg, who watched all this somewhat meaningless ritual, his round eyes thoughtful and uneasy, suddenly took the doctor on one side, and the two men had a muttered conversation at the far end of the long room.

Millie could not help overhearing some of it, because Dr. Crupiner was deaf these days and Henry was anxious to make himself understood.

"Twenty years ago," she heard. "Very sudden." And then after a pause, the awful word 'hereditary'.

Millie's trembling fit increased in intensity and her broad, stupid face looked frightened. They were talking about her poor papa. He had died very suddenly of heart disease.

Her own heart jumped painfully. So that was why Henry seemed so anxious.

Dr. Crupiner came back to her. She had to undo her dress and Dr. Crupiner listened to her heart with an ancient stethoscope. Millie, already trembling, began to breathe with difficulty as her alarm became unbearable.

At last the old man finished with her. He stared at her unwinkingly for some seconds and finally turned to Henry, and together they went back to the far end of the room.

Millie strained her ears and heard the old man's rumbling voice.

"A certain irregularity. Nothing very alarming. Bring her to see me again."

Then there was a question from Henry which she could not catch, but afterwards, as the doctor seemed to be fumbling in his mind for a reply, the chemist remarked in an ordinary tone: "I've been giving her Fender's pills."

"Fender's Pills?" Dr. Crupiner echoed the words with relief. "Excellent. Excellent. You chemists like patent medicines, I know, and I don't want to encourage you, but that's a well-known formula and will save you mixing up my prescription. Carry on with those for a while. Very good things; I often recommend them. Take them in moderation, of course."

"Oh, of course," said Henry. "But do you think I'm doing right, Doctor?"

Millie looked pleased and startled at the earnestness of Henry's tone.

"Oh, without doubt, Mr. Brownrigg, without doubt." Dr. Crupiner repeated the words again as he came back to Millie. "There, Mrs. Brownrigg," he said with spurious ollity, "you take care of yourself and do what your ɯusband says. Come to see me again in a week or so and ʏou'll be as right as ninepence. Off you go. Oh, but Mrs. ℨrownrigg, no shocks mind. No excitements. No little ᵤpsets. And don't over-tire yourself."

He shook hands perfunctorily, and while Henry was ɥelping Millie to collect her things with a solicitude quite ᵤnusual in him, the old man took a large, dusty book from ɥe shelves.

Just before they left he peered at Henry over his ₅pectacles.

"Those Fender's pills are quite a good idea," he ₑmarked in a tone quite different from his professional ɾumble. "Just the things. They contain a small percentage ɔf digitalin."

One of Mr. Brownrigg's least attractive habits was his ɱethod of spending Saturday nights.

At half past seven the patient but silently disapproving Millie would clear away the remains of the final meal of the ɟay and place one glass and an unopened bottle of whiskey ₐnd a siphon of soda on the green tablecloth.

This done, she would retire to the kitchen, wash up, and ƈomplete the week's ironing. She usually left this job until ᴛhen, because it was a longish business, with frequent ₚauses for minor repairs to Henry's shirts and her own ᵤnderclothing, and she knew she had plenty of undisturbed ᴛime on her hands.

She had, in fact, until midnight. When the kitchen clock ʍheezed twelve Millie folded her ironing board.

Then she went into the living-room and took away the ₉lass and the empty bottle.

She also picked up the papers and straightened the ɾoom.

Finally, when the gas fire had been extinguished, she ₐttended to Henry.

A fortnight and three days after her visit to Dr. ℂrupiner—the doctor, at Henry's suggestion, had ᵢncreased her dose of Fender's pills from three to five a ɟay—she went through her Saturday ritual as usual.

For a man engaged in Mr. Brownrigg's particular ₚrogramme to get hopelessly and incapably drunk once,

179

much less once a week, might well have been suicida lunacy.

One small glass of whiskey reduced him to taciturnity twelve large glasses of whiskey, or one bottle, made him limp, silent sack of humanity, incapable of movement o speech, but, quite remarkably, not a senseless creature.

It might well have occurred to Millie to wonder why he husband should choose to transform himself into a Thérès Raquin paralytic once every week in his life, but in spite o her awful stupidity she was a tolerant woman and honestl believed that men were odd, privileged creatures who too secret delight in strange perversions. So she humoured hi and kept his weakness secret even from her mother.

Oddly enough, Henry Brownrigg enjoyed his periodica orgy. He did not drink during the week, and his Saturda experience was at once an adventure and a habit. At th outset of his present project he had thought of forgoing until his plan was completed, but he realized the absolut necessity of adhering rigidly to his normal course of life, s that there could be no hook, however small, on which th garment of suspicion could catch and take hold.

On this particular evening Millie quite exhausted hersel getting him upstairs and into bed. She was so tired when i was all over that she sat on the edge of her couch an breathed hard, quite unable to pull herself togethe sufficiently to undress.

So exhausted was she that she forgot to take the tw Fender's pills that Henry had left on the dressing-table fo her, and once in bed she could not persuade herself to ge out again for them.

In the morning Henry found them still in the little box He listened to her startled explanations in silence and then as she added apology to apology, suddenly became himsel again.

"Dear Millie," he said in the old exasperated tone sh knew so well, "isn't it enough for me to do all I can to ge you well without you hampering me at every turn?"

Millie bent low over the stove and, as if he felt she migh be hiding sudden tears, his manner became mor conciliatory.

"Don't you like them?" he inquired softly. "Don't yo like the taste of them? Perhaps they're too big? Look here
180

old dear, I'll put them up in an easier form. You shall have them in jelly cases. Leave it to me. There, there, don't worry. But you must take your medicine, you know."

He patted her plump shoulder awkwardly and hurried upstairs to dress.

Millie became thoughtful. Henry was clearly very worried about her indeed, or he would never be so nice about her silly mistake.

Young Bill Perry, Brownrigg's errand-boy assistant, was at the awkward stage, if indeed he would ever grow out of it.

He was scrawny, red-headed, with a tendency to acne, and great raw, scarlet wrists. Mr. Brownrigg he loathed as only the young can loathe the possessor of a sarcastic tongue, but Millie he liked, and his pale, sandy-fringed eyes twinkled kindly when she spoke to him.

Young Perry did not think Millie was half so daft as the Old Man made out.

If only because she was kind to him, young Perry was interested in the state of Millie's health.

On the Monday night young Perry saw Mr. Brownrigg putting up the contents of the Fender's pills in jelly cases and he inquired about them.

Mr. Brownrigg was unusually communicative. He told young Perry in strict confidence that Mrs. Brownrigg was far from well and that Dr. Crupiner was worried about her.

Mr. Brownrigg also intimated that he and Dr. Crupiner were, as professional men, agreed that if complete freedom from care and Fender's pills could not save Mrs. Brownrigg, nothing could.

"Do you mean she might die?" said young Perry, aghast. "Suddenly, I mean, sir?"

He was sorry as soon as he had spoken, because Mr. Brownrigg's hand trembled so much that he dropped one of the jelly cases and young Perry realized that the Old Man was really wild about the Old Girl after all, and that his bully-ragging her was all a sham to hide his feelings.

At that moment young Perry's sentimental, impressionable heart went out to Mr. Brownrigg, and he generously forgave him for his observation that young Perry was patently cut out for the diplomatic service, since his tact and delicacy were so great.

The stores arrived. Bill Perry unpacked the two big cases; the smaller case he opened, but left the unpacking to his employer.

Mr. Brownrigg finished his pill-making, although he was keeping the boy waiting, rinsed his hands and got down to work with his usual deliberation.

There were not a great many packages in the case and young Perry, who had taken a peep at the mottled ledger some time before, thought he knew why. The Old Man was riding close to the edge. Bills and receipts had to be juggled very carefully these days.

The boy read the invoice from the wholesalers, and Mr. Brownrigg put the drugs away.

"Sodii Bicarbonis, Magnesia Levis," he read, stumbling over the difficult words. "Iodine, Quininae, Hydrochloridum, Tincture Digitalin . . . that must be it, Mr. Brownrigg. There, in the biggish packet."

Bill Perry knew he read badly and was only trying to be helpful when he indicated the parcel, but Mr. Brownrigg shot a truly terrifying glance in his direction as he literally snatched up the packet and carried it off to the drug cabinet.

Young Perry was dismayed. He was late and he wanted to go. In his panic he floundered on, making matters worse.

"I'm sorry, sir," he said. "I was only trying to help. I thought you might be—er—thinking of something else and got a bit muddled."

"Oh," said Mr. Brownrigg slowly, facing him with those hot, round eyes in a way which was oddly disturbing. "And of what should I be thinking when I am doing my work, boy?"

"Of—of Mrs. Brownrigg, sir," stammered the wretched Perry helplessly.

Henry Brownrigg froze. The blood congealed in his face and his eyes seemed to sink into his head.

Young Perry, who realized he had said the wrong thing, and who had a natural delicacy which revolted at prying into another's sorrow, mistook his employer's symptoms for acute embarrassment.

"I'm sorry," he said again. "I was really trying to help. I'm a bit—er—windy myself, sir. Mrs. Brownrigg's been

182

very kind to me. I'm sorry she's so ill."

A great sigh escaped Henry Brownrigg.

"That's all right, my boy," he said, with a gentleness his assistant had never before heard in his tone. "I'm a bit rattled myself, too. You can go now. I'll see to these few things."

Young Perry sped off, happy to be free on such a sunny evening, but also a little awe-stricken by revelation of this tragedy of married love.

Phyllis hurried down Coe's Lane, which was a short cut between her own road and Priory Avenue. It was a narrow, paper-baggy little thoroughfare, with a dusty hedge on one side and high tarred fence on the other.

On this occasion Coe's Lane appeared to be deserted, but when Phyllis reached the stunted may tree half-way down the hedge a figure stepped out and came to meet her.

The girl stopped abruptly in the middle of the path. Her cheeks were patched with pink and white and she caught her breath sharply as though afraid of herself.

Henry Brownrigg himself was unprepared for the savagery of the sudden pain in his breast when he saw her, and the writhing, vicious, mindless passion which checked his breathing and made his eyelids feel sticky and his mouth dry, frightened him a little also.

They were alone in the lane and he kissed her, putting into his hunched shoulders and greedy lips all the insufferable, senseless longing of the past eighteen days.

When he released her she was crying. The big, bright tears which filled her eyes brimmed over on to her cheeks and made her mouth look hot and wet and feverish.

"Go away," she said and her tone was husky and imploring, "Oh, go away—please, please!"

After the kiss Henry Brownrigg was human again and no longer the fiend-possessed soul in torment he had been while waiting in the lane. Now he could behave normally, for a time at least.

"All right," he said, and added so lightly that she was deceived. "Going out with Peter Hill again this afternoon?"

The girl's lips trembled and her eyes were pleading.

"I'm trying to get free," she said. "Don't you see I'm trying to get free from you? It's not easy."

Henry Brownrigg stared at her inquisitively for a full minute. Then he laughed shortly and explosively and strode away back down the lane at a great pace.

Henry Brownrigg went home. He walked very fast, his round eyes introspective but his step light and purposeful. His thoughts were pleasant. So Phyllis was there when he wanted her, there for the taking when the obstacle was once removed. That had been his only doubt. Now he was certain of it. The practical part of his project alone remained.

Small, relatively unimportant things like the new story the mottled ledger would have to tell when the insurance money was in the bank and Millie's small income was realized and reinvested crowded into his mind, but he brushed them aside impatiently. This afternoon he must be grimly practical. There was delicate work to do.

When he reached home Millie had gone over to her mother's.

It was also early-closing day and young Perry was far away, bowling wides for the St. Anne's parish cricket club.

Mr. Brownrigg went round the house carefully and made sure that all the doors were locked. The shop shutters were up too, and he knew from careful observation that they permitted no light from within to escape.

He removed his jacket and donned his working overall, switched on the lights, locked the door between the shop and the living-room, and set to work.

He knew exactly what he had to do. Millie had been taking five Fender's pills regularly now for eight days. Each pill contained one sixteenth of a gramme of Nativelle's Digitalin, and the stuff was cumulative. No wonder she had been complaining of biliousness and headaches lately! Millie was a hopeless fool.

He took out the bottle of Tincturae Digitalin, which had come when young Perry had given him such a scare, and looked at it. He wished he had risked it and bought the Quevenne's or the freshly powdered leaves. He wouldn't have had all this trouble now.

Still, he hadn't taken the chance, and on second thoughts he was glad. As it was, the wholesalers couldn't possibly notice anything unusual in his order. There could be no inquiry: it meant he need never worry—afterwards.

184

He worked feverishly as his thoughts raced on. He knew the dose. All that had been worked out months before when the idea had first occurred to him, and he had gone over this part of the proceedings again and again in his mind so that there could be no mistake, no slip.

Nine drachms of the tincture had killed a patient with no digitalin already in the system. But then the tincture was notoriously liable to deteriorate. Still, this stuff was fresh; barely six days old, if the wholesalers could be trusted. He had thought of that.

He prepared his burner and the evaporator. It took a long time. Although he was so practised, his hands were unsteady and clumsy, and the irritant fumes got into his eyes.

Suddenly he discovered that it was nearly four o'clock. He was panic stricken. Only two hours and Millie would come back, and there was a lot to be done.

As the burner did its work his mind moved rapidly. Digitalin was so difficult to trace afterwards; that was the beauty of it. Even the great Tardieu had been unable to state positively if it was digitalin that had been used in the Pommeraise case, and that was after the most exhaustive P.M. and tests on frogs and all that sort of thing.

Henry Brownrigg's face split into the semblance of a smile. Old Crupiner was no Tardieu. Crupiner would not advise a P.M. if he could possibly avoid it. He'd give the certificate all right; his mind was prepared for it. Probably he wouldn't even come and look at the body.

Millie's stupid, placid body. Henry Brownrigg put the thought from him. No use getting nervy now.

A shattering peal on the back door startled him so much that he nearly upset his paraphernalia. For a moment he stood breathing wildly, like a trapped animal, but he pulled himself together in the end, and, changing into his coat, went down to answer the summons.

He locked the shop door behind him, smoothed his hair, and opened the back door, confident that he looked normal, even ordinary.

But the small boy with the evening paper did not wait for his Saturday's payment but rushed away after a single glance at Mr. Brownrigg's face. He was a timid twelve-year-old, however, who often imagined things, and his employer, an older boy, cuffed him for the story and made a mental note to call for the money himself on the Monday night.

The effect of the incident on Henry Brownrigg was considerable. He went back to his work like a man in a nightmare, and for the rest of the proceedings he kept his mind resolutely on the physical task.

At last it was done.

He turned out the burner, scoured the evaporator measured the toxic dose carefully, adding to it considerably to be on the safe side. After all, one could hardly overdo it that was the charm of this stuff.

Then he effectively disposed of the residue and felt much better.

He had locked the door and changed his coat again before he noticed the awful thing. A layer of fine dust on the top of one of the bottles first attracted his attention. He removed it with fastidious care. He hated a frowzy shop.

He had replaced his handkerchief before he saw the show-case ledge and the first glimmering of the dreadful truth percolated his startled mind.

From the ledge his eyes travelled to the counter-top, to the dummy cartons, to the bottles and jars, to the window shutters, to the very floor.

Great drops appeared on Henry Brownrigg's forehead There was not an inch of surface in the whole shop that was innocent of the thinnest, faintest coat of yellowish dust.

Digitalin! Digitalin over the whole shop. Digitalin over the whole world! The evidence of his guilt everywhere damning, inescapable, clear to the first intelligent observer

Henry Brownrigg stood very still.

Gradually his brain, cool at the bidding of the instinct of self-preservation, began to work again. Delay. That was the all-important note. Millie must not take the capsule tonight as he had planned. Not tonight, not tomorrow Millie must not die until every trace of that yellow dust had been driven from the shop.

Swiftly he rearranged his plan. Tonight he must behave as usual and tomorrow, when Millie went to church, he must clear off the worst of the stuff before young Perry noticed anything.

Then on Monday he would make an excuse and have the acuum-cleaning people in. They came with a large machine and he had often said he would have it done.

They worked quickly; so on Tuesday. . . .

Meanwhile, normality. That was the main thing. He must do nothing to alarm Millie or excite her curiosity.

It did not occur to him that there would be a grim irony in getting Millie to help him dust the shop that evening. But he dismissed the idea. They'd never do it thoroughly in the time.

He washed in the kitchen and went back into the hall. A step on the stairs above him brought a scream to his throat which he only just succeeded in stifling.

It was Millie. She had come in the back way without him hearing her, heaven knew how long before.

"I've borrowed a *portière* curtain from Mother for your bedroom door, Henry," she said mildly. "You won't be troubled by the draught up there any more. It's such a good thick one. I've just been fixing it up. It looks very nice."

Henry Brownrigg made a noise which might have meant anything. His nerves had gone to pieces.

Her next remark was reassuring, however, so reassuring that he almost laughed aloud.

"Oh, Henry," she said, "you only gave me four of those pills today, dear. You won't forget the other one, will you?"

"Cold ham from the cooked meat shop, cold tinned peas, potato salad and Worcester sauce. What a cook! What a cook I've married my dear Millie."

Henry Brownrigg derived a vicious pleasure from the clumsy sarcasm, and when Millie's pale face became wooden he was gratified.

As he sat at the small table and looked at her he was aware of a curious phenomenon. The woman stood out from the rest of the room's contents as though she alone was in relief. He saw every line of her features, every fold of her dark cotton dress, as though they were drawn with a thick black pencil.

Millie was silent. Even her usual flow of banality had dried up, and he was glad of it.

He found himself regarding her dispassionately, as

though she had been a stranger. He did not hate her, h[e]
decided. On the contrary, he was prepared to believe tha[t]
she was quite an estimable, practical person in her ow[n]
limited fashion. But she was in the way.

This plump, fatuous creature, not even different in h[er]
very obtuseness from many of the other matrons in th[e]
town, had committed the crowning impudence of getting i[n]
the way of Henry Brownrigg. She, this ridiculous low[?]
woman, actually stood between Henry Brownrigg and th[e]
innermost desires of his heart.

It was an insight into the state of the chemist's mind tha[t]
at that moment nothing impressed him so forcibly as h[is]
remarkable audacity.

Monday, he thought. Monday, and possibly Tuesda[y]
and then. . . .

Millie cleared away.

Mr. Brownrigg drank his first glass of whiskey an[d]
soda with a relish he did not often experience. For him th[e]
pleasure of his Saturday night libations lay in the od[d]
sensation he experienced when really drunk.

When Henry Brownrigg was a sack of limp, uninvitin[g]
humanity to his wife and the rest of the world, to himself [he]
was a quiet, all-powerful ghost, seated, comfortable an[d]
protected in the shell of his body, able to see an[d]
comprehend everything, but too mighty and too importa[nt]
to direct any of the drivelling little matters which made u[p]
his immediate world.

On these occasions Henry Brownrigg tasted godhead.

The evening began like all the others, and by the tim[e]
there was an inch of amber elixir in the square bottl[e]
Millie and the dust in the shop and Dr. Crupiner ha[d]
become in his mind as ants and ant burdens, while [he]
towered above them, a colossus in mind and power.

When the final inch had dwindled to a yellow stain in th[e]
bottom of the white glass bottle Mr. Brownrigg sat ve[ry]
still. In a few minutes now he would attain the peak of th[e]
ascendancy over his fellow mortals when the body, s[o]
important to them, was for him literally nothing; not even [a]
dull encumbrance, not even a nerveless covering but [?]
nothingness, an unimportant, unnoticed element.

When Millie came in at last a pin could have been thrust deep into Mr. Brownrigg's flesh and he would not have noticed it.

It was when he was in bed, his useless body clad in clean pyjamas, that he noticed that Millie was not behaving quite as usual. She had folded his clothes neatly on the chair at the end of the bed when he saw her peering at something intently.

He followed her eyes and saw for the first time the new *portière* curtain. It certainly was a fine affair, a great, thick, heavy plush thing that looked as though it would stop any draught there ever had been.

He remembered clearly losing his temper with Millie in front of young Perry one day, and, searching in his mind for a suitable excuse, had invented this draught beneath his bedroom door. And there wasn't one, his ghost remembered; that was the beauty of it. The door fitted tightly in the jamb. But it gave Millie something to worry about.

Millie went out of the room without extinguishing the lights. He tried to call out to her and only then realized the disadvantages of being a disembodied spirit. He could not speak, of course.

He was lying puzzled at this obvious flaw in his omnipotence when he heard her go downstairs instead of crossing into her room. He was suddenly furious and would have risen, had it been possible. But in the midst of his anger he remembered something amusing and lay still, inwardly convulsed with secret laughter.

Soon Millie would be dead. Dead—dead—dead!

Millie would be stupid no longer. Millie would appal him by her awful mindlessness no more. Millie would be dead.

She came up again and stepped softly into the room.

The alcohol was beginning to take its full effect now and he could not move his head. Soon oblivion would come and he would leave his body and rush off into the exciting darkness, not to return until the dawn.

He saw only Millie's head and shoulders when she came into his line of vision. He was annoyed. She still had those thick black lines round her, and there was an absorbed

189

expression upon her face which he remembered seeing before when she was engrossed in some particularly difficult household task.

She switched out the light and then went over to the far window. He was interested now, and saw her pull up the blinds.

Then to his astonishment he heard the crackle of paper, not an ordinary crackle, but something familiar, something he had heard hundreds and hundreds of times before.

He placed it suddenly. Sticky paper. His own reel of sticky paper from the shop.

He was so cross with her for touching it that for some moments he did not wonder what she was doing with it, and it was not until he saw her silhouetted against the second row of panes that he guessed. She was sticking up the window cracks.

His ghost laughed again. The draught! Silly, stupid Millie trying to stop the draught.

She pulled down the blinds and turned on the light again. Her face was mild and expressionless as ever, her blue eyes vacant and foolish.

He saw her go to the dressing-table, still moving briskly as she always did when working about the house.

Once again the phenomenon he had noticed at the evening meal became startlingly apparent. He saw her hand and its contents, positively glowing because of its black outline, thrown up in high relief against the white table cover.

Millie was putting two pieces of paper there: one white with a deckle edge, one blue and familiar.

Henry Brownrigg's ghost yammered in its prison. His body ceased to be negligible: it became a coffin, a sealed leaden coffin suffocating him in its senseless shell. He fought to free himself, to stir that mighty weight, to move.

Millie knew.

The white paper with the deckle edge was a letter from Phyllis out of the drawer in the shop, and the blue paper—he remembered it now—the blue paper he had left in the dirty developing bath.

He re-read his own pencilled words as clearly as if his eye had become possessed of telescopic sight:

'Millie dear, this does explain itself, doesn't it?'

And then his name, signed with a flourish. He had been so pleased with himself when he had written it.

He fought wildly. The coffin was made of glass now, thick, heavy glass which would not respond to his greatest effort.

Millie was hesitating. She had picked up Phyllis's letter. Now she was reading it again.

He saw her frown and tear the paper into shreds, thrusting the pieces into the pocket of her cardigan.

Henry Brownrigg understood. Millie was sorry for Phyllis. For all her obtuseness she had guessed at some of the girl's piteous infatuation and had decided to keep her out of it.

What then? Henry Brownrigg writhed inside his inanimate body.

Millie was back at the table now. She was putting something else there. What was it? Oh, what was it?

The ledger! He saw it plainly, the old mottled ledger, whose story was plain for any fool coroner to read and misunderstand.

Millie had turned away now. He hardly noticed her pause before the fireplace. She did not stoop. Her felt shod slipper flipped the gas tap over.

Then she passed out the door, extinguishing the light as he went. He heard the rustle of the thick curtain as she drew the wood close. There was an infinitesimal pause and then the key turned in the lock.

She had behaved throughout the whole proceeding as though she had been getting dinner or tidying the spare room.

In the prison Henry Brownrigg's impotent ghost listened. There was a hissing from the far end of the room.

In the attic, although he could not possibly hear it, he knew the meter ticked every two or three seconds.

Henry Brownrigg saw in a vision the scene in the morning. Every room in the house had the same key, so Millie would have no difficulty in explaining that on awakening she had noticed the smell of gas and, on finding her husband's door locked, had opened it with her own key.

The ghost stirred in its shell. Once again the earth and earthly incidents looked small and negligible. The oblivion

191

was coming, the darkness was waiting, only now it was n[...] longer exciting darkness.

The shell moved. He felt it writhe and choke. It wa[...] fighting—fighting—fighting.

The darkness drew him. He was no longer conscious o[...] the shell now. It had been beaten. It had given up the figh[...]

The streak of light beneath the blind where the stree[...] lamp shone was fading. Fading. Now it was gone.

As Henry Brownrigg's ghost crept out into the cold [...] whisper came to it, ghastly in its conviction:

"They never get caught, that kind. They're too dull, to[...] practical, too unimaginative. They never get caught."

THE MIND'S EYE MYSTERY

"My dear Judith, it's the name I don't like to hear. I can't bear you using it. I realize you can't be talking about the same Laurie Butler, but if you're going to marry him, or even to bring him home here, you'll have to call him Laurence."

Mother, who is round and charming and normally reasonable had the grace to look uncomfortable as she regarded me through the looking-glass above her dressing table, but her eyes were almost frosty.

"I'm sorry," she said, "but that was the name of the child who killed Dorinda. She was your father's only sister and he worshipped her. I dare say the story is ancient history to you, but to Daddy and me it's only twenty-five years ago, and that isn't terribly long when you're fifty, as you'll find one day."

As I stood behind her I could see my startled face hovering in the dark mirror above her head. She and I are not very alike. I am long and skinny with Dad's Scottish colouring, and my modern hair-do looked flippant above her soft grey waves. She was bluffing, of course. I realized that. But I was shocked to see how much she cared. I put my arms round her neck and laid my cheek against hers.

"It's the same person, darling. He was only eight years

old then and he's thirty-three now. He's grown into the best man I ever met. I don't know if I'll marry him because he hasn't asked me yet, but I know I want to." I sounded breathless and even a little unsteady. I had not admitted quite so much to myself before. In the looking-glass I saw her bleak expression give place to a worried one.

"Oh, Judy," she said helplessly, "how perfectly awful, darling! What are we going to say to Daddy?"

I did not answer. It was a question I had been pondering over since I stepped on to the train which would bring me home to Meade for the weekend. I was at the university, on a refresher course, and even up there the position had appeared to be a little awkward. Home here at Meade, where it had all taken place, the atmosphere was very different. I saw that it could well seem rather shocking to the home folk that I should want to marry Laurie, of all men in the world. I believe that at that moment, if it hadn't been for the memory of his hurt face and shadowed eyes, I would have rushed back to London with my course at the University Hospital where we had met only half finished.

I am a child psychiatrist and I take my job with a passionate sincerity which would be rather a bore, I'm afraid, if the subject wasn't so desperately important. It was the reason why I went out of my way to get to know Laurie while I was working in the hospital where he was one of a team of research chemists. I knew who he was and I was interested to see what effect the experience in his childhood had had on him. I walked into it with my eyes open. The instant we met I was lost. When Laurie and I first saw each other something happened to both of us. There is only one thing certain about those cheerful idiots who inquire if one believes in love at first sight, and that is that they have never experienced it. It is not a phenomenon which leaves room for any doubt, my goodness!

After our first meeting Laurie and I simply managed to see each other all the time when we weren't actually working. We talked about every subject under the sun except two. We did not mention the shooting, although the shadow of it hung between us like a sheet of glass, and we did not actually talk of love. After a week the situation was unbearable and I fled to spend a couple of nights at home with the laudable idea of trying to clarify my mind. The

194

clearer it became the more wretched I grew.

The story of Dorinda's death was one of those mysteries whose solution appears only too obvious from the very beginning. My father, Dr. Davies, had been one of the more popular medical men in Meade. Laurie's father, Sam Butler, was the County architect. I was a few months old and Laurie himself was a child. We lived near each other and belonged to the same set. Dorinda Davies was just nineteen and beautiful. She had come to us to spend the summer, partly to help Mother with me and partly to take a share in the social season which in those far off times was gay enough to attract any young girl. From the outset she was a tremendous success. I grew up with a child's belief that she was the most dazzling heroine of romance who had ever lived, but if not quite that, it does appear that she was unusual, pretty, popular and vivacious.

The whole town was shaken when tragedy overtook her. Early one evening about eight weeks after her arrival her body was found in a meadow by the river on the outskirts of the town. She had been shot at close range with a light sporting gun, which lay in the grass a few yards from the body. Our family punt, in which she had been seen alone earlier in the day, was tied up to some willows near by.

The police identified the gun very quickly. It belonged to Mr. Butler. He and his wife were away on a weekend trip, but Laurie had been left behind in the care of a housekeeper and already he had been punished twice for shooting without permission. Also he had told several people that he wanted to bag a water-rat. After that, it was only a matter of hours before they discovered witnesses who had actually seen him trotting down to the watermeadows in the hot afternoon, the gun under his arm.

Old Inspector Andrews, who was in charge of the case, was a family man himself and it was said that the business broke his heart. He talked to Laurie and made up his mind that it had been an accident, and that the child was too frightened to own up. He thought the boy had been showing the gun to the girl when the shot was fired, and he did everything he could to make him admit it.

Unfortunately Laurie had a different story and nothing would make him alter it. He agreed that he had taken the gun, knowing that he was doing wrong, and that he had gone down to the river to wait for a rat. He was in position, he explained, crouched down by a tree stump, when Dorinda came drifting along in her boat, playing a portable gramophone. He called to her, asking her to be quiet and not to scare the rat, but he thought he frightened her, for she turned very red, he said, and was furious with him. She came into the bank and asked him if his father knew that he was out shooting. He had to confess that he did not, whereupon she insisted that he gave her the gun at once before he did any harm with it. He was not enthusiastic, naturally, but she was grown-up and quite capable of telling on him, so finally he gave way. He parted with his prize and according to him the last time he saw it was as it lay in the bottom of the skiff as she sped away downstream. After that, he said, there was no point in waiting, and so he came home and played in the garden until supper-time.

It was an inconclusive tale, highly unsatisfactory in the circumstances. The hideous fact remained, Dorinda was dead. No one believed Laurie.

Sympathy for both families was very great in the town and the Coroner's court, with a kindness more well meant than actual, brought in an open verdict. After a while Sam Butler resigned his job and the family moved elsewhere.

As far as I could gather afterwards, our lot behaved very well, but Daddy never made any bones about his beliefs. For him there was no mystery. Dorinda had been the victim of a tragic accident, and the Butler boy was a dangerous young liar with bad blood in him somewhere. So there it was.

I looked at Mother again. "You don't think Dad's attitude may have mellowed?" I began half-heartedly, but she silenced me.

"I know it hasn't. He was speaking about it only the other day. He surprised me. He's still very bitter about the lying. He feels that if only the child had been made to own up it would have settled things once and for all, and there wouldn't have been all the talk about the poor girl afterwards."

"Talk?" I murmured, surprised. "I thought she was supposed to be the complete innocent."

"Oh well, of course, she was." Mother's round face grew

even pinker. "No one could criticize her when she was dead, dear." She paused, honesty compelling her, no doubt, and added unexpectedly, "To be truthful, she was something of a nightmare to me. I was only five years older, you see, and I couldn't begin to manage her. Girls were wild in those days, too. However, don't you dare to repeat that. Daddy would never forgive me."

"I won't," I said hastily, but she had made me curious. "What brought the subject up?" I inquired. "You noticed that paragraph about Laurie's experiments, I suppose?"

"No, darling. I'm afraid I didn't." With extreme delicacy she managed to convey that whilst being on my side she still didn't like to hear the tabooed name on my lips. "We heard on the news that John Ryder, the painter, had died somewhere down in Cornwall, and we began to talk about him. He and his wife were staying at the Johnson's cottage down here when it all happened. He was very struck with Dorinda and he had asked Daddy if she could sit for him. There was some talk that the portrait might get hung in the Royal Academy and we were all wildly excited about it." She caught my eye and laughed. "We were a very ordinary lot of provincials, I'm afraid. Oh Judy, my dear, you're horribly right, it *is* a long time ago."

I kissed her and let the matter drop. Both she and Father are darlings and I adore them both, but their life in a small country town has not made them exactly flexible in outlook. With the years, to put it mildly, their ideas have tended to become set. Meantime, my own predicament had not grown any easier. I found I was searching my heart almost eagerly to see if I was missing Laurie any less, which was absurd. He filled my whole world and there was never going to be any escaping from him. I felt that in my bones.

I assumed Mother had decided to let well alone and would ignore our conversation, but on Sunday evening, just as I was in bed, she came trotting in with an envelope in her hand.

"Look, Judy," she began, sounding faintly conspiratorial although Daddy could hardly have heard her down three flights of stairs, "this is what I meant about Dorinda. See how lovely she was and how—well, how wild." She sat down on the quilt, opened the envelope and shook two photographs out on to my lap. I turned them over curiously. They were snapshots but they had been printed on square sheets of paper with official looking hieroglyphics printed under them. Each was a picture of the same girl in different poses, and one negative was very much clearer than the other. I saw that she had been a raving beauty of the period, very much more made up than I had realized was the fashion and there was certainly provocativeness in her attitude as she sat on the grass looking up and smiling. The other photograph, although it had been taken at the same time, since the dress and background were the same, was very blurred. One could only just make out her shadowed face as she leant back against a tree trunk, the leaves making patterns across her distinctive white skirt with a scalloped hem.

"You can guess she was a handful," Mother went on. "There were such a lot of men about then. Young husbands, and old ones, too. I had quite a time one way and another. The wives always came to me."

I could imagine that they would. It would hardly be much use going to the young baggage in the photograph. I felt I was getting a new angle both on Dorinda and on Mama. I turned the pictures over.

"What are these?" I inquired idly. "Exhibits at the Coroner's court?"

"I suppose they must be," she agreed. "The police gave them to your father when the case was closed. They were found in her camera, which was lying right there beside her in the grass. Two exposures had been made and so the police developed the film. That was her new dress. She'd never worn it before that day. See the scalloped hem? That's how they knew when the snap was taken. She'd only had the dress on for those three hours before she died.

"Really?" That was a piece of data I'd never heard. "Did they discover who took these, darling?"

"Oh, they were certain the boy did. I don't think he admitted it, but it was quite obvious that he met Dorinda and that they talked, and she asked him to snap her, and then he started showing her his gun and, of course, it went off. I always blamed the parents. Fancy going away for a weekend and leaving a gun where a child could reach it!"

I hardly heard her. I was looking at the photograph of the lovely face smiling so invitingly at the camera. The curve of the full throat was sensuous and the shape of the swelling breast just apparent under the silk dress.

"Have I seen this before?" I demanded. "I think I have."

"You may have done, dear. That was the one the police reproduced everywhere on the off-chance that someone would come forward to say they'd seen them together that afternoon. The other one wouldn't reproduce. No one did come forward, though. My word, she was a pretty girl, wasn't she?"

"Staggering, as far as I can see from these," I said and handed them back to her.

She studied them again and began to talk as people do about old photographs.

"If only this one had come out properly you'd see what I mean about her so much better," she rambled on. "It wasn't only her appearance. I don't suggest there was any harm in her but she did like to provoke people. This second picture shows that if you study it, but it's no good, the negative was over-exposed and I should say the child moved when he took it. All the same," she added brightly, "I do believe those old cameras took better pictures than the very expensive new ones."

I did not answer. I was still bothered by the first picture, the one the police had reproduced. Something about it had struck me as being curious but for the life of me I couldn't define it. Mother cut into my thoughts by suddenly gathering her papers and rising.

"I don't hold it against the little boy," she said in a sudden burst of confiding, "but, oh my pet, do get over it if you can. It's irrevocable, you see. At this distance nothing is true about a thing like that except what people believe. Daddy and I could forgive him but we could never get it out of our heads that he's naturally careless and tells lies. It isn't only us, either. The case made quite a sensation. You'll find that nearly everyone of our age or older will feel exactly the same way about it. You being you just turns it into a story people will want to tell."

She went on, leaving me so flattened that I did not notice until later that she had left the second photograph—the

199

bad one—on the bed. Without thinking I put it in my handbag which was lying on the side table, and switched off the light.

She was right; I could see that. I went back to the hospital and work and for a few more days Laurie and I kept up our pretences. I did not broach the subject because I was terrified lest anything should shatter the cloud-cuckoo-land dream in which I seemed to be wandering, but in the end matters came to a head. It happened almost casually, as such things so often do.

We had been for a long walk together and had come back through one of the pretty villages just outside the university town, and as we crossed a stone bridge over the river we paused to look down at the shallow water hurrying over the pebbles. I remember thinking that the spot was traditionally romantic and that Laurie was downright conventionally handsome, with his Nordic face and tow-coloured hair, and then I laid my hand on the parapet and he dropped his own over it.

"Oh, my dear girl," he said, in probably the most unromantic way such a declaration was ever dragged out of a man, "this can't go on. I shall be sick."

Fortunately I laughed so much it did not matter my eyes watering.

"That's exactly how I feel," I said.

He did not speak at once but went on holding my hand very tightly. Finally he turned me round to face him.

"How idiotic that it had to be us," he said. "You and me, I mean. You think I killed that relative of yours, don't you?"

It was not at all what I had expected and I was unpardonably clumsy.

"My dear," I said, "no one could blame a child of eight who—"

"That's not what I asked you, Judy. You've answered me all the same. You think I shot her. So does everybody else in the world."

I stared at him and for the first time doubt concerning the question entered my mind, and as it did so I realized what it was that had struck me as being so strange about

200

he snapshot Mother had shown me.

"Do you mean to say you didn't?" I demanded.

He gave me a queer sidelong glance under his lashes.

"I wish I thought I had," he said deliberately. "Unfortunately I don't. I never did. That makes me odd man out. Before God, Judy, if I shot that girl I did it in a brainstorm, and all my life since I've been terrified I'd have another."

I felt my heart turn over in my chest, I was so appalled by the revelation. The agony the child must have suffered, the horror of adolescence in such circumstances.

"Darling," I exclaimed involuntarily, "what a miracle you stood it. Of course, of course, you didn't kill her. She was going to meet somebody. That's why she was so angry when you appeared on the bank so inopportunely."

He stared. "That's what my father tried to believe. What put it into your head?"

"The photograph." The words came out of my mouth before even I realized their full implication. "That girl wasn't smiling up at a child when that snapshot was taken."

He frowned. "Wasn't she? I don't really remember the picture. I know there was one and I recall a rather kindly old copper trying to persuade me to say that I took it. But it didn't mean a thing to me. I was simply sticking to what I believed was the literal truth. Never, at any point in my life, have I been able to remember anything different from the story I told the police, yet now it does seem to me that if there had been any other possible explanation they would have discovered it. That's the mischief of the whole wretched situation. Nothing can ever be proved, and after all this time it's what everybody believes which is the reality."

They were so nearly Mother's words all over again I felt a wave of sheer dismay pass over me.

"But it's all wrong," I burst out, stammering in my excitement. "It's—it's monstrous! Don't let it make any difference to us, Laurie. Please darling, that would be wicked."

I heard him catch his breath. "You're the sweetest thing, Judy. I love you. I want to ask you to marry me more than

201

anything in the world, but I shan't because I know
couldn't stand the publicity all over again and I don't thin
you could."

"Publicity—" I began contemptuously but he cut m
short.

"My dear, you've no idea what it's like. It's not th
paragraphs in the newspapers, or even the re-hashing of th
whole dreary story which can only have the sam
hopelessly indeterminate conclusion—either I'm a liar or a
lunatic. It's the letters from people one's never heard of."

"Good heavens," I ejaculated. "Surely they didn't writ
to you as a child?"

"Did they not!" He was bitter. "My father and mothe
were almost driven to suicide. People wrote condoling, o
censuring, or suggesting idiotic solutions. Some wer
spiteful, some were ostensibly well-meaning, but they wer
all utterly relentless. I tell you, the public's reaction to
story which takes its fancy is fearsome. It can shake you u
horribly, especially if you don't know quite how guilty yo
are."

I said nothing. I was both scandalized and scared. Also
loved him so much that the prospect of losing him made m
feel positively faint.

"Are you sure people would still be interested after a
this time?" I ventured at last.

He grimaced. "Some hardly need a reminder. Last week
as you know, there was a couple of paragraphs about thi
job I'm on in two very solid and respectable journal
Today I got a cutting from the Meade Courier quotin
them and then recalling the whole of the old story, whil
three or four days ago there was an illiterate note from
some woman in Cornwall saying that her lodger, who ha
just died, had painted a picture of the 'lady you shot as a
little boy' and asking me if I would like to buy it as 'h
always said you ought to have it'. No, Judy, once ou
names are linked together we'd pull a hornet's nest abou
our ears and yet—oh God, my darling, what can we do?"

I put my arm through his possessively.

"Tell me about the woman in Cornwall. The lodger wa
John Ryder, I suppose?"

"That's the man." He held my arm tightly against him a
we strode on down the road together. "He was visitin

202

Meade at the time. I don't really remember him so well as I do his wife, who was a terrifying piece of work, Spanish or something, jealous as the devil. He was quite a well-known painter then, although I can't say I've heard of him since. All the same, it shows you how even disinterested people talk. It must be the element of mystery which fascinates them. Did the wretched child pull the trigger or didn't it? Unlucky, in this case there never can be any proof."

"Someone might confess," I suggested half-heartedly.

"After twenty-five years? It's not very likely." His quick smile faded and the long wrinkles appeared on his forehead. "Even so, you know, I think both the police and myself would need more than a mere statement to set all doubt at rest. Proof is the necessary item, Judy, cast-iron irrefutable proof. At this stage in the proceedings it's just not possible."

The world lay heavy between us for the rest of the walk home. I saw his point only too vividly. I was remembering the attitude of my own people. Whichever way I turned the same blank wall seemed to confront me and I had never felt so helplessly miserable.

All the rest of the day I turned the matter over and over in my mind, and by evening I was in the mood to catch at the most flimsy of straws. Laurie and I were in his study listening to some records when the idea which had been nagging me suddenly took shape. I got to my feet.

"Look," I announced. "I'm going to Cornwall to see that picture. Will you drive me?"

To my relief he laughed. I'd been afraid he might be angry.

"Anywhere in the world," he assured me. "There's nothing I'd like better. But if it's a matter of morbid curiosity I can satisfy that instantly. The lady sent the picture on approval with the letter. I hardly looked at it. It's in the cupboard, still in brown paper, ready to be returned."

We went across the room together and carried the square flat parcel to the table under the light. Laurie pulled off the wrappings and put his arm round my shoulders as we stood looking down at a canvas perhaps twenty inches square. The moment I saw it I stood transfixed, staring at it incredulously, hardly conscious of Laurie's voice con-

tinuing in the quiet room. When at last I got hold o
myself and turned to him he was still talking about th
painter and his landlady.

"She didn't actually say so but I gather he was definitel
odd at the end of the time," he was saying. "She say
something about him painting this picture over and ove
again and making her promise to give it to me when h
died. But, as she points out, since he owed her nearly
year's board she thought she was justified in trying for
sale. His wife must have vanished some time ago. There'
no mention of her. It's not a bad, old-fashioned factua
painting. What do you say? Shall I buy it and justify he
faith in writing letters to strangers?"

On the last word he looked round at me and caught m
expression.

"Why, Judy," he exclaimed, "what is it, my dear
What's the matter? You look as though you've seen
ghost."

"I—I have," I said huskily. "Laurie, this is it. This is th
answer. This is the confession and the proof."

"Proof? Darling, what on earth are you talking about
You're lightheaded, my poor pet. This is only a portrait o
Dorinda. I can't remember if it's very like her. I thought o
her as being older and more—more staid than this. There'
no significance here."

"Isn't there!" I exploded. "You don't understand. Thi
is the picture, the one which didn't come out properly, th
one the police couldn't reproduce because the negative wa
too bad. Don't you see, *he knew he had taken it*. He knev
it was not only in the camera but in his own mind's eyes
That's why he wanted you to have it. John Ryder sho
Dorinda. One can easily guess why. She was wanton an
reckless and he had a jealous termagant of a wife. This i
his confession. Moreover," I added, looking up into hi
disbelieving face, "as it happens, I can prove it." And
opened my handbag.

It was terrifying. The two pictures were almost identical
The shadow of the leaves made almost the same pattern o
the white skirt with the tell-tale scalloped hem which fixe
the time of wearing, but, whereas in the photograph th
face was almost lost in shadow, in the painting it wa
unbearably vivid. Every provocative line was clearl
204

emphasized and there was no doubt whatever about the mingled fear and attraction which the painter had felt for that impish face for ever implanted in his memory.

Laurie stood looking at the two for some time and then suddenly he put his arm round me.

"My God, Judy," he said and he sounded afraid. "I thought I'd suffered, but what hell it must have been for him."

I made no comment. How could I, with his lips over mine?

MUM KNOWS BEST

Mrs. Chubb's 'little room', which hung like a signalbox over the great circular bar of the Platelayers' Arms, wa unusually deserted for the time of day, which was six o'clock on a fine warm evening. Only two or three of the habitués were present, but Charley Luke, the D.D.C.I. of the district, was there, and so was his old friend Albert Campion, startled at the moment into mild astonishment.

Luke was speaking. "Mum? Of course I've got a mum." He was aggrieved and his diamond-shaped eyes opened as wide as his prominent cheek-bones would permit. "What do you think? That I sprang in full uniform from the head of an Assistant Commissioner?" As was his custom, he gave a brief pantomimic display to illustrate his words and managed to look for a second like a piece of early Greek statuary, boldly costumed by a spiv tailor. "Not on you life," he went on, settling down again on the table where he had been sitting. "I've got a mum, all right. Two jam pot high and boss of all she surveys. Perceptive, that's what mum is."

He hunched himself suddenly and, by peering at us from under his lids and pulling his lips down over his teeth, gave us a sudden startling glimpse of a new and doughty personality.

"What she knows, she knows she knows," he said. "She's got a twenty-two carat heart, was born within sight—much less sound—of Bow Bells, and takes a poor view of policemen."

Luke grinned at Campion. "Her dad was killed in the Melbourne Street Raid when he was a Sergeant C.I.D.; she married a Superintendent and then there's me coming along. She's had a packet to put up with."

"What exactly has she got against the profession?" inquired Mr. Campion with interest. "Always assuming, of course, that the question is without personal offence."

"Not at all, chum." Luke's magnificent teeth showed for an instant above the pewter rim of his tankard. "She thinks we're a weak-minded, unsuspicious lot, too slow to catch a pussycat. And so we are, by her standards. If she wore a helmet, none of you would go out without your rear lights, and she can smell breath over the telephone. I caught her out once though. Whenever she comes the acid, I promise to buy her a diamond necklace. That sends her back to the gas stove."

He presented his back to us, hunched and sulky, so that we caught an image of an angry, elderly person minding her own business grudgingly.

"It was before I got my step up," he said, referring to his Chief Inspectorship. "I'd just taken over this manor and I was going steady, playing myself in. As you know, this isn't a posh district exactly, but it's been posh and there are, so to speak, remnants of poshness scattered about." He waved a hand to the open doorway where the flight of stairs led down into the stucco wilderness of the area north of the park.

"I'd got my office nice and clean, decided which peg to hang my hat on, and started reading up the 'pending' file, when in came my first bit of homework, a nice respectable old housekeeper, all gloves and embarrassment, and would I please come and see her Dear Old Master who'd been made a fool of and wanted to speak to someone BIG. I hinted the D.O.M. might demean himself and come down to see the D.D.I., but that wouldn't do. The Dear Old Master was too old, too ill, too upset. It sounded as though he was dropping to bits, so I took my hat off the peg and

207

went down the road with her to inspect the ruin." He paused and his diamond-shaped eyes became reflective.

"I expected a nice clean house, you know," he went on. "But whacky! Luxury! Enormous great rooms full of gorgeous junk!" His long hands, which were never quite still when he was talking, drew some remarkably vivid shapes in the air. One received an impression of vast quantities of baroque furniture, statuettes, pictures and floating drapery. At the end of the swift performance he rubbed an imaginary piece of material between thumb and forefinger. "Velvet," he said. "Carpets, too. I was over my ankles in lush! Well, I saw the old boy and I thought he was one of his own idols until he spoke. He was sitting by the fire in a high-backed chair and he looked as if the last hundred years hadn't meant much to him. But he was very nice, you know. Very charming and even 'wide' in his own way. I took a shine to him. The story he had to tell was familiar enough—old-fashioned and not even out of the ordinary; but he told it very well and very politely, if you see what I mean—didn't expect ME to be a mug. He could laugh at himself, too. I've been hearing versions of the story all my life. The old chap had been out in his car with a chauffeur driving and they had crossed the park in a rainstorm. Presently, what should they see but a young woman, not too well dressed but quite respectable, caught by her high heel in a grating in the road. The old boy stopped the car and told his man to help her get free. After that they had to give her a lift home because the heel had come off. She gave a very decent address in this neighbourhood and they drove her to it, but didn't wait to see her go in."

He sighed and we shook our heads over the duplicity of young women.

"Meanwhile, of course," Luke continued, "on the drive he had heard The Tale. It was a good one. She was very young and she said she was a student at a dramatic school, that she lived with her mother who was a widow, and that she was determined to go on the stage. He asked her to tea one day in the following week and the old housekeeper, glad to see him amused, baked a special cake. So it went all through the season until he'd grown quite fond of the poppet. As far as I could hear he never gave her anything but cake and the visits were restricted to formal tea parties.

e was that sort of old boy. But the time came, naturally,
hen she did her stuff—'came to her bat', as we say in the
ade." Luke pushed his hat on to the back of his head and
linked at us innocently.

"It's wonderful to me," he announced, "how certain
ories just happen to work. Everybody's heard 'em,
omen are born knowing how to tell 'em, yet they never
il. Tell the truth—say, you've counted your money and
ou haven't as much as you thought—and no one will
elieve you. But come out with one of these old Cinderella
arns and Bob's your Uncle! You've got a happy and
ontented audience digging in its hip pocket. This girl told
e one about the ball—I believe she really did call it a
all—where she was to meet The Impresario. She'd got a
ress but—ahem—no jewellery." Luke favoured us with a
er of quite horrific archness, fluttering his lashes and
idening his mouth like a cat's. "He fell for it," Charley
ent on, "went through all the motions except one. He did
ot ring for the chauffeur and drive her down to Cartier's
r something suitable. Not at all. He trotted off to his
udy, unlocked the secret safe, and came back with
omething which must have startled her out of her wits. It
as a single string diamond necklace. Family stuff, worth
e Lord knows what. I had a full description of it,
omplete with weights of the individual stones and all the
est. He lent it to her for the evening. He told me that
ithout a tremor, but I could see he knew he'd asked for it.
Ie said she was so young and so guileless and had come to
e house so often—that's where she was so clever—that
e trusted her."

Luke wrinkled up his long nose with weary resignation.
After that it was just the usual," he went on, flicking away
e details with a bony hand. "No girl, tea party deserted,
o girl next day. Housekeeper consulted, talk, chauffeur
ent round to the house where they had taken her on the
irst occasion. Finds out she's not known there . . . All the
rdinary palaver. And there is my poor old pal without his
arklers and without his little ray of sunshine who, no
oubt, is shining somewhere else all up like a perishing
hristmas tree. That was where I came in." Luke shook his
ead. "The public believes in us if mum doesn't," he said.
Think of it. What an assignment!"

"So you didn't get the necklace back?" someone said.

Luke lifted up his hand.

"Don't hurry me," he protested. "Let me have my pleasure. I tried. We worked on it for months. The only description of the girl which we sifted—from the report of the three of them—housekeeper, chauffeur, and old boy—was that she was five foot one, two or three inches high; that she was pretty, innocent looking, 'like a flower', that her eyes and hair were 'blue and brown', 'hazel and black', 'brown and dark'. The diamonds were easier, but not much. It was a single string, you see. The value lay in the size and purity of the stones. The jewellers helped more than anybody. They all agreed that the necklace couldn't be disposed of over here without making a bit of a stir in the trade and that if it were broken up it would lose so much in value that they rather thought an effort would be made to get it to the Continent intact. We warned the Customs and shook up all the likely fences. I put the thing in the hands of a really good boy by name of Gooley, who was a sergeant of mine, and I got on with my other work."

Luke paused and accepted the cigarette Campion offered him. "It was one Sunday afternoon in August," Charley continued. "Hot? I thought I was being rendered down! I was sitting in mum's backyard reading the paper and trying to make a noise like someone weeding a path, when Gooley came through on the blower. He was in a terrific state. He thought he'd got her, he said, or he thought he knew where she was. In the last report I'd had from him he'd mentioned some rumours he'd picked up of a diamond necklace owned by a member of the chorus at the New Neapolitan. He'd followed these up like a sensible lad, but the show had closed, making the job more difficult. Now he had got wind of the string of ice again and had pinned it down to a troupe of seventeen dancers who were just going off to Holland. In fact, they were actually at Liverpool Street Station, waiting for the boat train which was mercifully late. He was ringing up from the platform and they were all in the tea-room, chattering like a parrot house and laughing as if they'd got something on their minds." Luke grinned at the recollection.

"Poor Gooley," he went on. "He reported that they were *all* covered with diamonds! He said he'd never seen such a laze. And he guessed that all the cheap jewellery counters f Western London must have been cleared. He was ertain that the real necklace must have been amongst hem, but for the life of him he didn't know where. He sked if he could pull them all in." The D.D.C.I. spread ut his hands. "I wasn't quite as senior as I am now," e remarked, "so before answering I asked for the name of he management. When I heard it I thought twice. The 'ustoms angle was difficult too. They'd help, of course, ut if the train was late and the boat was waiting they /ouldn't thank me if I sent 'em on a wild-goose chase. iooley was by no means certain, and being alone he ouldn't watch seventeen girls at once. 'We'll have to pick er out,' he said to me. 'Can't you bring an expert? He ould look the nceklaces over and pick the right one at nce.' "

Luke rubbed his hand over his forehead and we emembered the heat of the day. "Expert!" he said bitterly. 'Anyone who had brains enough to be an expert was out of London that afternoon. I only had half an hour. The old oy and his servants were away in Scotland and it looked s if I'd have to turn it up and let Gooley down. There /asn't a soul I could produce on the spur of the moment. 'hen I had a brainwave. 'Hold it,' I said to him. 'I'm oming and I'll bring someone who knows most things.' " 'Ie beamed at us. "I took mum," he said.

"It was quite ticklish work getting her there in time, but he arrived at last—little black hat crammed over her eyes, est coat buttoned up to hide her house dress, second best umbrella for defence. We found Gooley as arranged, by the ookstall. He was sweating with heat and anxiety, and his aw dropped when he saw who I'd got with me. 'Is hat. . . ?' he began. 'Greatest living expert,' I said hastily. Where are they?' He pointed to the upstairs tea-room. They're getting ready to make a move,' he said, 'train's due n ten minutes.'

Luke rubbed his hands with remembered excitement.

"We put mum in," he said. "Just like putting a ferret lown a hole. She went through the glass doors and we tood one on either side. The idea was for her to take ights, spot the real diamonds, and then nip out and tell us. 3ut there was nothing like that. Within a matter of minutes
211

there was the Ma and Pa of a row inside. We hadn't time to get in. As we moved, a girl came flying out into our arms, making a bolt for it. Seconds later, mum followed, very dignified except that there was a cup of tea all over her where the kid had chucked it the moment she had asked her to take off her necklace." Luke wagged his head. "Poor mum! She was very pleased with herself until we all four got back to the station, roused the jeweller from Crumb Street, and got him to take a squint through his spy-glass at the kid's necklace. Net value Five Guineas and he didn't know how they did it at the price, he announced. 'Cheer up, mum,' I said to her. 'How could you tell diamonds, duck? You never had any except the little black 'un you call your eyes. Besides, it wasn't as if it mattered. By that time the girl had broken down and come across with the whole story, and I'd got through to Harwich where they'd picked up the real necklace."

As he ceased to speak, Mr. Campion took off his horn-rim spectacles. "Oh, I *see*. Mrs. Luke picked the *girl*."

The D.D.C.I. nodded. "Seventeen lovelies, five others on the staff, and four schoolmistresses who had nothing to do with it," he announced. "Mum took one look round and picked the only wrong 'un in the room. She'd seen her picture in the sensational Sunday rag she takes. Couldn't think what the story had been, but she knew it must be a police case because that's the only news she reads. It was eighteen months before—but she remembered!" Luke chuckled. "All the girls were plastered with fake ice to assist their chum to 'fool the Customs'. The little thief had lent the real stones to the youngest of them all—a kid of seventeen—so that she could carry the can if there was any trouble. Or that was the idea. However, when mum made her entrance and picked out the real crook, she lost her nerve."

Luke glanced at his watch and drank up hastily. "And who shall blame her?" he inquired rhetorically. "Not Charles! Kitchen tiles to be laid tonight or else," he added briefly. "So long."

THE SNAPDRAGON AND
٠ THE C.I.D.

"Murder under the mistletoe—and the man who must have done it couldn't have done it. That's my Christmas and I don't feel merry, thank you very much all the same." Superintendent Stanislaus Oates favoured his old friend Mr. Albert Campion with a pained smile and sat down in the chair indicated.

It was the afternoon of Christmas Day and Mr. Campion, only a trifle more owlish than usual behind his horn-rims, had been fetched down from the children's party which he was attending at his brother-in-law's house in Knightsbridge to meet the Superintendent who had moved heaven and earth to find him.

"What do you want?" Mr. Campion inquired facetiously. "A little pocket conjuring?"

"I don't care if you do it swinging from a trapeze. I just want a reasonable explanation." Oates was rattled. His dyspeptic face with the perpetually sad expression was slightly flushed and not with festivity. He plunged into his story.

"About eleven last night a crook called Sampson was found shot dead in the back of a car in a garage under a

213

small drinking club in Alcatraz Mews, named the Humdinger. A large bunch of mistletoe which had been lying on the front seat ready to be driven home, had been placed on top of the body partially hiding it—which was why it hadn't been found before. The gun, fitted with a silencer, but wiped of prints, was found under the front seat. The dead man was recognized at once by the owner of the car who is also the owner of the club. He was her current boy friend. She is quite a well-known West End character called 'Girlski'. What did you say?"

"I said 'Oe-er'," murmured Mr. Campion. "One of the Eumenides, no doubt?"

"No." Oates spoke innocently. "She's not a Greek. Don't worry about her. Just keep your mind on the facts. She knows, as we do, that the only person who wanted to kill Sampson is a nasty little snake called Krait. He has been out of circulation for the best of reasons. Sampson turned Queen's evidence against him in a matter concerning a conspiracy to rob Her Majesty's mails and when he was released last Tuesday he came out breathing retribution."

'Not the Christmas spirit," said Mr. Campion inanely.

"That is exactly what *we* thought," Oates agreed. "So about five o'clock yesterday afternoon two of our chaps, hearing that he was at the Humdinger where he might have been expected to make trouble, dropped along there and brought him in 'to help our inquiries' and he's been in ever since. Well, now. We have at least a dozen reasonably sober witnesses to prove that Krait did not meet Sampson at the club. Sampson had been there earlier in the afternoon but he left about a quarter to four saying he'd got to do some shopping but promising to return. Fifteen minutes or so later Krait came in and stayed there in full view of Girlski and the customers until our ministering angels turned up and collected him. Now what do you say?"

"Too easy." Mr. Campion was suspicious. "Krait killed Sampson just before he came in himself. The two met in the dark outside the club. Krait forced Sampson into the garage and possibly into the car and shot him out of hand. With the way the traffic has been lately he'd hardly have attracted attention had he used a mortar let alone a gun
214

with a silencer. He wiped the weapon, chucked it in the car, threw the mistletoe over the corpse and went up to Girlski and the rest to renew old acquaintance and establish an alibi. Your chaps, arriving when they did, must have appeared welcome."

Oates nodded. "We thought that. That *is* what happened. That is why this morning's development has set me gibbering. We have now two unimpeachable witnesses who swear that the dead man was in Chipperwood West at six last evening delivering some Christmas purchases he had made on behalf of a neighbour. That is a whole hour after Krait was put under arrest. The assumption is that Sampson returned to Alcatraz Mews some time later in the evening and was killed by someone else—which I do not believe. Unfortunately the Chipperwood West witnesses are not the kind of people we are going to shake. One of them is a friend of yours. She asked our Inspector if he knew you because you were 'so good at crime and all that nonsense'."

"Good Heavens!" Mr. Campion spoke piously as the explanation of the Superintendent's unlikely visitation was made plain to him. "I don't think I know Chipperwood West."

"It's a suburb which is becoming fashionable. Have you ever heard of Lady Larradine?"

"Old Lady 'ell?" Mr. Campion let the joke of his salad days escape without being noticed by either of them. "I don't believe it. She must be dead by this time!"

"There's a type of woman who never dies before you do," said Oates with apparent sincerity. "She's quite a dragon I understand from our Inspector. However, she isn't the actual witness. There are two of them. Brigadier Brose is one. Ever heard of him?"

"I don't think I have."

"My information is that you'd remember him if you'd met him. We'll find out. I'm taking you with me, Campion. I hope you don't mind?"

"My sister will hate it. I'm due to be Father Christmas in about an hour."

"I can't help that." Oates was adamant. "If a bunch of silly crooks want to get spiteful at the festive season someone must do the homework. Come and play Father

Christmas with me. It's your last chance. I'm retiring in the summer."

He continued in the same vein as they sat in the back of a police car threading their way through the deserted Christmas streets where the lamps were growing bright in the dusk.

"I've had bad luck lately," he said seriously. "Too much. It won't help my memoirs if I go out in a blaze of no-enthusiasm."

"You're thinking of the Phaeton robbery," Mr. Campion suggested. "What are you calling the memoirs? *Man-eaters of the Yard*?"

Oates's mild old eyes brightened but not greatly. "Something of the kind," he admitted. "But no one could be blamed for not solving that blessed Phaeton business. Everyone concerned was bonkers. A silly old musical star, for thirty years the widow of an eccentric Duke, steps out into her London garden one autumn morning leaving the street door wide open and all her most valuable jewellery, collected from strongrooms all over the country, lying in a brown paper parcel on her bureau in the first room off the hall. Her excuse was that she was going to take it to the Bond Street auctioneers and was carrying it herself for safety! The thief was equally mental to lift it."

"It wasn't saleable?"

"Saleable! It couldn't even be broken up. The stuff is just about as well-known as the Crown Jewels. Big Jewels. Great big enamels which the old Duke had collected at great expense. No fence would stay in the same room with them, yet, of course, they are worth the earth as every newspaper has told us at length ever since they were pinched!"

"He didn't get anything else either, did he?"

"He was a madman." Oates dismissed him with contempt. "All he gained was the old lady's housekeeping money for a couple of months which was in her handbag—about a hundred and fifty quid—and the other two items which were on the same shelf, a soapstone monkey and a plated paper-knife. He simply wandered in, took the first things he happened to see and wandered out again. Any sneak thief, tramp or casual snapper-upper could have done it and who gets blamed? Me!"

He looked so woebegone that Mr. Campion changed the subject hastily. "Where are we going?" he inquired. "To call on her ladyship? Do I understand that at the age of one hundred and forty-six or whatever it is she is cohabiting with a Brig? Which war?"

"I can't tell you," Oates was literal as usual. "It could be the South African. They're all in a nice residential hotel. It's the sort of place that is very popular with the older members of the landed gentry just now."

"When you say 'landed' you mean as in Fish?"

"Roughly, yes. Elderly people, living on capital. About forty of them. This place used to be called 'The Haven' and has now been taken over by two ex-society widows and renamed 'The Ccraven' with two Cs. It's a select hotel-cum-Old-Ducks' Home for 'Mother's Friends'. You know the sort of place?"

"I can envisage it. Don't say your murdered chum from the Humdinger lived there too?"

"No, he lived in a more modest outfit whose garden backs on the Ccraven's grounds. The Brigadier and one of the other residents, a Mr. Charlie Taunton who has become a bosom friend of his, were in the habit of talking to Sampson over the wall. Taunton is a lazy man who seldom goes out and has little money but he very much wanted to get some gifts for his fellow guests—something in the nature of little jokes from the chain stores, I understand—but he dreaded the exertion of shopping for them and Sampson appears to have offered to get him some little items wholesale and to deliver them by six o'clock on Christmas Eve in time for him to package them up and hand them to Lady Larradine who was dressing the tree at seven."

"And you say that Sampson actually did this?" Mr. Campion sounded bewildered.

"Both old gentlemen swear to it. They insist they went down to the wall at six and Sampson handed the parcel over as arranged. My Inspector is an experienced man and he doesn't think we shall shake either of them."

"That leaves Krait with a complete alibi. How did these Chipperwood witnesses hear of Sampson's death?"

"Routine. The local police called at Sampson's home address this morning to report the death only to discover

the place closed. The landlady and her family are away f[]
the holiday and Sampson himself was due to spend it wit[]
Girlski. The police stamped about a bit no doubt, makin[]
sure of all this and in the course of their investigations the[]
were seen and hailed by the two old boys in the oth[]
garden. The two were shocked to hear that their kin[]
acquaintance was dead and volunteered the informatio[]
that he was with them at six."

Mr. Campion looked blank. "Perhaps they don't kee[]
the same hours as anybody else," he suggested. "O[]
people can be highly eccentric."

Oates shook his head. "We thought of that. M[]
Inspector, who came down the moment the local polic[]
reported, insists that they are perfectly normal and qui[]
positive. Moreover, they had the purchases. He saw th[]
packages already on the tree. Lady Larradine pointed the[]
out to him when she asked after you. She'll be delighted []
see you, Campion."

"I can hardly wait!"

"You don't have to," said Oates grimly as they pulled u[]
before a huge Edwardian villa. "It's all yours."

"My dear boy! You haven't aged any more than I have[]
Lady Larradine's tremendous voice, one of her chi[]
terrors as he recollected, echoed over the crowded firs[]
floor room where she received them. There she stood in []
outmoded but glittering evening gown looking as alway[]
exactly like a spray-flecked seal. "I knew you'd come," sh[]
bellowed. "As soon as you got my oblique little SOS. H[]
do you like our little hideout? Isn't it *fun*! Moria Spry[]
Fysher and Janice Poole-Poole wanted something to do []
we all put our pennies in it and here we are!"

"Almost too marvellous," murmured Mr. Campion i[]
all sincerity. "We really want a word with Brigadier Bro[]
and Mr. Taunton."

"Of course you do and so you shall! We're all waiting f[]
the Christmas tree. Everybody will be there for that i[]
about ten minutes in the drawing-room. My dear, when w[]
came they were calling it the Residents' Lounge!"

Superintendent Oates remained grave. He was startled []
discover that the Dragon was not only fierce but also wil[]
The news that her apparently casual mention of M[]

Campion to the Inspector had been a ruse to get hold of him shocked the innocent policeman. He retaliated by insisting that he must see the witnesses at once. Lady Larradine silenced him with a friendly roar. "My dear man, you can't. They've gone for a walk. I always turn men out of the house after Christmas luncheon. They'll soon be back. The Brigadier won't miss his Tree! Ah. Here's Fiona. This is Janice Poole-Poole's daughter, Albert. Isn't she a pretty girl?"

Mr. Campion saw Miss Poole-Poole with relief knowing of old that Oates was susceptible to the type. The newcomer was young and lovely and even her back-comb hair-do and the fact that she appeared to have painted herself two black eyes failed to spoil the exquisite smile she bestowed on the helpless officer.

"Fabulous to have you really here," she said and sounded as if she really meant it. While he was still recovering Lady Larradine led him to the window.

"You can't see it because it's pitch dark," she said, "but out there, down the garden, there's a wall and it was over it that the Brigadier and Mr. Taunton spoke to Mr. Sampson at six o'clock last night. No one liked the man Sampson. I think poor Mr. Taunton was almost afraid of him. Certainly he seems to have died very untidily!"

"But he did buy Mr. Taunton's Christmas gifts for him?"

The dragon lifted a webby eyelid. "You have already been told that. At six last night Mr. Taunton and the Brigadier went to meet him to get the box. I got them into their mufflers so I know! I had the packing paper ready too, for Mr. Taunton to take up to his room. . . . Rather a small one on the third floor." She lowered her voice to reduce it to the volume of distant traffic. "Not many pennies but a dear little man!"

"Did you see these presents, Ma'am?"

"Not before they were wrapped! That would have spoiled the surprise!"

"I shall have to see them." There was a mulish note in the Superintendent's voice which the lady was too experienced to ignore. "I've thought how to do that without upsetting anybody," she said brightly. "The Brigadier and I will cut the presents from the Tree and

Fiona will be handing them round. All Mr. Taunton's littl
gifts are in the very distinctive black and gold paper
bought from Millie's Boutique and so, Fiona, you mus
give every package in gold and black paper not to th
person to whom it is addressed but to the Superintendent
Can you do that, dear?"

Miss Poole-Poole seemed to feel the task difficult bu
not impossible and the trusting smile she gave Oates cu
short his objections like the sun melting frost.

"Splendid!" The Dragon's roar was hearty. "Give m
your arm, Superintendent. You shall take me down."

As the procession reached the hall it ran into th
Brigadier himself. He was a large, pink man, affabl
enough, but of a martial type and he bristled at th
Superintendent. "Extraordinary time to do your busi
ness—middle of Christmas Day!" he said after ac
knowledging the introductions.

Oates inquired if he had enjoyed his walk.

"Talk?" said the Brigadier. "I've not been talking. I'v
been asleep in the card-room. Where's old Taunton?"

"He went for a walk, Athole dear," bellowed the Drago
gaily.

"So he did. You sent him! Poor feller."

As the old soldier led the way to the open door of th
drawing-room it occurred to both the visitors that th
secret of Lady Larradine's undoubted attraction for hin
lay in the fact that he could hear *her* if no one else. Th
discovery cast a new light altogether on the story of th
encounter with Sampson in the garden.

Meanwhile they had entered the drawing-room and th
party had begun. As Mr. Campion glanced at the company
ranged in a full circle round a magnificent tree loaded wit
gifts and sparkling like a waterfall, he saw face afte
familiar face. They were old acquaintances of the dizz
nineteen-thirties whom he had mourned as gone for eve
when he thought of them at all. Yet here they all were, nc
only alive but released by great age from many of th
restraints of convention. He noticed that every type o
head-gear from night-cap to tiara was being sported wit
fine individualistic enthusiasm. But Lady Larradine gav
him no time to look about. She proceeded with her tasl
immediately.

220

Each guest had been provided with a small invalid table beside his armchair and Oates, reluctant but wax in Fiona's hands, was no exception. He found himself seated between a mountain in flannel and a wraith in mauve mink, waiting his turn with the same beady-eyed avidity.

Christmas tree procedure at the Ccraven proved to be well organized. The Dragon did little work herself. Armed with a swagger stick she merely prodded parcel after parcel hanging amid the boughs while the task of detaching them was performed by the Brigadier who handed them to Fiona. Either to add to the excitement or perhaps to muffle any unfortunate comment on gifts received by the

"Such a nice little man. Most presentable but just a little throughout and under cover of the noise Mr. Campion was able to tackle his hostess.

"Where is Taunton?" he whispered.

"Such a nice little man. Most presentable but just a little teeny-weeny bit dishonest." Lady Larradine ignored his question but continued to put him in the picture at speed, whilst supervising the Tree at the same time. "Fifty-seven convictions, I believe, but only small ones. I only got it all out of him last week. Shattering! He'd been so *useful* amusing the Brigadier. When he came he looked like a lost soul with no luggage but after no time at all he settled in perfectly." She paused and stabbed at a ball of coloured cellophane with her stick before returning to her startled guest.

"Albert. I am terribly afraid poor Mr. Taunton took that dreadful jewellery of Maisie Phaeton's. It appears to have been merely her own fault. He was merely wandering past her house, feeling in need of care and attention. The door was wide open and he found himself inside, picking up a few odds and ends. When he discovered from all that fuss in the newspapers what it was he had got hold of—how well known it was, I mean—he was quite horrified and had to hide. And where better than here with us where he never had to go out?"

"Where indeed!" Mr. Campion dared not glance across the room to where the Superintendent was unwrapping his black and gold parcels. "Where is he now?"

"Of course, I hadn't the faintest idea what was worrying the man until he confessed," the Dragon went on stonily.

221

"Then I realized that something would have to be done at once to protect everybody. The wretch had hidden all that frightful stuff in our tool-shed for three months, not daring to keep it in the house, and to make matters worse, the impossible person at the end of the garden, Mr. Sampson, had recognized him and *would* keep speaking. Apparently people in the—er—underworld all know each other just as those of us in—er—other closed circles do."

Mr. Campion, whose hair was standing on end, had a moment of inspiration. "This absurd rigmarole about Taunton getting Sampson to buy him some Christmas gifts wholesale was your idea!" he said accusingly.

The Dragon stared. "It seemed the best way of getting Maisie's jewellery back to her without any one person being solely involved," she said frankly. "I knew we should all recognize the things the moment we saw them and I was certain that after a lot of argument we should decide to pack them up and send them round to her. But, if there *was* any repercussion, we should *all* be in it (quite a formidable array, dear) and the blame could be traced to Mr. Sampson if absolutely necessary. You see the Brigadier is convinced that Sampson *was* there last night. Mr. Taunton very cleverly left him on the lawn and went behind the tool-shed and came back with the box."

"How completely immoral!"

The Dragon had the grace to look embarrassed. "I don't think the Sampson angle would ever have arisen," she said. "But if it had, Sampson was quite a terrible person. Almost a blackmailer. Utterly dishonest and inconsiderate. Think how he had spoiled everything and endangered us all by getting himself killed on the one afternoon when we said he was here, so that the police were brought in. Just the one thing I was trying to avoid. When the Inspector appeared this morning I was so upset I thought of you!"

In his not unnatural alarm Mr. Campion so far forgot himself as to touch her sleeve. "Where is Taunton now?"

The Dragon threshed her train. "Really boy! What a fidget you are! If you must know, I gave him his Christmas present—every penny I had in cash for he was broke again he told me—and sent him for a nice long walk after lunch. Having seen the Inspector here this morning he was glad to go." She paused and a gentle gleam came into her hooded yes. "If that Superintendent has the stupidity to try to find him when once Maisie has her monstrosities back none of us will be able to identify him I'm afraid. And there's another thing. If the Brigadier should be forced to give evidence I am sure he will stick to his guns about Mr. Sampson being down the garden here at six o'clock last night. He believes he was. That would mean that someone very wicked would have to go unpunished, wouldn't it? Sampson was a terrible person but no one should have killed him."

Mr. Campion was silenced. He glanced fearfully across the room.

The Superintendent was seated at his table wearing the strained yet slap-happy expression of a man with concussion. On his left was a pile of black and gilt wrappings, on his right a rajah's ransom in somewhat specialized form. From where he stood Mr. Campion could see two examples amid the rest; a breastplate in gold, pearl and enamel in the shape of a unicorn in a garden and an item which looked like a plover's egg in tourmaline encased in a ducal coronet. There was also a soapstone monkey and a silver paper-knife.

Much later that evening Mr. Campion and the Superintendent drove quietly back to headquarters. Oates had a large cardboard box on his knee. He clasped it tenderly.

He had been silent for a long time when a thought occurred to him.

"Why did they take him into the house in the first place?" he said. "An elderly crook looking lost! No luggage!"

Mr. Campion's pale eyes flickered behind his spectacles.

"Don't forget the Duchess's housekeeping money," he murmured. "I should think he offered one of the widows who really run that place for the first three months' payment in cash, wouldn't you? That must be an impressive phenomenon in that sort of business, I fancy."

Oates caught his breath and fell silent once more until presently he burst out again.

"Those people! That woman!" he exploded. "When they were younger they led me a pretty dance—losing things or getting themselves swindled. But now they're old they take the blessed biscuit! Do you see how she's tied my hands, Campion?"

Mr. Campion tried not to grin.

"Snapdragons are just permissible at Christmas," he said. "Handled with extreme caution they burn very few fingers it seems to me." He tapped the cardboard box. "And some of them provide a few plums for retiring coppers, don't they, Superintendent?"